Two Heirs for the Billionaire

Those Fabulous Jones Girls
Book Two

Mia Caldwell

CHAPTER ONE

SYLVIE FOUGHT BACK THE DESIRE TO kick Alan's shin. She hated it when he acted like a dick. It brought out The Ugly in her, and right now The Ugly wanted out to play.

Alan smiled, his bleached white teeth gleaming in the gloom of the cab's back seat. "Nothing like the city, is there, babe? Gets me pumped up. It's not boring like Zeke's Bend. Mmm, look over there." He pointed at the sidewalk where two pretty women were walking hand-in-hand. "Wonder if they'd like to have a third tonight. Har-har!"

Sylvie rolled her eyes. "If they did, they'd be more interested in me than you."

"Har-har! Good one. Maybe they'd take us both. I wouldn't mind seein' some of that." He peered out the cab window like a starving kid at a cupcake factory.

He was searching for more women to throw in her face. He'd been acting this way the entire trip. Sylvie wished she'd stayed home rather than giving in to his whining and coming to this boring conference weekend in Chicago.

As if she cared about the latest breakthroughs in chiropractic medicine. She didn't, not at all, never would, not if she lived to be a hundred years old. Sitting through the mind-numbing workshops and lectures had been worse than watching paint dry. She was a hairdresser and small business owner, not a chiropractor. That was Alan's job.

It was typically selfish that he'd wanted her beside him during the panels and classes. She could have been out doing something more fun, like being tortured on a rack or having her fingernails pulled out one by one. Yes, that would have been more fun than attending Dr.

Sleepmore's lecture on ... what was it? Damn. She couldn't remember. Something about toe bones. The memory of it was enough to send her into a doze.

If the boring conference wasn't bad enough, it was freezing cold, what with it being January. Not exactly the best time of year to visit the city.

And now, as if the whole day being a frozen yawn-fest weren't enough, Alan was ruining their night out by ogling every woman they passed. She'd about had enough. Sylvie Jones was not the kind of woman to let a man—

"Hot damn!" Alan interrupted. "Look at that one! You think those are fake or real? Eh, who cares? They're way bigger than yours. Har-har! Why don't we get you a pair? I'll pay half."

And she'd pay the other half? Hilarious. What the hell was wrong with her girls, anyway? Sylvie thought they were fine as they were. Thinking, however, was becoming a bad idea; the more she thought, the madder she got.

"Aw," Alan said, "are you pouting? Did I make you feel bad about your itty titties? Don't worry, babe. I don't expect you to compete with lookers like these in the city."

Sylvie's brain paused. It was like she'd blown a mental fuse. Itty titties? Can't compete with lookers? What the hell? Maybe he was on drugs or something.

No, Alan was just a jackass. It really was time to make a decision about him. It might not be the ideal time and place to do it, but if she waited, there was a risk she might reconsider. She shuddered. Gawd. She couldn't risk that.

Something snapped inside her and everything became easy. She realized the snapping sensation came from the severing of the invisible cord that connected her to Alan. Over time, the frayed cord had grown thinner and thinner, the fibers worn down by Alan's crappy behavior like the scraping of an emery board. This break had been a long time coming and there was no putting the pieces back together.

During their time together, she'd tried to repair the ongoing damage with assurances to herself like, "He didn't mean it," or "You're just being sensitive," or "Once you get him trained up properly he won't be such a prick."

But all those repairs had been for nothing.

Tonight, their connection was severed, forever broken by one shitty comment too many. Broken by Mr. Itty Titty himself. It was over, so far gone that she wasn't even sorry about it.

"Did you hear me?" Alan asked. "I said I'll pay half for a pair of new—"

"Fuck you, Alan," Sylvie said. She leaned forward and spoke to the taxi driver. "Pull over, please."

Alan laughed, his blonde hair falling across his forehead. He kept the front long, she knew, because it covered up his receding hairline, or, at least, he thought it did. The man was more vain about his hair than a shampoo model.

"Are we there already?" Alan asked. "Or are you upset and having a tantrum?"

What had she ever seen in this asshole? Had he always been this bad? No, he hadn't. Not in the beginning.

He'd been sweet and generous and he'd treated her well. She'd thought that was who he was. But he'd been lying, suckering her in for what? Did he think Sylvie was a doormat?

Maybe she had been, for a while. But no more.

She glanced out the window beyond Alan and saw they were passing a fancy hotel. She spoke to the cabbie. "Pull over right here, please."

Cursing in some language other than English, the driver swerved right, jerking to a halt beside the curb.

She thought he said, "Where who here crave wimmins." Or it might have been, "Here you are, crazy woman." It was hard to say which one was accurate.

The uniformed hotel doorman rushed out and opened the cab door.

Alan waved his hand at him. "No, go on. No one's getting out here."

"Fuck you, Alan," Sylvie repeated, enjoying the sound of it on her tongue. She wanted to say it again, but figured twice was sufficient. "I'm getting out."

"Calm down for God's sake." He sighed loudly. "You're always getting worked up over some dumb thing or other. I was just yanking your chain. Get a sense of humor, would you?"

The doorman leaned down and looked inside. "Welcome to the Grande City Hotel. Do you have luggage?"

"No," Sylvie said, "it will just be me."

"The hell it will," Alan said, then turned to the doorman. "Shut the damned door." To the cabbie, he said, "Get going or we'll be late and lose our reservation."

The cabbie looked at Sylvie. The doorman looked at Sylvie. Alan glared at the cabbie and tried to pull the door closed.

Sylvie was finished with it. She opened the door on her side of the cab and stepped out into traffic. A car whizzed by, laying on the horn. She didn't care. She dashed around the rear of the taxi to safety, then hopped onto the sidewalk, heels be damned, and marched toward the hotel, pulling her coat tightly around herself.

Alan jumped out of the cab and charged after her. He grabbed her arm and turned her around. "Stop acting like a spoiled child and get back in the taxi."

"Listen," she said. "If you want to keep that hand, you'd better let go of my arm. Let me go before I yell for the police."

"Quit exaggerating," he sneered, but he released her arm. "Okay, I get it. You're no fun tonight. Understood. Now get in the cab so we can, at least, get something to eat before you ruin the rest of this trip."

"Me? I ruined the trip?" Sylvie found she still had some outrage left in her and she found it annoying. "You are such a ... a ... I'm not going to say it." She took a deep breath then continued. "We're over, Alan. You can't throw other women at me and think I'm going to put up with it forever. You want to drag me down, but I know my worth, and I'm worth twice, no, four times what you are. Ten times. It's over."

He glared at her. "You really are out of your depth. Fine. Go on. You'll come running back. Maybe I'll be waiting for you and maybe I won't. Plenty more where you came from."

She stared at him and wondered how she'd ever found this spray-tanned, washed-up, fake-beachy-dude attractive. "That's big talk there, Alan. Face it, you've blown it."

She gestured up and down herself. "You had all this and you threw it away. You got ahead of yourself and forgot what's what. B-i-i-i-g mistake. Don't think for a minute that you're ever getting this back. It's gone. Forever. Watch it walk away."

She turned on her heel and sashayed to the front doors, letting the dickhead get a good rear view of what he'd never have again. Whatever it was that Alan was spewing behind her, she didn't hear it. He was nothing but a flea on the sidewalk—too little to be heard.

The doorman dashed up in front of her, opening the door for her in the nick of time. He gave her an approving smile and nod of respect as she passed.

Now there was somebody who knew what was up.

CHAPTER TWO

AN HOUR AND A HALF LATER, SYLVIE was nursing her second drink at the Grande City Hotel bar and had considerably cooled down.

The bar accomplished some of that with its old world charm, dark wood paneling, shiny brass fixtures, and gleaming mirrors behind rows of colorful liquor bottles. It had the feel of another era, a time when gentleman lounged in wingback chairs, smoked cigars and sipped fine scotch while reading a financial newspaper.

It hadn't taken long for Sylvie to regret rashly dumping Alan while on a visit to a strange city. All her things were in their hotel room, and although she had her own card key, it didn't mean she relished returning and spending the night with her now-ex. Too bad she couldn't have put up with him until the next day when they were back home.

Thank God, though, she'd insisted on carrying her own plane ticket. Or, more like, thank Momma. She was the one who'd harped at Sylvie about always having a way to get yourself home on your own.

Momma knew well the dangers of relying on a man to take care of her. Sylvie's father had dumped Momma, Sylvie, and her younger brother, Will, at a truck stop in Arizona when she'd been eight. That had been one terrifying vacation. No money, no transportation, no way home. Just a pile of luggage baking on the asphalt parking lot.

To this day, the smell of hot tar made her nauseous.

So, hell yeah she had her ticket home in her purse. She'd never be without a way home to Zeke's Bend.

She sighed and swirled her drink. She didn't feel the least bit buzzed. Maybe that was the problem. She needed to quit nursing the booze and get down to serious action.

She thought about calling her cousins and best friends, Phae and Neesa, to tell them what had happened. She knew they'd be thrilled that she'd dumped Alan, and that's probably what kept her from calling.

Her cousins never said it in so many words, but Sylvie understood their feelings about Alan weren't positive, and it wasn't just because Sylvie considered herself to be something of a psychic.

Okay, so she wasn't a great psychic, but sometimes, she'd get these premonitions, and when she got them, she obeyed.

A small voice inside her asked why she hadn't predicted Alan would turn into a top-notch asshole, but she brushed it aside. That didn't have anything to do with her being a little bit psychic.

So she wouldn't call Phae and Neesa because she wasn't in a place yet to hear the relief that would be in their voices.

She'd been approached several times in the past hour by men in the bar, some wanting to buy her a drink, all of them wanting to chat her up. Though their attention had made her feel good after Alan's putdowns, she'd brushed the men aside. It was too soon to be interested in anyone. She wanted to be left alone to ponder why she'd wasted so much time fiddling with a tool.

Maybe she'd head over to the restaurant, order some dinner. Maybe she'd pull out her credit card and book a night's stay in the fancy hotel if they had an available room. Talk about a splurge. She wondered how much a room cost in a place like this.

Maybe she'd ask the bartender the next time he came by.

A movement to her right drew her eye. She glanced toward the entrance and then did a double take.

A tall man stood in the arched entryway, and not just any man. A drop-dead gorgeous man.

He was crazy tall, almost basketball player height. It was impossible to know for sure, but she'd bet he was well over six and a half feet tall.

He was huge, like a giant who had wandered in out of a different dimension. His sheer size was both intimidating and awesome. The guy could seriously fill a doorway and command attention.

Styled cleanly and simply, his dark hair was brushed back and away from chiseled features. And his light tan didn't come from a spray can like Alan's; that was clear enough. It came from hours spent on exclusive beaches, from piloting fancy sloops and playing tennis at private clubs. That was a rich man's tan if she'd ever seen one (not that she'd seen many).

Oh, and he could dress, too. He wore an impeccably tailored dark suit and tie, every line conforming to his muscular body. Shiny black shoes sparkled on his long feet, and Sylvie couldn't help but speculate about the old adage of what big feet on a man were supposed to mean.

She didn't think any red-blooded woman could look at this man and not speculate about something. He stood with a loose and casual air that came from complete confidence, and his confidence was as much a draw as his appearance, perhaps more.

He scanned the room, his vivid green eyes piercing the dim lighting. It was like he owned the place, hell, like he owned the city, and everyone else was just a cold-water-flat renter.

When his gaze met Sylvie's, his arched brows shot up and a slow grin stretched across his sexy mouth.

Sylvie was taken aback. Was he smiling at her? Unlikely.

He began walking, his gait smooth and manly, like a debonair actor from an old movie. He held her gaze all the while as if he was heading for her.

Wait. Was he walking toward her?

Sylvie's temperature shot up. It couldn't be. No.

But yes. Yes, this Greek-god-statue of a man was coming straight at her. Gulp.

Never one to forget her raising, Sylvie returned the handsome stranger's smile.

He faltered for a split second. Was that a moment of uncertainty on those confident features? Surely not. She'd probably misread it. He was suave as ever now.

He came up and nodded once at the stool beside her. "May I?"

"Of course," she said. Like anyone would deny this guy anything. Up close, he was even taller and larger. Why was she feeling all funny inside?

The bartender popped up behind the bar as if from out of nowhere.

Sitting, the handsome man glanced at the bartender in brief acknowledgment. "I'll have whatever the lady's having."

The bartender nodded crisply and rushed off. She guessed that was rich white guy service in action. It was almost comical how eager the bartender was to please, and it helped snap Sylvie back to herself.

"Do people always wait on you like that?" she asked, gently teasing.

"Most of the time," he said. "I'd think it can't be much different for a woman as beautiful as you. Men must always be stumbling over themselves to give you whatever you want."

"They are. Just yesterday a man gave me a hundred-foot yacht. I had to return it, though. The color clashed with my ruby-encrusted bikini."

"A ruby-encrusted bikini. There's a mental image I won't soon forget."

"You might as well. I've already worn the suit once, and I *never* wear anything twice."

"Of course not," he said, grinning. "I'm crushed."

"Not for long, I'll bet. There have to be crowds of employees waiting just outside to cater to your every whim."

He chuckled, his eyes twinkling. "The service really got it right this time. I predict we're going to get along very well. I'm Heath, as you know. And your name is Kassy, yes?"

Sylvie had no idea what he was talking about. Service? He acted like he knew her, kind of. Like a blind date, maybe? Or a dating site?

He gave her a funny look. "You were waiting for me, weren't you? I was told I'd be meeting Kassy in a champagne silk dress and," he gestured at her, "that dress looks champagne to me."

"Um, yeah," Sylvie said, trying to think fast.

She was drawn to the guy, no doubt about it. And this was her one night out in the city to have fun before it was time to head back to Zeke's Bend and face her newly single status.

Whoever Heath (and what a yummy name that was) had arranged to meet, it wasn't Sylvie. But that didn't mean the woman couldn't be Sylvie now. Take a chance, have some fun, be dangerous, live on the edge.

She took a moment and glanced around the bar to see if another woman in a champagne dress was waiting nearby.

The bartender delivered Heath's drink with a quick bow then scrambled away again.

"I think he's afraid of you," Sylvie said, stalling for time. "Are you a secret agent type who seduces ladies and terrifies men? Am I going to be your sidekick while you stop a bad guy from blowing up the city?"

"It wouldn't be so bad a life." His tone was devastatingly flirty. "Adventurous missions, exotic locales and meeting beautiful women like you. It sounds like a much better alternative to what I actually have planned for us tonight. It's only a business dinner I'm afraid."

Sylvie frowned. What was it with men and business? From a chiropractic convention to a business dinner. Well, hurrah.

He laughed. "You look disappointed. Didn't your employer tell you why I was hiring you? I can't imagine your services are often required for saving the city from villains."

Hiring her? What the hell? He mentioned a service. Services? Her employer? She was beginning to put this together and—

"Do you think I'm a whore?" she blurted, her verbal filter dropped like a hot coal.

His thick brows shot up. "Of course not. I don't know what I could have said to give you that impression, but I certainly didn't intend it."

"Oh, well then, that's good. Because I'm not a whore."

"Of course not."

He took a long drink and studied her. She took a long sip of her own drink because right then, she seriously needed some liquid courage.

"I've used your employer before," he said. "It's strictly an escort service without the … well … without the happy ending, so to speak."

He looked uncomfortable, which amused Sylvie, who sensed that this man was rarely flustered.

Sylvie wasn't sure what to think. Here was a gorgeous, obviously wealthy man who hired an escort service to provide him with dates for business dinners. It didn't make any sense.

"Why would a man like you need an escort service to get a date?" she asked.

"What difference does it make? I don't mean to be rude, but do you always grill your dates like this and accuse them of thinking you're something you're not?"

"Maybe. Maybe not. But come on. You're not a paunchy, red-faced blowhard who has just enough money to drape a decent-looking woman on his arm every once in a while. You must be aware that women find you attractive."

His grin returned. "You think I'm attractive?"

"Quit playing around." She ran a fingertip over the rim of her glass, pretending to be cooler than she actually was. "Fess up. Why'd you hire me?"

"Honestly? Because it's easy. I don't know you. You don't know me. You won't get the wrong idea and think we're going to live happily ever after just because I asked you out once."

She considered his response. His honesty was plain on his handsome features. "You're rich, good looking, and women are always hoping you'll marry them if you so much as smile at them. That's what you're saying."

"I wouldn't put it that way, but, yes. I'm a busy man, and a simple transaction is the easiest and quickest way to handle things."

"Even your love life?"

"Who's talking about my love life?"

The way he said it sent a shiver down her back. "Your social life, then. You've turned it into a business exchange."

"This aspect of my social life, yes. It's a simple transaction."

Sylvie batted her eyelashes, deciding to go fishing. "It's not a cheap transaction, either."

"It's not. But seeing you, it's well worth every dollar and then some."

Hmm. She was in a dilemma. On the one hand, she wasn't a prostitute, not even a woman who'd prostitute her company. But on the other hand, this was the finest man she'd ever met and he was probably planning to take her to a fancy restaurant.

Wow. Tonight, she'd dumped one guy for acting like she wasn't good enough, and now here was another one thinking she was a hot paid escort.

The idea of a spontaneous adventure appealed to her. She realized she should set Heath straight, but this could be a story she could tell her friends for ages.

She could hear it already, how she'd pretended to be an escort and gone to dinner with a rich, devastatingly handsome man. Everyone would ooh and ahh and ask what she ate, if they danced, and what it was all like. They'd want to know how much he paid for it all, too.

Really, if she played along, what was the worst that could happen? She might have to eat snails or something like in *"Pretty Woman."* It didn't sound so bad.

She took a few more hasty glances around the room and didn't see anyone in a champagne silk dress. The real Kassy had missed her chance.

She smiled and gave her companion her full attention. "I'm definitely worth every penny, Heath."

He held out a big, manicured hand. "I look forward to spending time with you this evening, Kassy."

"And I, you."

She took his hand, and when her skin touched his, she nearly yanked her hand back in surprise. A brilliant, electric buzz passed between them, something akin to static electricity, but not that. Something else. Something she'd never felt before.

She blinked. He blinked.

His eyebrows shot up again. He'd felt it, too.

Tonight had taken a fascinating, tingly turn.

CHAPTER THREE

HEATH BLINKED. SOMETHING ELECTRIC had passed from Kassy straight up his arm and down his spine. Something that made his loins tighten. Something he'd never felt before.

When Kassy pulled her hand away, he realized she was flustered. She must have felt it, too. Interesting. No, more than interesting. Strange.

He watched her pick up her drink and take a sip, her full upper lip wrapping over the brim of the glass. Damn. He couldn't look away. He tried to focus on her elegant, tapered fingers, the long, silvery nails sparkling in the low lighting. Nope. He had to watch her mouth, those sexy lips.

He sipped his own drink but didn't taste it. Who was this woman?

He'd used this particular escort service several times in the past, and he'd always been pleased enough. The women they sent were always intelligent, educated, good-looking and decent conversationalists.

In general, they were everything they should be to pass as a legitimate date, and most of them only did this work part-time as a way to afford college or as extra income to support a fledgling career in some field or other.

But this woman, Kassy, she was a world apart. When he'd spotted her from the doorway, he hadn't dared dream this vision was his date for the evening.

To say that she was built was an understatement. She had curves in all the right places, with wide hips and a nipped-in waist that couldn't be hidden even when she was sitting.

Her silk dress hugged her shapeliness and snugged up against a generous bosom that was just the right heaping handful size. And those legs, those long, shapely, creamy mocha legs that were silkier looking than her dress, ending in delicate feet slipped into heels that displayed her dainty, painted toenails—she was more than right, in every way.

She was a vision of femininity from another time. Her gently curling hair and her wide-set eyes, her full lips and defined cheekbones, all combined into a devastating assault on his senses.

She was, without doubt, the most beautiful woman he'd ever seen. And that was what he thought before she smiled at him.

When Kassy smiled at him, it was like he'd been punched in the stomach, briefly knocking the air out of him. It was a thousand watt flash that lit up his world like a floodlight in a blackout. That smile was everything, kind and spunky, smart and teasing, welcoming and warm, and perfectly devastating.

It made him want to know her. To know her well.

In fact, the actual words that passed through his befuddled mind had been, "That's the woman I'm going to marry."

What an idiot he was. He hadn't even spoken to her yet. How stupid was it to think such a thing? He wasn't some country bumpkin on his first trip to the city getting his first look at a beautiful girl.

He was one of the most sought-after men in his social sphere. Women threw themselves at him. He could have his pick, and he did pick, plenty. He just always wound up tossing them back.

He'd certainly never had the clichéd, "I'm going to marry that woman" moment you heard long-dead actors talk about in scratchy black and white movies. Not until tonight. Not until Kassy.

Of course, this was silly, and it didn't matter. She was a beautiful woman, and Heath had a lot on the line tonight. The deal with Yurovize could be a game changer, and this meeting over dinner would likely determine the final score.

He was rattled, that was all, overly emotional on an important night.

"So how much did you pay for me?" Kassy asked, snapping him out of his reverie.

"I beg your pardon?"

"You know. What did my company charge you for, well, my company?"

"I'd think they'd tell you."

She had an adorable twinkle in her expressive brown eyes. "No. I mean, yes. But, for all I know, they're not being honest and are pocketing more than their share. I like to check up on them every so often. It's good business and you seem like you wouldn't mind telling me, so—"

"I'd say I'm not paying nearly enough."

"Oh, so that's how it is."

"That's how it is," he said, enjoying the quirk of a smile playing at the corners of her lips.

"I bet you think it's impolite to talk about money."

"Good God, no. All I do all day long is talk about money."

"Hmm. I was going to ask what you do, but that comment makes me want to see if I can guess."

Heath glanced down. Her dress had ridden up slightly and he could just see the rounded curve of her knee. He fought back the urge to stroke that accidental reveal. "It isn't a secret."

"No, don't tell me. Wait, here's a thought. How about if I'm able to guess what you do, you'll tell me how much my company's charging you for tonight?" She smiled.

Heath's stomach tightened. Damn. What had she said? Her knee had distracted him. Oh, yeah, she was making a deal. "All right, Kassy. I'll agree to that. But you have to be specific and get it just right."

"Oh, I'll get it just right," she said, with full-on innuendo.

He almost groaned. His phone vibrated in his pocket. Saved in the nick of time. "Excuse me, but I'd better check this."

She nodded politely and looked away, idly running a fingertip around the rim of her glass. So sexy. Could this woman do anything that wasn't sexy?

He pulled out his phone. It was a text from his assistant. Yurovize had to cancel the meeting. Supposedly their lead negotiator's flight had been re-routed due to a storm and he wouldn't be able to make the dinner in time. Hell.

Heath considered the likelihood that they were telling the truth. Stanford Tilling, the lead negotiator on this deal, was the slipperiest sort of operator. This was probably a power play to force Heath into a new timeline of their choosing.

He shot back a message to his assistant telling her to contact Tilling's people and find out how late he'd be arriving. Then Heath gladly turned his attention to more pressing matters: the lovely lady perched appealingly on the barstool beside him.

"That was my assistant," he told her. "Looks like my meeting may be delayed."

"Oh." Her lovely face fell. "Does that mean dinner is off?"

"Certainly not." He checked his watch. "If fact, if you'd like, we could head over to the restaurant now. It's right here in the hotel. Have you eaten here before?"

"No, I haven't had that pleasure."

"It's one of the best in the city. Just say the word and we're there. I'm sure our table is ready."

"Wonderful. I guess. Or not. I mean, this was supposed to be a business dinner, and I hate to tell you this," she lowered her voice and fluttered her long lashes charmingly, "but I don't have much to say about business in general. Not tonight anyway."

"I couldn't be more pleased. Suddenly, business is the very last thing on my mind."

"Oh, my. What's the first thing on your mind?"

He smiled. "Honestly? Do you want to know?"

"I do."

"I'm wondering how it would feel to hold you in my arms."

Kassy looked shaken, her flirtatious demeanor startled away for a split second. She recovered quickly. "There's only one way to find out."

Damn. He wasn't expecting that. He leaned forward, gladly planning to take her up on her offer.

She held out a dainty hand and stopped him cold with an arched eyebrow. "Silly man. I meant if there's time, I might be open to some dancing later. But you'll have to feed me first before I can decide anything."

He laughed. "Fair enough." He stood up and held out his arm. "Shall we?"

She smiled at him, and once again, he was blasted with a wave of premonition, a sense of having known her forever, of wanting to keep on knowing her forever, of knowing her in the most intimate of ways.

Kassy slid gracefully off the stool, picked up her purse, then placed her hand on his arm. Another electric spark shot through him.

He decided that the second they were seated in the restaurant he was texting his assistant to tell Tilling the meeting was off. Heath wouldn't be waiting around for him.

As of this moment, Heath had far more important things to do. Like dining and dancing with a beautiful woman.

This particular acquisition couldn't wait.

CHAPTER FOUR

AS SYLVIE AND HEATH STUMBLED INTO the elevator after dinner, Sylvie couldn't help but think that this was one of the best nights of her life. Heath had been charming, charismatic, and attentive throughout dinner. It was hard to remember that this evening with him was just a one-time deal.

Heath cozied up next to her in the elevator and she thought again about their initial conversation. She had told him in no uncertain terms that this was a hands-off transaction. But as she watched him press the button for the floor to the penthouse, she had to think about what she wanted to do next.

"So where do you think you're taking me now?" she asked in a teasing tone. She didn't know if her attraction was growing more intense because of all the flirting or because of all the expensive wine and champagne she'd consumed at dinner.

"I promised you dancing and I know of a place where we can have a dance floor all to ourselves," he said with a confident smirk.

Sylvie didn't see the point of beating around the bush. "Does this private dance floor happen to be in your room? I'm kind of psychic, you know. And I'm getting a powerful vision that you're trying to seduce me."

"I told you that I wanted to hold you in my arms," he said in a sultry tone. "I haven't yet had the pleasure of enjoying that feeling. Can you blame a guy for wanting to have the freedom to fully explore a unique opportunity without being in front of prying eyes?"

He was so close to her that she could feel the vibration of his words, and they sent shivers through her. Sylvie wanted this man, and she was tipsy enough to admit it. Would it be so wrong to let the night continue in its natural ebb and flow?

She wasn't naïve. It wasn't as if Alan was the first man she had slept with, although the list of men before him wasn't all that long. Still, Sylvie understood how these things worked. If she went up to Heath's room, there would be certain expectations.

She tried to draw up a mental pro/con list in her head, but there was a fuzzy fog in there that made it a little difficult to concentrate. After several moments of hard effort, there was barely anything in the con column other than Heath thought she was someone else.

Meanwhile, in the pro column, the list rambled on for ages. At the top of that list was that a fling with a hot, rich guy was the perfect chance to put Alan behind her for good.

Sylvie felt reckless. Random sex with a sexy, filthy-rich, ultra-attractive man. How many times would this kind of opportunity come her way? Unique opportunity, indeed.

The elevator doors opened, and Heath put his hand on the small of her back and gently guided her forward, as if she needed any coaxing. He led her out of the elevator and into the hallway. A key appeared in his hand as they stepped towards a wide set of double doors. He paused before he unlocked the door and looked at her with a questioning glance. The moment of truth had arrived.

"I'm not stepping over any boundaries here, right?" he asked.

It was only the second time that evening that Sylvie had seen Heath appear the slightest bit uncertain. She adored him for asking the question, for making sure she understood what he wanted.

He was rather gallant, she thought. He had commanded the wait staff around them at the restaurant with barely any effort. They had waited on their every pleasure and whim, particularly Sylvie's, and that was because Heath subtly shifted their attention to her.

Sylvie wasn't used to that kind of attention from anyone. Being with Heath had made her feel like a woman who was worth something, like a queen. Nothing like how Alan made her feel. Heath seemed to respect her, and he had abided by every wall that she had put up to keep the evening firmly in appropriate territory.

The irony now was that she was the one who was ready to break down all the walls and leap forward into the unknown without a backward glance.

So the answer to his question was, no, he wasn't stepping over her boundaries.

"You're not," she finally said. "If nothing else, I think that I'd like to hear some music. But I should pick it. I'm not so certain about your taste after what you told me earlier."

They both started to laugh.

It had been a game she'd created once they sat down to dinner. She was curious about Heath but didn't want to pry too much, fearing her curiosity might lead to him returning the favor. She didn't want him to ask her anything that would indicate she wasn't Kassy, the escort, after all.

So she created a game called "Private Yet Public." The point of the game was to answer all personal questions in the most specific way possible without giving away information about your actual identity.

She had learned a lot about Heath just playing that silly little game, including his irrational love of heavy metal 70s bands.

Heath finished laughing and then took her by the elbow before pulling her toward him. "The only music I plan to play is slow and sensual. It is guaranteed to make sure your body is as close to mine as possible. That's not so bad, is it?"

Sylvie forgot to breathe for a moment. He was so tall and commanding that she wanted to sink right into him. But she caught herself at the last moment. There was still time to step away and confess to Heath who she really was. Then she thought for the hundredth time that this type of thing would never happen to her again.

Tomorrow, she would go back to Zeke's Bend and her salon, and she'd be plain old Sylvie Jones again. Eventually, she would have to find someone new to settle down with now that Alan was out of the picture.

There was no one in Zeke's Bend that could hold a candle to Heath, the gorgeous billionaire. It was thoroughly depressing to think about her future right now, so why not enjoy playing the part of Kassy the escort a little bit longer? Kassy's life certainly appeared a lot more exciting than Sylvie's.

Sylvie didn't know if Heath was really a billionaire. They had joked about it at dinner because he obviously had more money than Sylvie would ever see in her lifetime. She had tried to guess what he did in her "Private Yet Public" game and still hadn't quite hit on it.

He said that she had to guess exactly what he did in order for him to tell her how much he was paying for her services for the night, and so far, she had missed the mark. It wasn't for lack of trying.

Turned out, though, that she didn't really care at the end of the day. She was far more curious about Heath, the man, than Heath, the billionaire.

"One last chance if you want to get away," Heath said.

The funny thing was that as he spoke, he held her elbow, effectively making it so that she couldn't move away from him right then even if she wanted to. She discovered she didn't mind it all.

And that seemed to be her answer.

Sylvie slowly shook her head as she licked her lips. She had been dying all night to have Heath lean over and kiss her. Her body shook in anticipation. She thought that moment might finally have arrived, but then he stepped away from her and opened the door to his room.

Sylvie was shaken to her core. She couldn't remember ever having felt this kind of wild physical attraction. She craved him like she craved the air that she breathed, and for some reason, she thought that it was possible he felt exactly the same way.

She had barely stepped fully into the room before her mouth fell open. This wasn't a room. This was a suite of rooms. Directly across from her, there was a bank of floor to ceiling windows showcasing a dazzling view of the skyscrapers of downtown Chicago. With the lights off, it felt as if they were standing in the middle of a sea of stars.

From somewhere off to her left, she heard a soft melody fill the air, and then Heath was behind her, grasping her hips and pulling her backward. She melted into him.

He started to move against her in time to the rhythm of the music, and she swayed as she leaned back against him and let her head fall against his shoulder.

Moving in unison, he propelled her slowly forward, crossing the room towards the lights. He murmured something in her ear, but she didn't really understand what it was. She was lost in the music and the feeling of intense heat wafting off of Heath's body to warm her skin through the thin fabric of her dress.

"Feeling you here in my arms is everything I imagined it would be and more," Heath whispered into her ear.

She let her head fall to the side to give him better access, which seemed to be exactly what he wanted her to do. The warmth of his breath caressed the side of her neck and sent a tickle of electricity down her spine.

She brought her shoulders up in a helpless shrug of delicious anticipation. His lips skimmed her earlobe. She said nothing. She didn't trust herself to say anything for fear of it coming out as, "Take me now."

Sylvie was many things. Confident. Sexy. Sometimes even brazen. She knew she was attractive to the opposite sex. She had enough experience with men to know that. But if she opened her mouth to say something right then, she wasn't sure that she wouldn't say something she would immediately regret.

She didn't want to come across as wanton or anything remotely like a prostitute. She was supposed to be playing the part of a celibate escort, after all. The moment was so pure and so sweet that she didn't want to ruin it by saying anything crass, even if it was exactly what she wanted him to do to her.

"Is this all right?" Heath asked. His voice was low, and she sensed the tight leash of control that he had on his need. Even now, he was concerned for her and wanted to make sure that she was completely with him.

His gentleman-like behavior made her want him all the more.

"Yes," she said softly.

"I'm not crossing any boundaries you don't want me to cross?"

She couldn't help but sigh with a low chuckle. Boundaries. It was something that they had talked about in a teasing fashion multiple times during their dinner. Every time one of them would get too close to an answer that would give away too much personal information, they'd say the buzzword "boundaries."

The thing was, they both understood the score if things continued down this path. It was a one-night thing.

Heath had hired Kassy to make sure that he looked good in front of his business associates. After Heath had canceled his business dinner, she thought for sure he'd disappear. But he hadn't. He wanted her, and it didn't matter if he called her Kassy or Cupcake. The woman he wanted was Sylvie Jones.

CHAPTER FIVE

IF THIS WAS A ONE-NIGHT THING, SYLVIE was going to make it the best night of her life. No more boundaries, at least in a physical sense.

Sylvie turned and wrapped her arms around Heath's neck. She stared up at him, and she could feel the intensity of his gaze on her face, searching in the dim light.

"What do you say we push those boundaries a little bit further?" she asked in a throaty whisper.

This seemed to be exactly the right thing to say to spring Heath into action. His hands roved everywhere all at once, and she delighted in the feeling of his hands exploring her body. He whispered how much he loved the ampleness of her curves even as his lips and tongue traced the lines of her neck.

When his mouth finally settled on hers, she felt as if she was being kissed for the first time in her entire life. The kiss set ablaze every fiber of her being. She knew that he felt it too judging by the hardness that she felt against her belly. It stoked the fire inside her core. She wanted him. She wanted every part of him.

Heath pushed her back against the glass, and the chill of the hard surface didn't stand a chance against the rising heat in Sylvie's blood. She felt like she was wearing too many clothes, despite the fact the champagne dress that had initially drawn his attention to her, was tight and fit her body like a glove.

Heath seemed to have the same idea about her wearing too much. He grabbed hold of the zipper on the back of her dress and pulled it down, even as his other hand tugged the hem of her dress up towards her waist.

She pulled at the buttons of his shirt to get them undone as quickly as possible. It was the craziest thing. She had just met him, and yet she felt as if she had known him forever. She didn't question the feeling, the rightness of touching him and exploring his body.

Sylvie intuitively knew that not everything in life made complete sense. You made the best decision you could with the information you had in the moment. And in this moment, she just knew that this was right, and she wasn't a person to argue with that.

Heath made short work of the lace panties underneath her skirt. Normally, she would be embarrassed about such a thing, but Heath seemed to enjoy luxuriously running his hands across her rounded thighs and kneading her bottom.

He murmured his approval at the softness of her skin. She leaned her head back and enjoyed the sensations that rolled through her body. When he fell to his knees in front of her, she wondered what was going to come next.

Sylvie gasped when Heath grabbed the back of one of her knees and hauled it up to hook it over his shoulder. She knew that she was exposed to him in the most vulnerable way possible, but she barely had any time to think about that before his mouth found her most intimate of places at the apex of her thighs.

She moaned in heady pleasure as his expert tongue delved between her folds and found that sensitive spot that drove her wild.

It wouldn't take much more to push her over the edge. Surely, he could sense that. In a way, she'd been on the verge of a mind-blowing orgasm ever since meeting him.

When his fingers joined his mouth between her legs, the pleasure began to spin out of control. Heath had created a firecracker of need inside of her that threatened to blow. She needed a release, and before she even completed that thought, the climax exploded inside her.

She didn't recognize the sounds that were coming out of her mouth, and they echoed in her ears, driving her wild. Then Heath picked her up as if she were nothing more than a rag doll, and they crossed the room with her legs wrapped around his hips.

Heath strode into the bedroom and gently tossed her onto the bed on her back. She stared up at him, aftershocks still tingling through her system.

He had a look of satisfaction on his face. "I want to see that again."

Sylvie knew she should be embarrassed, but she wasn't, especially when she knew it wasn't over yet. She couldn't help but stretch as she watched his admiring look drift down over her half-naked body. She sat up, and he reached behind her to fully undo the zipper of her dress, and he whipped the dress off her body, tossing it across the room in triumph like the spoils of a battle.

"I've been admiring these curves all night long," he said as his hands roamed up and down her body in appreciation.

His hands settled on her breasts as he squeezed them gently, and she arched her back offering them up to him. It had been too long since a man had made her feel like this. Hell, a man had *never* made her feel like this. Sylvie grew more anxious now. She wanted to have all of him.

Heath joined her on the bed. His kiss was gentle, but then his fingers tightened on her hips. She knew the tight control he had displayed, so far, was fraying.

She scratched her nails down his back, setting loose something animal-like inside of him that excited her. When he climbed between her legs, she was ready for him.

"Now, Heath," she said, her voice husky with desire.

He needed no more invitation.

He drove into her in a slick and forceful entry. Sylvie saw stars. As he moved inside her, the only thing she could think was that this was exactly the kind of stuff that dreams were made of.

She was ready to burst again before long. His passionate, hard thrusts had her on the verge in record time, and she dug her nails into his shoulder to urge him on, ever faster and harder.

She knew the moment that Heath joined her in her climax, his moans of ecstasy joining hers in a perfect harmony.

She wrapped her legs around his waist drawing him as close to her as possible. He let out a low groan when, at last, it was over. Then he fell forward on top of her. She couldn't help but think there was nothing quite like the weight of a man on her body; this man, in particular. Though he was huge, his weight on her could never be too much.

A few minutes later, Heath propped himself up on his elbows. He planted small kisses on her neck and around her mouth. She felt him stiffening inside of her again already, and a small smile tugged at the corner of her mouth.

"How about we play another game?" Heath asked.

"What did you have in mind?" Sylvie sighed as his lips found her nipples.

"For every orgasm I give you, you scream my name. If we hit ten, you have to prank call the front desk of the hotel with whatever I tell you to say, no matter how embarrassing."

That such a man had a prankster side was incredibly appealing to Sylvie. Her laugh turned into a low moan as his fingers found that sensitive ridge between her thighs again.

"You're on," she purred.

If she had ten orgasms before the morning, she didn't think there was much she wouldn't do for him.

CHAPTER SIX

HEATH SAT AT THE BREAKFAST TABLE feeling satisfied about the extent of the breakfast spread in front of him. He didn't know what Kassy liked to eat, so he had ordered one of nearly everything on the menu. The wanton decadence of the display pleased him. It was fitting after the night he'd just had.

He glanced toward the bedroom and wondered what Kassy could be doing in the bathroom. She'd been in there a long time, long enough that he had been able to order room service and have it delivered while he waited. He grumped and wondered what *did* women do in bathrooms that took so damned long, *anyway*?

He smiled at himself. Truth was, he missed her. He wanted her out here so he could feed her and then maybe undo all the primping she was undoubtedly doing in the bathroom right then.

A disconcerting thought crossed his mind. He hoped that she didn't regret what had happened in the night. For his part, he was entranced with her.

He loved that she seemed game for whatever crazy scheme he came up with. The early morning prank call to the front desk using a dramatic fake accent had been especially amusing, but she had to pay up on their bet.

Heath couldn't help but remember what he thought the first moment he laid eyes on her. He had thought "I'm going to marry this girl." Now he was starting to wonder if maybe, just maybe, there might have been something more to that than silly fancy. Perhaps the universe was trying to tell him something.

Kassy had surprised him at dinner with her sense of humor and her silly game of "Private Yet Public." He had learned enough about her to make him sure he wanted to know more. He wanted to get very specific now, especially after what happened between them during the night.

In particular, he wanted to know the specifics surrounding her being an employee of an escort service. He figured she was probably a graduate student at one of the local universities putting herself through college by being an escort.

If they went out again, and he planned on it, he wanted to make sure that she didn't have to subject herself to that kind of work anymore. He knew the escort service carefully screened all clients, but there was always a risk. It was one of many things he wanted to talk to her about before he left Chicago.

The bathroom door opened, and Heath looked up expectantly. What he saw surprised him. He had awoken with a slightly tousled, wide-eyed, sexy-as-hell woman in his arms. He loved it.

Kassy, on the other hand, had been mortified. She'd scampered out of bed and grabbed her clothes up before making a mad dash into the bathroom, saying something about needing to get cleaned up.

He thought, at the time, that she wanted to brush her teeth or something like that; women were peculiar about those kinds of things. He had never imagined that she would reappear fully dressed and seemingly ready to run out the door. She looked stunningly beautiful, but she was wearing far too many clothes again.

She wasn't going to leave, was she?

"I wasn't sure what you might like," he said as he held up the bowl of dressed fruit and waved at some Eggs Benedict. "So I tried to cover all the options."

She smiled hesitantly and shook her head slowly.

"I didn't expect us to eat it all," he soldiered on. "I was thinking that we might save some for later. I've already devised a new game for the leftovers if you're interested. That is, assuming you don't have anywhere to be today."

Kassy looked uncertain. Heath felt an unaccustomed pang of dread grow in his stomach.

He thought that they'd had a great time together, and he wasn't ready for it to end yet. Now, it looked as if there was something else going on that he hadn't anticipated. She might want to leave.

Since when did women want to leave Heath's bed before he was ready to let them go? He'd had to work up all sorts of tricks over the years to get them out, most of them involving vague, fake promises of getting together at some vague, hazy future date.

"You'll have to eat those yourself," Kassy said. "I've got to get out of here. The agency is gonna be wondering where I am if I don't check in soon."

Damn, she did want to leave. Figured. He was irked. Heath wasn't used to not having complete control of a situation.

He raised an eyebrow. "Does this kind of overnight thing happen often?"

Kassy's expression darkened. "I told you I'm not a whore. This has never happened to me before."

He realized quickly that he'd let his annoyance get the better of him. He stood and tried to reach out for her, but she slipped away.

"I'm sorry," he said. "I didn't mean to offend you, and I didn't mean it that way. I just thought that maybe you thought that I wanted what others might, and I don't know …" God, he was rambling. He had to get a grip. "I thought we had a great time last night, and I'd love to see you again the next time I'm in town."

She wasn't looking on him with any greater favor.

"My flight isn't until tonight," he continued. "And since my business here in Chicago got canceled, my day is open. How about we spend it together? Maybe you can show me around. I haven't played a tourist here in years."

Kassy pulled the corner of her lip into her mouth and seemed to be biting down on it hard. It made him want to reach over and kiss her silly.

"We talked about boundaries remember? This was just a one-night thing. You're from out of town, and I'm sure you're not going to be here for business again anytime soon. And I have a life, you know, commitments and so on."

Heath was surprised by her reaction. It made him concerned that he had completely misjudged the situation. "I come to Chicago on business quite a bit. You'd be surprised. C'mon, Kassy. You know you want to spend the day with me." Heath pulled out his most charming smile.

Kassy looked hesitant again. Then it seemed as if her back straightened. She had made up her mind about something, and Heath sensed that regardless of whether he wanted to know her decision or not, Kassy was the kind of girl who would tell it to him straight.

"Look, I had a really great time last night. I did," she said. "But whatever else you're thinking could happen between us just wouldn't work because we're from two different worlds. I'm an escort, and you're a rich guy. This isn't *Pretty Woman*, you know. This is real life."

Heath wasn't about to take that for an answer. It made no sense to him. If he liked her and she liked him, there was a way to make it work.

Heath used his best negotiating tone of voice, patient, metered, rich, and understanding. "I know this whole thing has pushed you outside of your comfort zone, Kassy, and it's probably because you're afraid you'll get in trouble with your employer because of last night. Honestly, I hate the idea of a woman like you having to do work like this at all. I'll give you the funds to help you pay for school or whatever else you need the money for so you don't have to do this kind of work anymore. I want to help you, truly."

She didn't seem impressed at all with his negotiating skills. "So even though I told you I'm not a whore and that I don't take money for sex, you're going to treat me like one anyway?" Kassy's hands settled on her generous, delectable hips. Standoff.

This discussion was going downhill quickly.

"That's not what I meant at all. I'm sorry. This is coming out all wrong. I want to be your benefactor," he said in a rush.

He picked up a stack of hundred dollar bills that he'd had the hotel manager deliver with breakfast. He held the gold-clipped bundle out to

Kassy. "Here. Take this. I just want to help you get ahead any way I can."

Heath moved toward her, but she stepped backward, eyeing the money like it had fangs. Heath paused and put up his hands in a conciliatory gesture. "It's just some money. It won't bite you. Use it to get a new apartment. Clothes. Whatever you want. It doesn't have to be school, if that's not your thing. What is your thing, anyway?"

"Ohhhh, I get it," she said, giving Heath a short-lived glimmer of hope.

It was a very short-lived glimmer.

"So you want to be my sugar daddy," she said, her fine brows bunching. "And what would that make me? Not a whore. I'd be a gold digger now. That's just great. Not much of a step up. How about a kept woman? Maybe I could be a kept woman? Is that what you're thinking?"

Heath ran his hand through his hair. Everything had gone from bad to worse. He dropped the cash on the table. "You're misunderstanding me, dammit. I'm trying to do a nice thing here."

She stared at him, her sweet lips slightly open, her eyes wide. "You don't have any idea what's wrong with any of this, do you?"

"I guess not."

She looked like she was going to say more, but then she took a deep breath and let it out in a lengthy, long-suffering sigh. "I don't know how a man gets to be in your position in the world and be so … so … unaware."

Heath was shocked. He wasn't unaware. He was trying to be a nice guy. What was unaware about that? "Can we just start over, maybe? You could go back in the bathroom and do some more of whatever it was you were doing. Then you can come out and I won't offer you money this time. How's that?"

He could see she didn't want to, but she smiled all the same. His gut clenched. Every time that woman smiled the world became a better place.

"Fine," she said. "But I'm not going back into the bathroom. I really do need to leave."

"Okay, if that's how it is. I'm almost afraid to ask, but could I, at least, have your phone number?"

"You already have my number, silly," Kassy said.

She used a cool tone that made him suspect she was avoiding the topic. Then he realized what she meant. Of course, he had the number for the escort agency. Cold.

He had wanted her personal number, despite the fact that they had said all along that there was not going to be anything personal about this transaction. The Private Yet Public game. That was coming back to bite him in the ass in a big way.

"Okay, I'm getting the hint," he said. "I'm coming on too strong, and you're uncomfortable. You probably have something already planned for today that I'm interfering with, and you don't want to tell me what it is because it would give something away about you. I get it, and it's okay. At least, let me walk you out."

He didn't want to let her go yet, but he couldn't hold her in the suite. He was starting to get concerned that he wasn't going to be able to see her again.

Kassy finally looked at him with an open expression. "Okay, you can walk me downstairs if you want."

He felt his heart beating hard against his rib cage. At least, he'd have a few more minutes to convince her to tell him how he could contact her again, outside of the escort service. This was all ... disconcerting.

Heath wasn't used to losing something he wanted. He had built his company through a series of mergers and acquisitions that were far more complex than the situation in front of him. And yet, he hadn't had a moment's control of the current conversation since Kassy had left their warm bed.

He'd turn it around, though. He'd tackled harder, tougher foes in business. Of course, he was going to be able to work this out. He just had to find the right lever for the negotiation.

"Great," he said. "Hang on just a second, I'll be right back." He gestured at his robe. "I just need to put some clothes on."

He probably set a new world record for getting dressed. All he could think about was what he was going to say to Kassy to convince her to see things his way. This wasn't a one-night thing for him. Not anymore. Maybe it never had been and he'd just been too stupid to realize it.

Fully clothed, he re-entered the living room and immediately discovered he'd made a fatal miscalculation.

The room was empty.

CHAPTER SEVEN

HEATH MADE HIS WAY OVER TO THE door and caught sight of a handwritten note sitting on the table beside it. The bundle of money rested beside it.

> *I figured out what you do. You show girls a good time.*
> *I have to admit — you are quite the expert.*
> *Thanks. Kassy*

Heath would have laughed at her witty implication if he weren't so shocked. She'd slipped out on him. What did it mean?

Surely she wasn't going to turn her back on what happened between them last night. There had been a real connection between them, something she couldn't possibly ignore.

He was ready to chase after her when his phone rang. Heath recognized the number on the screen. It was the escort agency. His heart did a little flip.

He answered the call. "Hello?"

"Mr. Collins, this is Maggie from Expert Escorts. We're so sorry about what happened last night. We will, of course, give you a full refund for the error."

He scowled. "What are you talking about? A refund for what error?"

Was it possible they knew that Kassy had slept with him? That was definitely against the rules. He hadn't intended to get her in trouble.

"Kassy was in an accident last night," Maggie said. "It was completely unavoidable. We didn't find out until this morning that she had been admitted to the hospital. That's the reason that we didn't contact you sooner. We're so sorry for this oversight, Mr. Collins."

"Is she okay?" he asked, stupidly responding while he tried to get his head around what Maggie was saying.

"Oh, the doctors believe she'll make a full recovery. You're so kind for asking."

"Yes, uh … well …"

"Mr. Collins, you are absolutely one of our most respected customers. I apologize profusely for any inconvenience that this may have caused you. If you'll give us another chance, your companion during your next trip to Chicago is on us."

Heath assured her he was fine and ended the call. He stared at the phone dumbly.

If the woman he had spent the night with wasn't from the escort agency, then who the hell was she?

He realized now that he truly was letting Kassy, or whatever her real name was, slip through his fingers. She'd left and he had no idea who she was.

He had to catch her.

He bolted out of the room for the elevator. Heath slammed his fingers against the elevator call button. He cursed the entire time he waited. How could he have been so blind?

"Kassy" had been so engaging and funny and smart. She was totally unlike all of the other dates that he'd ever hired from the escort agency. From any agency. Of course, she wasn't an escort. But why didn't she tell him the truth?

He frantically got into the elevator as soon as it got there and then moaned in frustration every time it stopped all the way down to the ground floor. He darted ahead of the people in front of him as he ran to the hotel entrance looking anxiously from side to side for the woman that he only knew as Kassy.

The doorman acknowledged Heath as soon as he stepped onto the sidewalk. "Is there something I can help you with, Mr. Collins?"

"There was a woman who was just here. She was wearing a champagne colored dress. I don't know about her coat. Damn. She may have checked it last night. I'd say she's late twenties. Beautiful. Gorgeous, big brown eyes, killer smile. Did you see which way she went?"

"I have seen her, Sir. I just whistled over a taxi for her," the doorman said. "I didn't overhear where she said she was going, though. I'm very sorry."

Heath stood there in shock.

Kassy was gone. Just like that, disappeared, consumed in the mass of people streaming through the great city.

Gone.

After a few moments, he realized he undoubtedly looked like a buffoon standing there in the middle of the sidewalk with his mouth hanging open. He made his way back into the hotel wondering what he was going to do.

He was just entering his room when it came to him. He was Heath Collins.

He was filthy rich and had practically unlimited resources at his disposal. One little woman shouldn't be that hard to find.

He started to walk more confidently as he headed to the wall of windows overlooking the city. As his gaze swept over all the buildings and people, he saw "Kassy" in his mind's eye.

No matter where she was off to, no matter where she ended up, he would find her. And then he would have her.

This transaction and their game weren't over yet, not by a long shot.

IT WAS HARD FOR HEATH TO BELIEVE that it had been nearly a year since he'd last seen the mystery woman, Kassy, in Chicago. He sat in his office overlooking downtown Seattle and sighed. It was a typical overcast, rainy, late January afternoon.

It was even cooler this year than years past, and everyone was complaining about it. It had been over a week since the sun had last peeked through the clouds, but the weather matched Heath's mood perfectly.

He should have been on top of the world. He was on the cusp of the largest acquisition in his company's history and was being heralded across the world by financial analysts and industry experts as being one of the savviest businessmen in the country. As soon as this deal closed, he would be bona fide filthy rich.

A year ago, when he canceled the business dinner in Chicago to spend time with Kassy, the executives at Yurovize thought that he was possibly pulling out of the deal. It had started a flurry of frantic emails and urgent conference calls that Heath had leveraged to his full advantage.

In the end, when he finally did sit down to meet with the Yurovize team in person, he had been able to negotiate a far better purchase price than expected. His financial future was set. And he owed it all to Kassy. Or whatever the hell her name actually was. Not-Kassy.

He'd soon have more money than he would ever know what to do with. It was unsettling to know that despite this impossible wealth and power, he couldn't find the one thing that he wanted most in the world.

It was simple. He just wanted to know the woman's name. He figured the least he could do was send her a thank you note.

Dozens of times he'd written the note in his head: Dear Not-Kassy, Thanks for the best night of my life, and for making me a billionaire. Best wishes for the future to you and yours. Sincerely, Heath Collins.

That night with her had taken on the aura of a dream. He often wondered if the time that they'd spent together was as perfect as he remembered, or if time had idealized it, created a perfect fantasy out of what was actually merely satisfactory.

Her face was burned into his memory, and he was certain he would recognize her laughter anywhere. He could still feel her curvy body writhing beneath him when he entered her, and he could still hear her calling out his name as he brought her to the heights of ecstasy.

But all those memories added up to nothing in the bigger picture. He didn't have her real name. Without it, he would never be able to find her.

It hadn't been for a lack of trying. His accounting team was mortified at the amount of money he had thrown at a variety of private investigators to try to find out who the mystery woman was.

He had only bare-bones facts to guide them, her approximate age, height, weight, and body type. He'd paid dearly for a member of the hotel's security staff to obtain several grainy photos from the hotel's cameras. But the quality was so poor that the still shots were of no use for identification purposes.

The only other clues he had were the generic things she'd told him throughout the course of their silly game at dinner. He had thought at the time, it was amusing to hear how different they were from each other; but later, her disappearance made everything she told him that much more important.

She came from a big family and had grown up with a myriad of cousins to play with, unlike Heath. Her parents were divorced. Heath's were still married. She said she'd always aspired to own her own business, but she wouldn't tell him what kind. Heath had admitted he was a CEO, but he hadn't told her what his company did because of their ongoing bet.

In her spare time, Not-Kassy loved reading fashion magazines and keeping up with current fashion trends. His personal assistant did all of his shopping. She loved her parents. He tolerated his. She had grown up in a small town while he had grown up in the city.

It seemed at every turn, they were opposites, and yet, Heath had never felt so perfectly in tune with a person as he did with her. And that's why he had been dead set on finding her. He didn't care how much it cost.

All of the little things he did know, when combined, should have been enough to provide a reasonable profile to assist in finding her. Chicago was a big city, but it wasn't that big. He had scoured the city and its environs and still could not find her. Every lead ran straight into a dead end.

The most recent private investigator had kicked his case file back to him within minutes of receiving it. He said he knew that Heath had already hired all of his competitors, and they had all failed to find what Heath sought.

In the process of conducting search after fruitless search, Heath's rants had become legendary in PI circles. So now, no PI anywhere in or around Chicago wanted anything to do with him for any amount of money. Heath was fresh out of options.

It had been a year, and Heath sensed that he'd reached the end of the proverbial road. He was going to have to give the search up and do something he never did.

He was going to have to admit defeat.

She was gone from his world forever. That idea gnawed at his insides, but there was nothing to be done about it.

He nursed a scotch on the rocks from his private collection as he gazed out the window. He didn't break into the expensive liquor very often. Usually, it was just for celebrations. But the mood in his office that day felt more like a funeral.

He simply had to wrap his brain around the fact that he was never going to find Not-Kassy. He wasn't a man who easily admitted failure, but this time, one curvy, sexy woman had gotten the better of him. If it were a game, she'd have won hands down.

He glanced at the stack of paperwork on his desk. He was going to have to sign the papers on the acquisition soon to make it official, and for the first time in his life, the idea brought him no joy. His victory tasted like sawdust in his mouth.

He swept the documents into his briefcase. It was the biggest deal of his life, and he had to make sure he read and understood every word. They weren't the kinds of documents to sign when he was distracted.

He'd take them home and try again tonight after a long, hard workout. He wanted to have a clear head.

He stopped by his assistant, Jamie's, desk on the way out. It was late, and he was surprised that she was still there. Jamie looked up as he approached her, and he could tell that she had probably just closed her browser window given the quick click of the mouse.

He didn't care if she was surfing the internet at work. Jamie was the best assistant he had ever had, and she got things done. He didn't think of his employees as mindless robots. He understood that they had lives outside of work, even if he didn't.

"Hey, Jamie. Can you let the Yurovize contacts know that I'll be signing the contracts tonight? I plan to have the paperwork over to their lawyers in the morning. We should be good to go then, and the acquisition should be final in less than a week."

"Will do, Mr. Collins. You finally heading out?" Jamie asked.

"Yeah, I think after this deal is done, I'm finally going to take that vacation everyone's been bugging me about."

Jamie looked surprised. Heath was surprised that he'd said it, too, and hadn't realized he'd been thinking about it. How long had it been since he'd taken time off? Ten years?

He'd been entirely focused on building his business empire and increasing the size of his bank account. The deal with Yurovize ensured that vision had finally been achieved, but where had it left him? With a gaping hole where a relationship could be.

Hell, when he stopped and thought about it, he could have even had a kid or two by now. Not that he'd ever envisioned himself being a family man. Undoubtedly, he would be a terrible parent since his own had set such a poor example for him.

"Well, you just let me know where you want to go, and I'll book it right now," Jamie said. "I'm assuming money is no object, so you should spoil yourself. You've earned it."

"How about Fiji?" Heath was being facetious. He had read somewhere that Fiji was one of the most expensive places in the world, at certain exclusive resorts. The scotch was settling in and had given him a warm and relaxed feeling that he welcomed.

He peered over Jamie's shoulder as she opened up her Internet browser again. He saw that she was on an unusual-looking page that appeared to have a list of recipes.

He knew Jamie enjoyed cooking and considered it a serious hobby. She joked about trying to audition to compete on reality TV shows. He remembered her briefly mentioning something about entering an online recipe contest a while back.

She had been really excited about it, and he felt like a jerk for not asking her about it sooner. "Whatever happened with that recipe contest you entered?" he asked.

Jamie looked up at him and smiled widely. "Funny you should ask. I didn't make first place, but I did take third. I won a hundred dollars. My picture's on the site and everything. Here, let me show you."

Jamie's fingers skimmed across the keyboard as she entered a URL in the browser, and it popped open a new page.

At the top of the page was a bold headline announcing the winners of Grandma Ethel's Favorite Down-Home Recipe Contest. Heath's eye was drawn down to a middle-aged, paunchy man holding a pie. First place. He scanned down to see Jamie's photo.

He didn't make it past second place. He forgot to breathe.

Jamie started chattering about some special ingredient that she added to her recipe to give it its unique flavor twist, but he wasn't listening to her.

He zeroed in on the photo of the second place winner. It was her.

The woman who'd been haunting his dreams for nearly a year. She was real and every bit as beautiful as he remembered. She was smiling in the photo and he wanted to reach into the picture and stroke her downy cheek. Not-Kassy. Finally.

No, wait. Her real name was bolded under the photo. If eyes could stumble, his would have done so as he sought to find what he'd been longing to discover for months.

Sylvie Jones.

He rolled the name around in his brain, tasted it on his lips. Sylvie Jones. Sylvie.

It was perfect. Beautiful. It seemed only right that she should be named Sylvie.

He didn't realize he had said her name out loud until Jamie gave a small sigh.

"I know, right? Isn't she just the cutest thing? And those babies! I could squeeze those chubby cheeks and eat them right up!" Jamie exclaimed. "I don't even mind that I lost to her."

Heath realized then that Sylvie held a pair of bundles in her arms. He blinked, then wiped his eyes before he squinted at the picture again.

She held two small babies in blue blankets. Babies. Small babies. His mind blanked.

It took a few moments before he realized that Jamie was still talking.

"Do you see that she placed for a take-out Chinese casserole? How brilliant is that? Second place was five hundred bucks. I should've thought of something like that. Genius idea. Way better than Mr. Puffy's pie that got first. I mean, a mincemeat pie? Who cares? But I'd love to try out that Chinese concoction."

Jamie rambled on, but Heath stopped listening again.

He read the rest of the caption:

Sylvie Jones and her three-month-old twin boys, Quentyn and Jadyn, from Zeke's Bend.

He felt as if his world went in and out of focus, and he wondered for a moment if he were going to lose his footing.

"Jamie," he said, his voice sounding distant even to himself, "these pictures. When were they taken?"

"Oh, well, I sent mine in after they told me I'd won third. They asked for a recent photo, so I took a new one and sent it in."

"When?"

"Just a few days ago. No more than a week," she answered. "Why do you want—"

"When do you think the other winners sent theirs in?"

Jamie gave him a sideways look. "I have no idea. How could I?"

"Right, right. So you wouldn't know if theirs are recent, too."

"Nooo," she said, her expression increasingly concerned. "I wouldn't know."

Heath was a whiz with numbers, always had been. The math took less than three seconds to calculate. Three-month-old twin boys, and he had last seen Sylvie a week or so shy of a year ago.

It couldn't be.

But the numbers added up.

Jamie stood up abruptly and put her hand on his shoulder. "Mr. Collins, are you feeling okay? You look a little pale. Maybe going somewhere you could get a tan would be a good idea. Gosh, I'm babbling. I'm sorry. It's just I don't know what to do. Is something wrong?"

Heath didn't have the wherewithal to say anything other than the truth. "Damned if I know."

CHAPTER EIGHT

IT WAS THE END OF AN EXCRUCIATINGLY long workday at Shear Stylin', and Sylvie was beat. She and her business partner, and aunt, Meg Jones, were cleaning up the shop. Sylvie had bought the business and the building it was located in from her cousin, Phae Holmes. It had been a dream come true when it happened.

Sylvie finally owned a business that was all hers, and she knew she was good at it. She enjoyed making the women in Zeke's Bend feel stylish and attractive, plus she got to stay up-to-date on all the latest town gossip.

Of course, she was always pretty sure she was on the verge of going broke. Phae, who used to keep the books for them, teased her that it wasn't true, but Sylvie thought Phae might be holding out the bad news because of how much she loved Sylvie.

She did admit that business had been booming. She and Meg had a similar sense of fashion and style and complimented each other well, which meant they were starting to be in high demand around Zeke's Bend. They even had a few regular customers coming in from Rollinsburg, the larger city nearby.

It was critical that Sylvie make a good living because she was a single mom now. Profits meant that she could provide for her boys without too much worry. But it also meant that her second job of being a mom started the moment her first job ended each day.

She wouldn't change it for all the world, though. Her baby boys, Quentyn and Jadyn, were the lights of her life. She couldn't believe how much her life had changed when her twins came into it, and as crazy as everything could get at times, all the change was for the better.

"Am I going to see those beautiful bouncing baby boys before I go home today?" Meg asked as she swept some hair trimmings into her dustpan. "We need to set up a playdate for them soon."

"You know they're still too young for a playdate," Sylvie said with a laugh. "Your son looks at them and can't figure out why they don't sit up and play with him."

"Who said it was a playdate for the kids? I'm talking about a playdate for their mommas," Meg said with a wink. "We could bake something delicious. I know. You could make me that casserole you won all that money for."

"Oh God, don't talk about that contest. Or Take Out Chinese casserole. You know what a hot topic it's become. Aunt Chelly and Aunt Charmaine are now complaining to everyone who'll listen that it was their idea."

Meg laughed. "What does your momma say?"

"You know her. She gets in their faces and scares them half to death and then they go running off to Aunt Elfleda, and then there's all sorts of hell to pay." Sylvie sighed. "I recognize that the universe is a wild and wooly place, but damn, I'd like to win five hundred bucks and not be thrown into the middle of a family feud because of it."

"You know I'm on your side," Meg said. "And I'll make Leon be on your side, too. He has to obey me or face my wifely wrath."

Sylvie snorted. "Have him rub his rabbit's foot for me and ask that all this craziness goes away."

"Nah. Can't do that. He'd take it to mean I put stock in his superstitious nonsense, then I'd never get any peace. I'd have to avoid black cats, throw salt over my shoulder if I do something or other, turn around fifty times if I open an umbrella, do a country line dance if I see a brown beetle."

Sylvie laughed. "You've got some stuff in there I've never heard of."

"And not a bit of it any sillier than what that man of mine believes."

"And you love him for it."

Meg waved a hand dismissively. "Somebody's got to do it."

Sylvie smiled, knowing well that her Aunt Meg was crazy about her Uncle Leon. "Tell you what. Let's make a plan for a night next week. I'll bring the stupid casserole."

"Yay. That sounds wonderful. I'll make some egg rolls to go with it."

"They're already in the casserole."

Meg eyed her askance. "Seriously?"

"Yep."

"That's … interesting. What else is in it?"

"You'll find out."

Sylvie thought she heard her aunt mumble, "I'm not sure I want to." Sylvie loved her family's honesty.

She also appreciated how much her family supported her and made sure she got out of the house now that she had twins taking up all her spare time. She sensed, though, that part of the reason was that they felt sorry for her.

Sylvie wasn't all that fond of people feeling sorry for her, and they were wrong to do it. She, herself, was nothing but thankful to have her children, and mostly didn't mind that they took up all her time.

"Momma should be here any minute with the boys," she said, perking up at the thought.

She knew her voice sounded exhausted. If she could, she would quit her job and stay at home with the boys full-time, never mind how much she loved running her business.

The twins were only three months old, and they were changing every single day. She loved to see how their little personalities were emerging, and she was afraid that she was going to miss something significant because she was at work.

Outside, they were identical, but inside, they were very different.

Quentyn was the serious one. When he had come into the world, she had almost been afraid that there was something wrong with him. He had done nothing but study the doctors and nurses and observe his new surroundings as if he needed to take it all in before he passed judgment. Sylvie called him her old soul.

Jadyn was the complete opposite of his twin brother. He came into the world with a lusty cry, and he was happy and bubbly almost all the time. He had smiles for her every time he saw her.

She couldn't help but think how close the twins would be as they grew up together. She was intrigued with their very twin-ness, seeing them as almost mystical in their connection. To Sylvie, they were further proof that the universe was a deep and mysterious place. Her gratitude knew no bounds.

She was incredibly grateful for her family, too. So many of them stepped up to help her when she found out she was pregnant. It had been a true blessing, and she knew she wouldn't have been able to get by without them.

Still, she heard the gossip around town. Everyone thought it was terrible that Alan, the twins' presumed father, wasn't involved in his children's lives or helping Sylvie out in any way, financial or otherwise.

When Sylvie walked down the street, she knew people looked at her and gossiped behind her back. It was something she had to accept, living in a small town, but sometimes, it grated on her nerves. She tried not to let it mar an otherwise wonderful experience.

She personally didn't want Alan involved. In fact, she didn't want any part of him in her life, in any way whatsoever. Since she broke up with him in Chicago, her opinion of him hadn't wavered. Alan was not a good person, and she didn't want him near her babies.

The truth was, though, and it was the deepest secret she'd ever held in her life, she wasn't sure that Alan was the father of her children.

The truth was, they could be Heath's, the exquisite result of what was undoubtedly the best night of her life.

There was a beauty in that thought that appealed to Sylvie's nature. Her twins were so beautiful and perfect; they had to come from a special moment, didn't they?

In all ways, she hoped they were Heath's. Every time she looked at them, when Jadyn would smile or Quentin would look at her with a faint frown as if he wasn't sure what to think, she recognized the handsome man she met a year ago.

Oh yes, she remembered him well. It didn't matter that it had been a one-night thing. Her memory of their hours together was still vivid, as if it happened last week and not nearly a year ago.

Sylvie understood, however, that no matter how much she wanted to believe fate brought them together, and that Heath was the father of her children, she couldn't be positive. Wishes weren't proof, and DNA didn't care about fate.

As for doing a paternity test, it was out of the question since she had no access to Heath or Alan's DNA. The only thing she actually could do was move on, let the gossips do their worst, and accept that she'd likely never know the truth.

So she focused on her new life and her little boys, and she was content. At least, that's what she tried to be.

The bell above the front door tinkled, announcing a new arrival. Sylvie's cousin and best friend, Neesa, bounced into the shop.

"Where are those babies?" Neesa said with an excited squeal as she clapped her hands together. "I haven't seen them in three days! They've probably grown a foot by now."

Neesa loved kids. She continually begged to babysit for Sylvie, which Sylvie would gladly have taken her up on more often if Sylvie had more of a social life. But she didn't. She knew, though, if she wanted to run over to Rollinsburg to do some shopping or get a few extra hours of shut-eye on a Sunday morning, Neesa was always there for her.

Sylvie chuckled and repeated what she had just told Meg. "Momma should be here with them any minute. They might be growing fast, but it's not that fast."

"Momma Jones is hoarding them! I'm going to give her a piece of my mind." Neesa crossed her arms over her chest in fake outrage.

Momma Jones was what all her cousins called Sylvie's mother, Sachet, even though her mother had married Eli Ford years ago. To everyone in town, Sachet would always be a Jones. Luckily, Eli didn't seem to mind. He was an easy-going type, a good man, unlike Sylvie's own father.

Neesa plopped into one of the stylist chairs and spun it around in a lazy circle. "I was thinking that you might want to go out and get a drink with friends tonight. I'd be happy to watch the kids for you."

"Go out with who? Almost all my friends are presently here in this room, except Phae," Sylvie said as she finished cleaning up her station. "And Phae can't go drinking, not in her condition."

"You need to start dating again, Sylvie," Neesa said. "Geez, get with the internet age. I'll help you come up with the perfect dating profile. I've found a few dates on that newest site, DatingBlues.com. It wouldn't hurt you to show some interest in the opposite sex again. The boys need a male role model in their lives."

Sylvie snorted. "Between my brother, my stepfather, and all our cousins, the boys have plenty of role models all over town. They need me at home with them. That's where I belong. Besides, who in their right mind would name a dating website DatingBlues? Sounds like all you can hope to find there are losers and broken hearts."

Sylvie knew she shouldn't make fun of Neesa's suggestion. It wasn't easy being a single gal in Zeke's Bend and the situation was made much harder when you were a Jones and related to half the male population. She had to grudgingly admit that at least Neesa was putting herself out there. Sylvie just couldn't bring herself to even think about dating. There was just no time for it. And besides, what single young man would look twice at her once he found out she had twin infants?

Anyway, the only thing she wanted to do every night was crawl into bed and snuggle with her boys. She wanted to enjoy that while they were still young enough not to push her away. The thought of adding anyone else to the mix felt too hard. Besides, she didn't need a man in her life to take care of anything.

Sylvie had it covered.

CHAPTER NINE

"I'M OFF TO RESTOCK," MEG SAID, heading to the back room. "And quit being an ass about internet dating. Everyone does it."

"Like she knows. She's almost always been married for fifteen years," Sylvie mumbled, careful to make sure Meg didn't overhear.

"You're lucky she didn't hear that," Neesa said with a grin. "She'd kick your casserole all the way down the street."

Sylvie rolled her eyes. "Enough with the casserole. I wish to hell I'd never entered that contest."

The bell over the door jingled again, drawing their attention. To their surprise, their other best friend and cousin, Phae, walked through the door.

Phae, the former owner of the shop, sold it to Sylvie for a couple of good reasons. Other than the fact that she wasn't too interested in cutting hair for a living, she was a newlywed and recently announced that she and her husband Kent were expecting.

The whole family loved Kent and they all were excited for Phae. That included Sylvie. She loved seeing how happy Phae was these days and was thrilled that her boys would have a cousin to grow up with just like she had grown up with Neesa and Phae.

Some of her favorite memories of her childhood were sitting at her kitchen table, talking and laughing with her cousins while Momma stuffed them full to bursting with her homemade chocolate chip cookies.

"Thought I'd find you both here," Phae said with a wide smile.

Sylvie wasn't sure if Phae was even aware that she had put her hands on her belly and was absently rubbing it. It was one of the first overt signs of pregnancy, and one that Sylvie remembered fondly.

She had loved every minute of her pregnancy with the twins. Well, almost every minute, if you left out the morning sickness, the aching feet, the hurting back, the constant peeing, the ... yeah, so maybe she hadn't loved every minute, or even close to it.

Neesa looked forlornly at Phae's slightly rounded tummy. Phae was just finishing her first trimester and with her tall, athletic form, she barely even showed.

"I want a baby too," Neesa said in a familiar refrain.

"Oh, trust me, you don't want to go through any of this," Phae said. "It seems like Kent has to hold my hair back out of my face every time I turn around so I can throw up, and I'm so bloated I can't stand it. I can't keep anything down, even though I'm starving all the time. I look hideous. This is definitely no picnic."

Sylvie hid her smile behind her hand. Phae didn't know even half of what she was in for. It was all worth it, though.

Phae might complain that she felt unattractive, but her inner glow made her even prettier than ever. Her handsome husband fell all over himself to make sure she was comfortable and happy.

It was still odd for Sylvie to watch their interactions. Phae had always been the fiercely independent one of their trio, and then she had attracted a man who had finally softened her up; in a good way.

Sylvie wouldn't have expected Phae to be the first one of them to settle down either. Sylvie couldn't help but wonder if she'd change like that once she found *the one*, too ... if she ever found *the one*.

"I don't care that it's not a picnic," Neesa said. "You can't get something so wonderful for nothing, you know."

"The twins should be here any minute, Neesa. I would think spending this much time with them would take care of some of that baby craziness you've got going on in your head," Sylvie scoffed. "Enjoy the fact that you still get to sleep through the night uninterrupted. I'd kill for a full eight hours of sleep."

"Not a chance. They're sweet as can be, and you know it, Sylvie. Being around them just makes me want a baby more. I can't believe the two of you are going to be moms before me! Neither one of you even liked babysitting when we were kids," Neesa said.

That much was true. When anyone in the family had been on the lookout for a babysitter, Phae and Sylvie would conveniently find a way to make themselves scarce. But that was more because they knew that Neesa loved doing it.

She saw a shadow fall across the big bay front window of the shop. She recognized the hat before she even got a clear view of the man wearing it. "Oh no. I see we're about to get more company," she said with a sigh.

Although Sylvie sounded slightly snarky about it, secretly she loved having her family around. Even after the shop closed for the night, that didn't stop any of her relatives from stopping by and saying hello.

Case in point, another one of her cousins, James, walked through the door a minute later. James was the sheriff of Zeke's Bend. He could also always be counted on to act like an overprotective big brother to the three girls. It was a role he took seriously, sometimes too seriously.

"Evening ladies," James said with a tip of his hat.

Sylvie often thought it was a shame that James was still single. He was a great man, and fine looking, too. If he found a girl of his own to settle down with, she thought he might stop butting into her business. She loved her cousin, but his meddling ranked right up there with her mother and brother on the side of extremely annoying.

"What's going on, Sheriff?" Sylvie asked. She spun around in her chair a little bit and tried to crane her neck to see further outside the window. She was anxiously waiting for the arrival of her boys.

"I'm glad I caught you here before you closed down for the night, Sylvie," James said. "I wanted to let you know that I saw Alan strutting around town showing off a brand-new sports car. I caught him speeding on the highway heading out of town toward Rollinsburg. I had to give him a ticket, and since that's the third one this year, it's going to be a pretty steep fine. He wasn't thrilled about that."

Sylvie, Phae, and Neesa all laughed as James regaled them with the story of Alan's outrage and how he threatened not to vote for James in the next election.

What was so hilarious about that was that no one ever bothered to run against James. He was the most popular and effective sheriff the town had ever had, and everyone knew it. Even Alan.

Meg walked out from the back room and asked what all the chatter was about.

"James gave Alan a speeding ticket," Phae said. "Serves the jackass right. I still can't believe he left you high and dry. He hasn't come around to see the boys once since they've been born. What kind of man walks around ignoring the fact that he has two kids living in the same town? Has he offered even a cent of support?"

Sylvie's laughter died instantly. The conversation had wandered into dangerous territory.

Although she had come home from Chicago fully expecting to tell her friends all about her wild adventure as the escort Kassy, for some reason she had held the story back. Later, when she missed her period and found out she was pregnant, she was glad she'd kept her one night fling a secret.

How would she have explained that to her family? They had all been so thrilled by the news that she had broken up with Alan. At least, her mother had been thrilled until Sylvie told her she was pregnant. Then the tables quickly turned to guilt and overbearing, unwanted advice about her unwillingness to include Alan in everything having to do with the babies.

"If Alan wants to spend his money on a fancy new car, that's totally up to him. I haven't spoken to him since I dumped him, and that's fine by me." Sylvie didn't want to talk about Alan anymore. It was a regular argument with her family that was wearing thin.

"Well, not only did he buy a new sports car, he was tooling around in it with that blonde bimbo that he says is his new assistant," James said with an outraged expression finishing his story with a flourish.

The other women groaned. Sylvie still didn't quite understand exactly what it was about Alan that was attractive to the opposite sex. Over the last year since she had dumped him, she'd come to the realization that she must've been temporarily insane to stay with him as long as she had.

She thought it had been the evening with Heath that had really opened her eyes to how bad Alan was for her, even though Phae and Neesa had been trying to tell her just that in the nicest way possible for years.

Now Sylvie knew she deserved someone better. She had briefly experienced what that could be like, and it was something she wanted again. But it would have to be with someone who liked kids because that point was non-negotiable.

Sylvie was so caught up in listening to James's story that she didn't hear the squeak of the wheels of the stroller until they were right behind her. She realized that Momma and the babies had snuck in the back door, and, by the expression on Momma's face, she had heard at least part of the Alan story, too.

Momma spoke in her usual haranguing tone that set Sylvie's nerves on edge. "I can't believe you are just fine with letting that man make a fool of you. You don't think people are talking about it all over town?"

CHAPTER TEN

EVERYONE IN THE ROOM FELL QUIET. Instead of letting herself be drawn into an argument that had been debated to death, Sylvie knelt down to look at her baby boys in the stroller. A wave of calm washed over her just seeing their faces. They looked like angels, and her heart warmed.

Ignoring her mother, she leaned over and brushed both of their foreheads before giving each of them a small peck on the cheek. She was hesitant to wake them, but she wanted to spend some time with them.

The time from after the shop closed until they went to bed, and in the morning before work, was really the only time she had with them during weekdays, and she hated to waste a moment. She sure wouldn't waste any on a distasteful topic like Alan.

"I'm not going to get into this discussion with all of you again," Sylvie said finally, knowing they were all waiting for her to speak. "Whatever was between us is over now. I don't need him to be involved, and I don't need him to take care of the boys and me. I can do that on my own, and I guarantee it's better for all of us."

"Amen, sister," Phae said. "But it wouldn't kill him to kick in some bucks, especially since you won't let any of the rest of us give you anything."

Sylvie scowled at her. "I said I'm not going to discuss it."

"It isn't right for a man to not take responsibility for his children," Momma said.

Damn. It was the beginning of a litany that Sylvie had listened to ever since she'd told her mother she was pregnant. Sylvie understood that the reason her mother was so adamant about the topic went back to her first husband abandoning them all those years ago. Clearly, her mother had never gotten over it.

There had been a brief period of time that Sylvie had considered moving away from Zeke's Bend once she realized that the babies could be Alan's or Heath's. How irresponsible was it that she didn't know who was the father of her children? Sometimes, she felt like a guest on a daytime talk show. She was sure that's how everyone would see her if they knew the truth.

Her desire to stick it to Alan in Chicago had literally changed her life. In the end, she decided it was easier to let everyone assume the babies were Alan's. Unfortunately, the result of that decision was that she had to listen to her family continually pester her about Alan's deadbeat dad-ness. Sometimes she wondered if it was worth it.

Neesa bustled up behind her and started to coo over the babies. As if on cue, Phae and Meg started to fuss over them as well. Sylvie took a step away from the stroller regretfully and found James watching her with a raised eyebrow.

"What?" she asked raising her chin.

"You can't blame folks for wanting Alan to take responsibility. They're his boys too, Sylvie. I know if it were me, I would want to be involved somehow in taking care of them, even if it was just financially."

"You and Alan are nothing alike," Sylvie said.

She had been secretly relieved that despite the fact that the timing of her pregnancy meant Alan was the likely father, he'd never reached out to her. She wanted it to stay that way. If he came around demanding a paternity test, she didn't know what she would do.

"Trust me, James, I've got this. The more you insist on Alan getting involved, the more you make me feel like I'm not doing a good job taking care of my children. You're making me feel bad."

James raised an eyebrow. "Don't try the guilt thing. You know what we think about you. You're a wonderful mother, etcetera, and so on."

"Gee, thanks for the praise. Now tell me again how I can't do this alone."

"I never said you can't do it alone. I said you shouldn't have to."

"That's right," Momma Jones chimed in.

Sylvie squared off, hands on hips. "I'm tired of this. I swore I wouldn't have this argument again and now here we are. Same old, same old. The bottom line is that it's my decision. Case closed."

She addressed the rest of the room. "And speaking of things that are my decision, I would like to be able to spend time alone with my boys tonight. Thank you, everyone, for stopping by, but the party is over."

It took her another ten minutes to finally flush everybody out of the shop. Her mother left grumbling about sports cars and the price of diapers.

Sylvie reminded Meg about covering the early appointments the next morning. Sylvie was looking forward to sleeping in and spending some time with the boys before she had her first appointment at ten.

Sylvie gave Neesa and Phae a kiss on the cheek as they headed out onto the sidewalk.

James gave her a strong hug and whispered in her ear that he hoped that she would reconsider her decision about Alan. She brushed the comment aside and pushed him out the door. He mumbled something about wanting some casserole, which Sylvie also ignored.

She closed the door and locked it. Now, all she had to do was shut off the lights, and they could escape to their cozy apartment that was located behind the shop at the rear of the building.

She walked back over to her sleeping babies and stared at them in the stroller. She wondered again if she truly was doing the right thing by them. She thought so.

Alan had been a lousy boyfriend, and she suspected he would be an even worse father. There was no way that she was going to expose her boys to a man who would probably run off like her father had run off and left her mother.

No, her boys deserved better than that. She would always be there for them, and she would always take care of them, no matter what.

She reached over and stroked both of their cheeks again. Sylvie breathed their baby scent, loving the way they smelled. It had a calming effect on her.

"I know, boys. I wish I knew who your father was, too. If it's the person I think it is, he might've made a great dad. But don't worry about a thing. We're in this together, you and me. I love you both to the moon and back. I'll never let anyone hurt you."

It was a promise she had every intention of keeping.

HEATH STOOD OUTSIDE THE SHOP CALLED Shear Stylin' and gazed at the scene on the other side of the window in disbelief. He had been standing outside on the sidewalk for almost an hour trying to decide the best way to make his entrance.

It was a charming shop with a bright blue awning and a painted wooden door with small inset windowpanes. A big window had a display of hair products and stylish wigs perched on old-fashioned head forms.

The shop sat on a busy street in downtown Zeke's Bend. There was an air of the past about the place. Sandwiched between a highly decorated antique store and a small pharmacy that advertised a soda fountain on their sign, Shear Stylin' fit right in.

Heath was surprised when a small crowd gathered inside after Sylvie's shop closed. He wondered what was going on.

He stepped back and moved over to the antique shop next door when everyone but Sylvie started filing outside. Pretending to be perusing an item in the shop's window, he hoped they believed he truly was interested in porcelain figurines of praying, big-headed children. Or maybe he didn't hope that. It was awkward, to say the least.

Heath wondered if there had been some kind of disturbance at the shop considering one of the people exiting was a policeman. He hoped everything was okay. As soon as the coast was clear, he cautiously made his way back to the beauty shop window.

Sylvie stood in the middle of the room bent over a stroller, and he felt a stab of anxiety in the pit of his gut again.

There had been an instant connection between them from the first moment he saw her in the hotel bar. He even entertained the idea that she was *the one.*

His search was finally at an end, and he was on her doorstep, determined to find out if that assessment might have been correct. If he didn't, he knew he'd regret it the rest of his life.

But then, there were the small bundles in the stroller to consider. They forced him to pause.

He had agonized for days about how he would approach this moment. The final signatures on the acquisition and resulting celebration by his company's board had gone by in a blur. For something he had worked on for so long, it had paled in comparison to the possibility of what he saw in front of him now.

He had so many things that he wanted to say to Sylvie, but he didn't want her to think he was some kind of crazy stalker. Of course, she could think that about him anyway, considering he had found her when she had obviously not wanted to be found.

The fear that she might not be so happy to see him had made him nervous. Fear was not an emotion Heath was accustomed to feeling.

He considered turning around and going home for the hundredth time since he'd arrived in Zeke's Bend. But he needed to see her face again. And he couldn't come all this way and not, at least, say something to her. Anything.

He had never backed away from a challenge in his life. He simply had to ball up the nerve to knock on the door and speak to her. He had to know if what he'd felt between them in Chicago was real or if he had just built the entire evening up in his mind into something akin to a mythic legend.

He took a deep breath. It was now or never. Heath smoothed his shirt down his chest then stepped over and rapped on the door.

Through the small panes of glass, he saw Sylvie turn toward the noise. She had an irritated expression. She marched over to the door and yanked it open.

He'd never know what she'd meant to say because she never said it.

Her eyes focused on him and her mouth fell open.

She went as still as a statue.

CHAPTER ELEVEN

THEY STOOD THERE STARING AT EACH other. Sylvie didn't smile or acknowledge him in any way, but she didn't walk away either. He could almost see her mind working, overwhelmed by him suddenly showing up, and was figuring out what it might mean.

As for Heath, seeing her up close like this, smelling her sweet perfume and gazing on her lovely face ... he knew that he was going to react the exact same way he had in Chicago if she smiled at him.

She was as breathtaking as he remembered in her fitted skinny jeans and smart navy blue blazer. The thin sweater she wore underneath was the same color as the dress she had worn in Chicago.

Her fashionable stacked sandals gave her another inch, and he thought that she might just make it to his chin. His eyes took in every inch of her form, and he committed her image to memory in case she kicked him out of her life and he never saw her again.

His eyes locked on hers even as her hand came up to cover her open mouth. He heard her take a breath that seemed to originate from the very deepest part of her core.

The door stood open, and they could have reached out and touched one another, but it was as if there was an ocean between them. Neither of them said anything.

He had come all that way. He had searched for her for so long. Heath needed her to speak first.

Finally, it was as if she gave in to his silent demand. "Heath."

His name on her lips was music to his ears. Her voice was a golden melody of a favorite song that had played in his head for the better part of a year.

"Sylvie. Sylvie Jones," he said.

He had done nothing but say her name, and she flinched slightly. She nodded. "How did you find me?"

"You didn't make it easy."

"No, I guess not."

"We have some unfinished business, you and I."

He let the words hang in the air between them. An odd sense of vulnerability swept through him. Had he completely misjudged what he thought had transpired between them?

He had chased this woman halfway across the country, a woman he had a one-night stand with a year ago. If he had told anyone who knew him what he was doing, they would probably have said he was certifiably insane.

Heath Collins was the one who was pursued, never the pursuer. But then again, Sylvie didn't know who he was, did she? He'd never told her his last name, not that he recalled anyway.

"I just assumed you would never want to see me again considering our business transaction was over. Remember?" she asked, speaking smoother now. "It was just one night, and we talked about boundaries. You didn't owe me anything else."

It was impossible for him to tell if she regretted their night together or not. Sylvie appeared to have mastered the art of the poker face.

He had been clear in the hotel room the morning after, that he wanted to see her again. It didn't make any sense why she was so against the idea until he learned that she had lied to him about who she was.

"The transaction we discussed was with the escort service. A service that, as it turns out, you weren't an employee of after all," he said.

Sylvie glanced down at her feet. "You made an assumption that night at the bar, and I didn't correct you."

"Why?" It was one of the many questions that had plagued Heath since he had found out that she had lied to him.

She kicked a toe at the floor. "I was having a crummy night on top of a rotten weekend, and I was in the middle of drowning my sorrows when you approached me. I didn't see the harm in a little flirting. Then you said that you wanted to take me out for dinner and dancing, and I thought it would be fun, even if you thought I was someone else. I guess I just wanted an adventure, something good to remember from my trip."

"And was it good?" He held his breath again as he waited for her answer.

A ghost of a smile crossed her face. "There were moments. I forgot how you were always begging for compliments."

Was that flirting? He could work with that.

"How did you find me?" Sylvie asked again.

"I came across your picture on the Internet. You took second place in an online recipe contest."

She groaned. "I swear to God, that recipe will be the ... er ... never mind."

"You didn't want to be found."

"Honestly? I don't know what I wanted, then or now. You've taken me by surprise."

Heath searched for a way to put her at ease. "Cooking wasn't on your list of hobbies when we played the game."

Sylvie nodded and smiled. And with that smile, Heath knew he was lost.

There it was, the same intense attraction he'd experienced when he first set eyes on her. He decided he would gladly give up every dime of his fortune if she'd smile at him like that every day for the rest of ... he pulled up short, realizing he was getting carried away.

"I believe I said something about eating being a hobby of mine, though. A man's gotta eat." Heath said patting his stomach.

Sylvie cut a glance behind her at the stroller before looking back at him. He sensed that the ground he'd just won in this invisible battle was about to be lost.

"I've come all this way. Can I come in?"

He had done his research on Sylvie before visiting Zeke's Bend. He knew that she owned the building. Her shop was in the front, and her apartment was in the back.

Getting her to talk to him seemed like the best place to start. He wanted to know her side of what had happened in Chicago.

He also wanted to know exactly what the situation was with the three-month-old babies that were currently sleeping soundly behind her.

Sylvie caught the direction of his glance and moved to block his view of the stroller. It was almost as if she thought he was going to do something to them, which was absurd. Did she really think that she had to protect them from him?

He had so many questions. She just needed to let him in.

"I don't think that's a good idea, Heath. I don't even know you. Not really."

"You know me well. I might even say, intimately." It might have been a bit unfair to remind her that they had slept together, but they had seen each other naked for Christ's sake. She definitely knew him, and she knew him in ways no other woman ever had.

Sylvie took a step backward. Away from him. He was losing her.

He stuck out his hand. "I'm Heath. Heath Cartwright. There. Now we know each other."

He didn't give her his real name, and he didn't lie without good reason. He'd given it much thought since he'd found his mystery woman, and had decided to go with a fake last name.

Women were always chasing him because of his money. He didn't think that Sylvie was a gold digger type, but until he got to the bottom of what had happened in Chicago and what the story was with the babies, he needed to be cautious.

Sylvie stared at his offered hand as if she didn't know what to do with the gesture. After a moment, she carefully put her hand into his, and the electric tingle he remembered rushed through him. By the way her eyes widened, he knew that she felt it, too.

The attraction between them was still there, and it hadn't lessened. Not one bit.

"Well, Mr. Cartwright, it's nice to officially meet you, and I appreciate you stopping by," she said, sounding brisk and business-like. "But I've worked all day and it's late. I have things that I need to attend to. I'm sure you understand."

He couldn't bear the idea of losing her again, but, at least, this time, he knew where to find her. He had to find some way to get her to talk to him. Showing up on her doorstep unexpectedly might not have been the best move. He needed to give her a bit of time to adjust.

"I'm in town for a few days," he said. "I was driving through on my way to a meeting in the area and thought I'd stop by since Zeke's Bend was on my way. How about coffee or lunch tomorrow? I'd love to have a chance to reconnect."

After seeing her again, that "reconnect" innuendo was the understatement of the year.

"Why?" Sylvie's eyes widened again, and she looked so confused. He wanted to take her in his arms and kiss her silly.

He wanted to tell her that he had never felt this way about another woman. But he didn't. He was a master at mergers and acquisitions, and it wasn't time for that play yet. He could wait.

"I didn't like the way things ended between us."

"My note offended you?"

"Of course not, you're charming."

She studied him, her nose scrunching up. She was hesitant, that much was obvious, and she was weighing her options. Heath had no idea which side of the scale he was falling on.

"I guess we can meet for lunch tomorrow. There." She pointed at the café directly across the street behind him. "Be there at twelve-thirty."

Heath was elated. He had won this round and was one step closer to his goal.

Of course, if anyone had asked what his goal was at that point in time, he wouldn't have been able to articulate it. He just wanted to give the two of them the time and space to figure out if there really was something between them or if it was nothing, or if it was passing.

He started to turn, and that's when he realized he had to ask one more question that had been weighing on his mind. "I saw you have children ... from the picture on the Internet. They're beautiful. How old are they again?"

It was a simple question that had a loaded answer. Sylvie ducked her head and looked away from him.

"It's late, and I have to get the boys fed and into bed. I'll see you tomorrow at the café across the street. Twelve-thirty."

She began to close the door and he had no choice but to step back if he didn't want to get a face full of wood and glass. Sylvie closed the door without looking at him and he heard the lock click into place. She turned away.

There was nothing for it but to leave.

He had been afraid of Sylvie's answer to his question about the babies. The fact that she had avoided answering suggested she had something to hide.

And that something might mean his life was about to change forever.

He didn't know how he felt about that yet, but he was willing to see where things were going to take him, especially if it meant Sylvie would be in it.

For now, he was cautiously optimistic. He would see her again tomorrow, and he'd get to the bottom of everything. Heath began his short walk back to his hotel, not far away, a stylishly restored multi-storied affair from the thirties.

No matter how good their mattresses, he doubted he'd get a wink of sleep that night.

CHAPTER TWELVE

SYLVIE SET HER WINEGLASS DOWN ON the nightstand and crawled into her bed exhausted but feeling good. Well, as good as she could feel considering the confrontation that had happened with Heath.

She had forced that out of her mind so she could be fully present with the boys as they went through their usual nightly routine. She had fed them, given them their baths, and gotten them dressed for bed. Then she read them a bedtime story and sang them to sleep.

That time with them was by far her favorite part of the day. Her next favorite time was waking up in the morning and hearing their coos and fussing through the baby monitor. While she wouldn't trade that for anything, seeing Heath again had awakened other desires that she thought had long gone dormant.

Sylvie adjusted the baby monitor on the nightstand and listened to the boys' even breathing for several minutes. She waited to hear if either of them stirred, indicating that she would need to get up to go check on them. It was a minor miracle when they both fell asleep at the same time, but that night it was as if the boys knew she needed some time to think.

If she were honest with herself, Sylvie was shaken to her core that Heath had found her. And he'd shown up on her doorstep right after she told the boys she thought he would make a great father. Was the universe trying to tell her something?

She didn't know Heath at all, so she couldn't say why she thought that about him. Perhaps it had to do with the little psychic tingle she felt when she thought of him. She'd always trusted that tingle and it rarely led her astray.

She sensed that Heath was a man of integrity, a man who knew how to treat a woman right. It said a lot about his character that he'd never intentionally treated her like the escort he thought she was.

Sylvie stretched across the bed and pulled her laptop off the nightstand. She sipped her wine, her liquid courage and nerve-soother all in one. She flipped the laptop open and then clicked on a folder on the home screen that she only let herself look at every so often. The folder was labeled "Chicago."

She double clicked the folder and started a methodical review of the contents inside. Then she saw the URL that she was looking for, titled: *"The 20 Richest Men You've Never Heard Of."*

She clicked the link.

Only when she was feeling particularly lonely and at her lowest did Sylvie allow herself to visit the page. Sometimes, it was a mistake because it made her feel worse. But usually, it ignited memories of that night so long ago, and it made her dream of what might have been.

Sylvie scrolled down to number ten on the list. The tenth richest man no one had ever heard of: Heath Collins, reclusive billionaire, complete with a grainy picture. The poor quality of the photo couldn't hide the good looks of the man who'd stood in her doorway that evening.

Heath Collins — not Heath Cartwright.

She wasn't sure why he'd lied to her about his last name. Perhaps he was trying to ferret out if she had done any digging on him after their night together? But then again, why?

Sylvie knew that she couldn't really be mad at him for lying about his last name. She had lied to him about who she was altogether. The whole situation was a mess of epic proportions.

And if the question of the hour was why did he lie, then the second question was, why didn't Sylvie call him on it? She had no idea. She just didn't.

She read the bio underneath his picture again, even though she had it memorized. It gave a summary about how Heath amassed his fortune. He was something of a shark when it came to acquiring companies that were in financial trouble and then turning them around.

She knew his most recent deal involved a company called Yurovize. It was probably completed by now and would shoot his net worth into the stratosphere, meaning multiple billions.

Sylvie couldn't wrap her head around half such a sum. Most months, she was lucky to have enough money to cover her bills, bills that amounted to laughably nothing in Heath's world. He probably spent more on manicures in a month than Sylvie spent on utilities.

She and Heath were worlds apart in so many ways. She remembered feeling that way the morning after in Heath's hotel room; cold, harsh reality had reared its ugly head.

It didn't start out that way. Sylvie had gotten in the shower thinking about how amazing the night with Heath had been. But as the cobwebs of sleep disappeared, she realized that her dreamy lover still thought that Sylvie was Kassy, the escort.

He'd told her the whole point of using an escort service was because he wanted to avoid romantic entanglements. And now there she was, daydreaming about getting all hella tangled up with him. She realized she'd probably made a horrible mistake by sleeping with him.

For a brief moment, she'd considered telling him the truth. She wasn't an escort. She was just Sylvie from Zeke's Bend, a small town girl who'd come to the big city and wound up in the bed of a drop-dead gorgeous, rich guy. Now she had stars in her eyes and wanted more … more of the incredible man who'd just given her the night of her life.

If he knew who she really was, what she really wanted, the whole fairy tale charade of her special night would crumble. He'd see she was no different from the other women who threw themselves at him, the women who expected an engagement ring after one date, as he described it.

Standing in that huge shower, being buffeted by multiple streams of water, the fixtures glimmering and the tiles shining, she felt like the country bumpkin she truly was.

She and Heath had nothing in common. How could they? He wouldn't want anything to do with her, especially when he found out that she was nothing but a hairstylist from a small town in the middle of nowhere. He was the flyer; she was the flyover.

That's when she'd given herself a harsh reality check. They came from two different worlds and there couldn't be anything else between them. Besides, he'd said he didn't want any commitments, and he wasn't going to start wanting them with someone like Sylvie.

She could hear Momma's disappointed voice moaning in her head, asking her if she had taken some drugs and gone plain crazy.

All she wanted at that point was to get the hell out of the suite before Heath discovered she'd been lying.

She hadn't expected him to stop her from leaving, to put on a huge breakfast spread and invite her to spend the day with him. She didn't understand that move at all.

Why he would want to spend more time with someone whose time he had to pay for to begin with? She figured he felt sorry for her, especially once he offered her money to take care of whatever phantom financial situation he'd invented for her in his mind.

It didn't surprise her too much that Heath wanted to swoop in and save her. He seemed like that kind of guy. The only problem was that Sylvie didn't need saving, and he pissed her off by offering to pay her, by coming too close to turning the whole encounter into a cheap and offensive exchange. That wasn't how she wanted to remember their time together.

Sylvie knew then that she had to get away. So she'd played it cool and acted like she didn't care what happened or if she ever saw him again, even though it killed her to see the disappointment on his face when he realized she was going to leave.

Deep down, she didn't want to leave either. But as soon as he left the room to change, she seized the opportunity to run before she did something stupid like telling him the truth. She was afraid that she wouldn't have been able to deal with his rejection. One break-up a weekend was her limit, thank you.

The joke was on her at the end of the day, though. She'd gotten pregnant, and the timing worked out that it had happened during her trip.

If only she knew who the father of her twins was.

If it was Alan, she would be devastated. If it was Heath, she wasn't sure, but there was a good chance that she could end up equally devastated.

She remembered running across the link to the "20 Richest Men" list when she was seven months pregnant. Finding Heath's last name and realizing she could contact him about her pregnancy was shattering.

She had cried for days because she didn't know what to do. In the end, she'd taken the coward's way out and done nothing.

Eventually, she found that she could justify her inaction. Heath had so much money; he could do whatever he wanted. He could decide that he wanted her babies. It would be so easy for him to have her declared an unfit parent. She wouldn't be able to fight him since she didn't have his kind of money to hire the best cutthroat lawyers.

She conveniently overlooked the fact that Phae was now loaded and would move heaven and earth to help Sylvie keep her babies. But Sylvie's justification didn't sound so hot when she thought about Phae, so she told herself she could never let Phae do that for her (which wasn't at all true — Sylvie would do anything and accept anything to keep her babies, but never mind).

Heath didn't seem like the type of guy who would take her children away from her, but learning he was a father might shift everything. She hadn't wanted to risk it by getting in touch with him. And anyway, she told herself, she had no solid proof that he was the father.

She reopened the "Chicago" folder and allowed herself to skim through the other URLs that had given her small glimpses into Heath's life over the months.

He kept an extremely low profile in the media. But there were still some pictures of him here and there and some mentions in business articles. She had collected everything in her Chicago file.

She sipped the rest of her wine. Her favorite pictures of Heath were the ones where he was caught with just a hint of a smile. She liked to pretend that he was smiling at her.

The photos she liked least were the ones where he had some slinky model-type beside him. She would study the women and couldn't help comparing herself to them, and she always felt she came out unfavorably. Thankfully, there weren't many pictures with Heath and dates. He wasn't a social type.

She closed all of the files and cursed herself. She couldn't believe that she had agreed to have lunch with him. It would end badly.

She cursed her mother for convincing her to enter the online recipe contest. When Sylvie found out that she'd won second place and the contest committee asked her to submit a photo for the announcement, Momma had also been the one who had insisted she send one that included the babies.

She'd been reluctant but had done it against her better judgment. It was silly how something so innocuous was probably going to blow up her whole life.

Of course, having somehow stumbled upon the contest page, Heath would have seen the photo, too. He was a smart guy, and the math around their ages added up to one big question mark.

He asked her how old the boys were because he was trying to figure out if they were his. She couldn't answer that question, which is why she had avoided it altogether.

She just wanted him to go away. No, that wasn't true. She wanted to grab his face and kiss him until neither of them could breathe. But she couldn't do that either. She had responsibilities to think about, and their names were Quentyn and Jadyn. She had to tread lightly when it came to Heath.

She'd agreed to lunch to appease him and hopefully satisfy his curiosity enough to make him go away and leave her alone. She was certain after they had lunch, and he realized how small-time she actually was, he wouldn't want to spend more time with her anyway. On top of that, she had the additional baggage of two babies.

Heath was a billionaire and could have any woman he wanted. He could lead the most glamorous of lifestyles if he chose. He wouldn't want anything to do with Zeke's Bend.

He would probably think it was a blessing to know that the twins weren't his. She was going to have to figure out some way to make him believe it wasn't even a possibility they could be his children.

She set her empty wineglass and laptop back on the nightstand and switched off the light. She settled into bed, noting the emptiness around her.

Sylvie couldn't help but remember that night so long ago. Lying there in the dark, she imagined that she could still feel Heath's hands on her body. The way he took control during their lovemaking — it still curled her toes.

She hadn't been with anyone since Heath.

But now, he was here and a teensy, tiny part of her wondered if maybe everything she imagined could go wrong might turn out to be right. Maybe he hadn't just accidentally found her and just dropped by to check in. Maybe he'd been looking for her all this time. Maybe he'd been desperately seeking Sylvie for nearly a year. Wouldn't that be something?

It was a such a fanciful, romantic notion that she let her mind wander, imagining Heath ordering private eyes around, shouting at them to find his mystery woman, or else! Eyes closed, she snuggled under the blanket and smiled at her own silliness.

If she were going to play the fantasy game tonight, she decided she might as well go all the way. She imagined Heath meeting her at the cafe and the moment he saw her, sweeping her off her feet and kissing her passionately. He'd tell her how much he longed for her, how much he wanted her. How no other woman had ever made him feel the way Sylvie made him feel.

Sylvie giggled. How ridiculous. That was never going to happen.

But it sure was fun to think that it might.

Chapter Thirteen

HEATH WAS NERVOUS IN A WAY THAT he couldn't remember being nervous since his very first business deal. He'd been twenty-two. Looking back on it, he realized that he hadn't known what he was doing.

Somehow, though, he'd managed to walk into that boardroom and charm the pants off every person in the room. He always recalled the deal fondly. It was the first time that he'd been completely out of his league and still managed to achieve his goal.

He made his first million dollars that day. Not too shabby for a kid who once thought he'd never amount to anything on his own. Persistence and a lot of hard work were the keys to success, something he'd had to learn on his own. His parents had never set any kind of example for him.

Heath's parents had been fairly generous with their money in his childhood but not so generous with their time or attention. He grew up under the watchful eyes of a series of nannies. They were all warm and kind to him, but they hadn't been his mother.

As soon as his parents deemed him old enough to handle it, they'd sent him off to boarding school where he lived for nine months of the year. It didn't take long before school was more his home than the place where he went on holidays to visit his parents when they weren't busy traveling. And they were pretty much always busy traveling.

Since he'd left home, he had maintained only a cold, distant relationship with them. He didn't think he had spoken to either one of them in well over a year, and he had stopped wondering long ago if they cared about him. The only thing he wondered now was why they bothered to have a child to begin with; he had never fit into their lives.

These were the thoughts that ran through his mind as Heath anxiously made his way to the café. He was excited to see Sylvie again, elated that his feelings for her hadn't dimmed with time.

But there was an elephant in the room that needed to be addressed: the babies. Maybe, *his* babies.

He didn't know how he would react if he was bold enough to ask her the question and the answer was yes, they were his children. He didn't have the least idea what to do with a baby, let alone two of them.

It had been a restless night's sleep. He dreamed about baby bottles, the sound of babies crying in the distance and the sensation of cold marble tile under his feet as he went in search of them.

This whole idea of being a parent had surfaced old resentments towards his parents that he thought he'd long since buried.

His earliest memories involved endless questions to his nannies about when his parents would be home. They were always traveling, always without him.

When they did return home, he mostly saw them from a distance at events like dinner parties and summer BBQs in the Hamptons. Heath's parents would parade him in front of their friends, pretend to be family people when nothing could have been further from the truth.

Heath understood now that it was a game to them, and to their guests. None of them knew the first thing about family. And because of that, neither did Heath.

He couldn't quite find it within himself to be completely dismissive of what his parents had done. Perhaps it was because of the dramatic change in his own lifestyle since his company had taken off. He was rich and successful, and most everything he had touched in the last fifteen years had turned to gold.

His work took him all over the world, and he enjoyed waking up in Seattle and going to bed in Singapore if he wanted. Right now, he could call up his private jet and fly anywhere in the world. He could have nearly any woman that he wanted on his arm. He could do or see anything that he wanted to see.

His parents hadn't done too poorly by him if his success was any reflection on how they'd chosen to raise him. He wasn't sure they deserved any credit, though. Not that credit mattered.

When he thought of his life, he wondered what it would be like to insert children into his lifestyle, and he'd wondered before he'd learned about Sylvie's twins. He couldn't be sure, but he didn't think the two would mix well.

Yet even with all of the billions in his bank account, he was alone. That was the cold hard truth of things. He'd thought he'd accepted that, just as he'd stopped blaming his parents for their neglect. But maybe, he wasn't as accepting as he thought.

Perhaps loneliness was why he had obsessively sought out Sylvie after his intense connection to her. He was tired of being alone.

And it was time to face that, at some point, he was going to get old. He chuckled to himself at that. He was still labeled one of the top eligible bachelors under 40. But there was plenty missing in his life. He marveled that it was possible to have so much money and yet feel so unfulfilled. This wasn't how things were supposed to work.

It was confusing. He wasn't ready to try to wrap his brain around all of it yet, especially when he didn't have all the facts. He told himself to live in the present.

Right now, in the present, he had a lunch date with the most beautiful and fascinating woman he'd ever met. He would focus on that, on learning about her.

He was glad that the cloak of lies surrounding their first meeting was gone. Now they could just be two people who had met each other and had a great time once. They could open up to each other without having to worry about keeping their true identities a secret. At least, that's what he hoped was about to happen.

He brushed aside the fact that there was still one lie left between them: his last name.

Heath got to the cafe fifteen minutes early. The place was bustling with customers, most of them people who worked nearby and were on their lunch hours. Almost all of the tables were full.

It took him a few minutes, but he managed to find a small table set back in the corner of the restaurant. He was glad that the table's location offered some privacy because he didn't want to be interrupted. He looked forward to having Sylvie all to himself.

He enjoyed the atmosphere of the small-town cafe. The walls were adorned with landscapes that were clearly painted by amateurs, an eclectic assortment of items like stuffed fish, baseball caps and old tin cans, hung beside signed photos of celebrities Heath didn't recognize.

The booths and tables were old but in good repair. Older men perched on stools at the counter, drinking coffee and talking politics.

A waitress with bleached helmet hair, wearing blue jeans and a t-shirt, sidled over to him and gave him a toothy smile. She winked and flirted and gave him a glass of water and a menu. Heath ordered some coffee and was relieved when one of the regulars called out to her and she left.

He watched the door with a devotion that would have put a lonely hound to shame. He didn't bother looking at the menu and only drummed on it with his fingertips. He wasn't hungry, despite the fact that he hadn't eaten breakfast.

When Sylvie walked into the restaurant ten minutes later, he sat back in his chair to admire the view. She wore a light blue sweater dress that hugged her full hips, landing just above her shapely knees and setting off the deep color of her skin perfectly.

Her lips had the faintest dash of rose-colored sheen. Her hair curled and brushed against the tops of her shoulders, and he had an overwhelming desire to touch her. He squelched that desire and stood to greet her.

He smiled at her and felt a rush of pleasure when she smiled tentatively back at him.

"Sylvie, I'm so glad you came. It's nice to see you again," he said. He hoped his tone was as earnest as he meant it to be.

"It's nice to see you, too." Her voice was even and neutral, not quite what he was hoping for.

There'd been a small part of him that had hoped she'd jump into his arms and tell him how much she missed him. He recognized that was irrational, but Sylvie brought out that side of him.

Heath pulled out her seat for her and gently pushed it in as soon as she settled into it. He resumed his seat across from her and studied her face expectantly. When it became obvious she wasn't going to say anything else, he felt the need to fill the air between them.

"I hope there's something on the menu that you like. Lunch is on me."

She frowned. Immediately, he reviewed his words and wondered what he'd said wrong.

"That's not necessary," she said. "I can pay my own way."

Heath cursed himself. She was there less than a minute, and he already stumbled into a minefield.

He remembered then how sensitive she was when he offered her money in Chicago. He just wanted to make her comfortable with him, but he couldn't seem to find the right thing to say. It was an awkward situation and he needed to do or say something to relieve the tension.

"You look lovely today," he said. "Robin egg blue is my favorite color, although champagne is a close second."

A brilliant smile crossed her face. "Thank you," she said primly.

Heath wondered if she remembered that he had told her his favorite color during their game that night. If she did, there was a chance she wore the dress for him, which would be a promising signal.

Sylvie opened the menu, briefly studied it, then closed it. "So you said you were on your way to a business meeting in the area? Where? I might know it."

Here again was another potential minefield. He'd come to Zeke's Bend specifically to find Sylvie. Here he'd been congratulating himself for putting an end to the lies between them, and here was one popping up at a most inconvenient time.

He decided in a moment of clarity that it was best to finally tell her the truth. There was no way they could have any kind of relationship if they didn't start sorting out the fact from fiction.

He set down his menu and dove in. "The truth of the matter, Sylvie, is that I came here—"

The flirty waitress chose that moment to show up at the table.

"Hey Syl," the waitress said, holding out a pot of coffee over the cup and saucer that was part of the table's setting. "Yes?"

"Yes, please," Sylvie said. "What are the specials today, Rita?"

Rita rapidly rattled off a mile long list of entrees, including a number of side dishes and a veritable smorgasbord of desserts.

"Umm," Sylvie said, looking off into the distance with an adorable concentration, "I think I'll have the chicken and dumplings. I shouldn't, but ... I can't help it."

"I know, darlin," Rita said. "You want sweet tea with that?"

"Duh," Sylvie said, making Rita snort.

"And how about you, Mr. Sexy?"

Heath blinked. Was she talking to him? She was definitely looking at him.

"She means you," Sylvie said with a sparkle in her big brown eyes.

"Right," he said. "I'll have what the lady's having."

"I bet you do," Rita said, smirking.

CHAPTER FOURTEEN

SYLVIE STIFLED A LAUGH BEHIND HER hand as Rita sashayed away.

"I don't even know what the hell that meant," Heath admitted.

"Don't worry about it. It's just Rita," Sylvie said, snatching up some creamer packets. "So, you were saying something about why you came here."

"Right, right. So, I think I should be honest about it. I actually came to Zeke's Bend to see you. Specifically to see you."

Did her hand tremble slightly when she tore open the creamer packets? He thought it had and wondered what it meant.

"Okay ..." her voice trailed away. "Why?"

"I know that we left things in a way where we both could walk away and forget the night we shared."

Sylvie's gaze flicked around the cafe. "Shh! Keep your voice down."

"I didn't realize I was being loud."

"You're not, but these people in here all know me, and they're all wondering what I'm doing here with you. Some of them have the hearing of a bat."

"Bats are pretty much deaf, aren't they?"

"No, they're pretty much blind. They hear with echolocation."

"Right. Okay, so the bat people are probably listening in."

Sylvie grinned. "Exactly. So, shh."

"Then I'll keep my voice down when I say," he leaned forward and said in low tones, "I couldn't forget the night we spent together. It was one of the best nights of my life. Perhaps *the* best."

Sylvie lost her grin and looked down at her napkin. She plucked at a corner.

Heath forged ahead. "I was truthful with you that morning when I said that I wanted to spend the day with you so I could get to know you better. You're not like other women I've met. There's something about you. I hoped you might feel the same about … me." Damn, that last part had been hard to say, but he was relieved to get it out.

"I would really like to start things over between us," he rushed on. "That is, if you'll just give me a chance." There. His confession was complete. Now all that was left was her reaction.

Sylvie sat there as if she was processing his words. He watched the flicker of different emotions cross her face. It seemed as if she might be happy about what he said, but then, suddenly there would be a slightly darker look that must mean she was unhappy about something he said.

He decided he wasn't going to say anything else. He had laid his soul bare to her. Now it was up to her to decide if she wanted to get to know him, too, or if he was going to be leaving town empty-handed and alone. There were certain rules to these kinds of exchanges, and for them to work, it couldn't be one-sided.

He held his breath when he saw her mouth open to reply.

"Well, well. Young Sylvie. Where have you been hiding?" The old, tinny voice over his left shoulder interrupted his entire thought process.

Sylvie quickly stood up and kissed the cheeks of the two elderly women who stepped up beside their table. It was as if they had appeared out of nowhere.

"Aunt Charmaine. Aunt Chelly. I didn't know that you were going to be in town today," Sylvie said.

Unless he missed his guess, Sylvie seemed relieved at the interruption. He caught the curious glances in his direction from Sylvie's aunts, and he looked at her expectantly with a raised eyebrow.

Sylvie waved at him, almost dismissively. "This is Heath Cartwright. Heath, these are my great-aunts, Charmaine and Chelly Jones."

Heath stood and gave the two ladies a slight bow. "My pleasure, ladies."

He was rewarded with two giggles. If there was one thing that Heath could normally do when he wanted, it was charm the socks off a woman. It didn't matter her age. Although Sylvie seemed to be immune today.

He held out his hand to each of them in turn and kissed the tops of their wrinkled knuckles. They smelled of roses. He sat back down.

"Where you been? I haven't been able to get in for an appointment with you in over a week," one of the women asked Sylvie. Heath had no idea if it was Charmaine or Chelly.

Sylvie grimaced. "I'm sorry, Aunt Charmaine. I've been busy, and I'm getting new clients in from as far away as Rollinsburg now. I'll let Meg know to make time in the schedule for you when you call. I've been meaning to call you anyways to schedule time for tea."

"I guess I can see why you've been busy." The other aunt, Chelly, gave Heath a sly look. "You should come around for tea this Sunday. Aunt Elfleda has been looking for you, too."

Heath wasn't sure if that was a cue of some kind, because the two women split apart as a wheelchair scooted in between them. An even older, even smaller elderly woman sat in the chair, her back ramrod stiff.

She gave Heath an appraising once-over before turning to Sylvie. "Sylvie Jones. Who's that?" She pointed a long, bony finger at Heath.

"Heath Cartwright."

"Is that so?" Aunt Elfleda said, as if his name was somehow suspicious, as if it had been up to something when no one was looking. "You look familiar. And didn't there used to be a fellow on TV with that name?"

Heath was stumped. Sylvie knitted her brows. Chelly and Charmaine giggled.

"You're thinking of Hoss, Elfleda. On 'Bonanza,' it was Hoss Cartwright," Charmaine said.

"Nope!" Aunt Elfleda pursed her lips. "I guess I know what I'm thinking. Heath Cartwright. He was the big one. I liked him. I always liked me a big man, one who can split a couple ricks of firewood and still have enough energy left to ring your clock."

Sylvie rolled her eyes and Chelly and Charmaine tittered and nodded like bobbleheads.

"You got a voice, Heath Cartwright?" Elfleda demanded.

"Yes, Ma'am," he answered quickly. He stood and did the bowing thing again.

"Hmm, I kind of liked that," Elfleda said. "You'll do ... for now. Come to tea on Sunday."

And with that, Elfleda spun her wheelchair ninety degrees and tore off down the center aisle of the cafe. More than one person had to leap out of her way or risk getting run down. Chelly chased after her, calling out that she'd get the door.

Charmaine stayed behind for a second and gave Sylvie a hard look. "I haven't forgiven you for taking my recipe," she said. "But you know I have a hard time holding a grudge. So anyway, that's why I want an appointment. So we can let bygones be bygones."

Sylvie opened her mouth then snapped it shut again. She blew out a short breath then said, "That's ... kind of you. I'm glad it's all settled then."

"Oh, it's not all settled. But it's enough to be getting on with." She rushed away without a response, calling out to Chelly to wait for her to help Elfleda.

Elfleda, meanwhile, had screeched to a halt in front of the cash register and was digging out change from a giant coin purse, throwing Chelly and Charmaine's front door plans to the winds.

Sylvie watched her aunts jostle one another at the door. "In case it wasn't obvious, Great Aunt Elfleda rules the Jones family."

"I imagined as much. I meet a lot of people in charge in my line of work."

"Yeah, well, Elfleda's more dictator than anything else. She drives me nuts sometimes."

As if she could hear them, which was impossible since she was all the way in the front of the building, she swung her wheelchair around to face them. She stared them down.

"And Sylvie," she called, her voice carrying surprising well for being so elderly, "Don't forget to bring those babies with you to tea!"

With that command complete, she whirled toward the door which was being held wide by both Chelly and Charmaine.

Sylvie sighed. "Like I was going to leave the babies at home alone or something? Gawd, she never quits."

She didn't stop watching the front until Elfleda and the other two women were gone.

She slid back on her seat. "I'm sorry about that. My grandpa used to say you can't swing a cat in this town without hitting a Jones. The Jones family is quite a big thing in Zeke's Bend."

"What's a big thing?" he asked.

Heath was intrigued. This seemed like much safer territory for discussion than Sylvie's babies or the reason for him showing up in Zeke's Bend. He had not forgotten, though, about his confession, and that he was still waiting for Sylvie's response.

"If you go back several generations, one of my ancestors founded Zeke's Bend," Sylvie said, a note of pride in her voice. "He had a large family, and after a bit of time more folks started settling in this area. Everybody started marrying each other and having kids and pretty soon most of Zeke's Bend was made up of the Jones family, or relatives in one way or another. But not really. To folks from out of town, it just may feel that way."

Heath was going to ask her what that meant when another woman appeared beside the table. This one he recognized. She had been at Sylvie's shop the night before. She rubbed her belly as she looked between Sylvie and Heath with an amused smile.

"Sylvie," she said.

All she said was Sylvie's name, and yet it felt as if she said, at least, three or four more sentences that Heath couldn't comprehend, but he could see that Sylvie understood. She seemed to slip a little bit further down in her chair.

"Phae," she answered.

Heath looked back and forth between the women. There was some sort of tennis match going on that he couldn't quite see or understand, but he knew it was happening. Phae stood there with a cocked eyebrow looking at Sylvie. Sylvie looked back at Phae with a closed expression. It was as if each of them was waiting for the other to say something.

Sylvie was the one who finally caved. "This is my friend, Heath Cartwright."

Phae turned to look at him. "Well hello, Heath. My name is Phae Holmes, once Jones."

Heath was trying to figure out if he was supposed to know who Phae was or not. He could see a slight resemblance between Phae and Sylvie, and he was starting to make some connections now. In fact, he couldn't help but be aware that there were a lot of other people around the cafe who suddenly seemed to be very interested in the activity at their table.

"Hello, Phae. It's very nice to meet you." He stuck out his hand, and Phae accepted it. Then all three of them stared at each other.

"Surely you have to get back to work now, don't you Phae?" Sylvie said.

If Phae was expecting an invitation to join them, it didn't appear to be coming any time soon.

Sylvie looked at Heath. "Phae is my cousin. She and her husband run a nonprofit down the street. They're *very busy* this time of year."

Heath had to grin. It was obvious that Sylvie was trying to make her cousin leave. Just when it looked as if Phae would concede, another woman popped up beside her. This woman was cute as a button with long braids down her back. She was smaller than Phae and Sylvie, but her face lit up with a warm smile that made Heath instantly like her.

"Hey, Sylvie. It's so nice to see you here," she said.

Heath was starting to wonder if he had stumbled into some kind of comedic play when he wasn't looking. Sylvie appeared frustrated at the turn of events. "Nice to see you too, Neesa. This is my friend."

Heath stood up again. He was starting to understand how this was going to work. Clearly, if Sylvie's relatives had the run of the town, this was probably what he could expect through the rest of lunch. He stuck out his hand. "Hello Neesa, I am Heath Cartwright. I'm a friend of Sylvie's just in town for a little bit."

Neesa shook his hand with a vigorous pump. Phae had a sly smile on her face, and Heath was starting to wonder what Sylvie's relatives were thinking about him and Sylvie. She clearly introduced him as her friend for a reason.

He supposed it made sense. She couldn't exactly introduce him as the man she had a one-night stand with in Chicago last year. Still, it felt a little bit awkward because he definitely didn't want to be just friends.

"I suppose you're a cousin of Sylvie's, too?"

"Oh, has she talked about me? Don't listen to anything she says. It's all lies," Neesa said.

The three women looked at each other and burst out into laughter. Heath sensed it was an inside joke that he didn't understand. Having such an array of family a stone's throw away was something totally outside his realm of experience.

He was curious about Sylvie's large extended family. It would be interesting learning more about all of them. But really, he'd prefer to learn it later … much later.

Phae and Neesa asked a few more leading questions which Sylvie neatly ducked, then with a quick goodbye to Heath, both cousins hooked arms and strolled away to the front of the cafe. They picked up a couple of orders to go and then were gone.

"I don't know how much lunch you're going to be able to eat," Sylvie confessed. "We can pretty much expect that someone from my family is going to pop up at this table every couple of minutes the rest of the time we're here. I should have picked a different spot for lunch."

"How about we try our little get to know you a little bit better conversation somewhere else?"

"No. I've got myself all set for those chicken and dumplings." Sylvie craned her neck and looked toward the kitchen. "Where are they, anyway?"

Rita saw her looking and ambled over. "Family reunion over? You ready to eat?"

"You know our reunions are never over, cuz." Sylvie glanced at Heath. "Rita's a Jones, too."

"I only married into it, though," she said. "Don't know what I was thinking."

The two women laughed.

"Okay, so I was keeping your stuff warm," Rita said. "I'll bring it out."

"Yeah, make it quick before anyone else comes in."

"Like quick will make a difference," Rita mumbled as she left.

Heath thought he'd give it another try. "Seriously, we could have her bag up our lunches to go. I have a nice room over at—"

"Please," Sylvie interrupted. "Don't even try."

"It would be perfectly innocent."

"Mmmhmm. Doesn't matter. No time. I have a life and a business to run. You wouldn't believe my schedule. And anyway, you're just passing through, as I recall."

"No," Heath said, "actually, I'm not if you think about what I told you a few minutes ago." Heath wasn't sure if she was deliberately acting as if she couldn't remember his confession or not. There was a lot of noise in the café, and they had been interrupted so many times.

"I'm flattered, Heath. But I really don't understand why you came looking for me."

Rita came back by, dropping off bowls of steaming dumplings and two tall glasses of iced tea. They thanked her.

Heath refused to be distracted again. When Rita was gone, he said, "You said you don't understand why I came looking for you. Your favorite color is yellow. Your favorite game when you were a kid was dominoes. You said you learned to fish before you learned to walk. You said you had a big family and loved every single one of them, even the annoying ones. Your favorite music is jazz. Your first concert was Kids on the Block. You want to skydive someday."

Sylvie listened wide-eyed, her spoon full of chicken and dumplings paused halfway between bowl and mouth.

"These are all things that I remember we talked about," Heath continued, "and every single one of them was something that resonated with me. I might not have known your real name, Sylvie, but I felt like I knew who you were. And I wanted to spend more time with that woman. I came halfway across the country to see you. What else do I have to say or do to convince you?"

Once again, Sylvie looked as if she was going to respond when this time a good-looking younger man appeared next to her and leaned down to give her a kiss on the cheek.

Heath wanted to growl in frustration and a bit of jealousy. What now? Who was this guy?

Sylvie jerked away from the man. "Don't sneak up on me like that! You nearly made me drop my spoon."

He scowled at Heath. "So who's this?"

"Don't be rude," she said. "Heath, this is my little brother, Will. Will, this is Heath. Be nice."

Will opened his mouth to speak, but Sylvie cut him off.

"Heath is my friend," she said as if repeating something by rote. "He's only in town for a couple of days. He's someone I met a little while ago when I was traveling. No, he doesn't know everyone in town. Yes, he's single. You don't need to know anything else, so don't bother prying."

Heath watched a very large woman come down the main aisle. She was headed straight for them. She stopped beside Will and, hands on wide hips, gave Sylvie a hard look.

Sylvie squirmed under the woman's glare.

"Single?" the woman said a bit more forcefully than she probably had to.

Heath was amazed that she could have heard that part since she wasn't close to the table yet when Sylvie said it. Then he remembered Sylvie's comment about ears like bats. He almost grinned.

Sylvie looked heavenward and said, "This is my mother, Heath, Sachet Jones-Ford."

Now it was making sense, Heath thought. He stood and greeted Sachet, but unlike the other Jones women, she wasn't impressed if her sour expression was anything to go by.

As he sat down, he realized a hush had fallen over the cafe.

Sylvie's mother turned her attention back to her daughter. "If you're looking to spend time with a single man, don't you think you should be spending it with the father of your children?"

No one in the cafe spoke or moved. Even Rita had stopped, standing there with wide eyes, frozen in the act of delivering the plates she was holding.

Everyone was watching Sylvie.

Heath had no idea what Sachet was talking about. There was someone everyone acknowledged as the babies' father? This woman's snide comment seemed to indicate just that. Heath experienced a boggling sensation of disappointment.

Sylvie lifted her chin. "Momma, Heath and I are having lunch, or we're trying to. It's just lunch. And we haven't had a chance to say much of anything to each other with everyone showing up."

"Well, I just got a call from Charmaine telling me that you were here showing off some type of gigolo," Sachet said, her glare at Heath deepening.

"What?" Sylvie half-shrieked.

"Momma, that's going too far," Will said, looking deeply embarrassed. "Come on, let's go."

Sachet eyed her son. "I say when things have gone too far."

"Then you'd best start talking," Will said. "But not here. Sorry, Syl. Come on, Momma. We're supposed to be having a nice lunch."

He nodded at Heath, gave Sylvie a quick squeeze on the shoulder, then pulled a grumbling Sachet away toward a booth at the front of the cafe.

Sylvie put her head in her hands and stared down at the table. "This is a disaster."

"I say we reconsider our options and get the hell out of here before someone else shows up," Heath said.

Sylvie raised her head. "I wouldn't blame you if you ran out of here like your butt's on fire."

"My butt's fine, thank you," he said.

She gave him a weak smile. "I'd have a good comeback for that if I weren't drowning in humiliation."

"Hey, I wish I had so much family that gave a damn about me. I can't point to a single person, so I'm actually jealous of you."

"You're just saying that."

"Nope. Hey, this may be the longest stretch of conversation we've had since you got here."

She nodded. "Yeah."

"Maybe we'd better get out while we can."

"I'm not leaving my chicken and dumplings," she said.

"I wouldn't ask you to."

"I think you might actually get me, Heath Cartwright."

"That's Hoss to you, little miss."

Her laughter was the sweetest sound he'd heard in ages.

CHAPTER FIFTEEN

SYLVIE WASN'T SURPRISED THAT RITA didn't care that they picked up their bowls and spoons and carried them outside. Heath had called to her that they'd bring them back when they were finished. Rita, who rarely cared much about anything, shrugged in unconcern.

Sylvie ignored her mother and brother on her way out, and for that matter, all the other busybodies who'd been listening in on her mother's rude comments.

Heath draped his arm around Sylvie's shoulders as they exited the cafe, and she found that she didn't mind at all. She could use some comfort after that crazy display.

They strolled down the street, eating dumplings. It wasn't too terribly cold and it was cozy watching the steam rise off their bowls. Eventually, they found a seat on a bench in the town square park.

Heath asked her questions about Zeke's Bend. It was fun to regale him with stories that she remembered from her childhood. He seemed to be interested and never acted bored like she'd expect someone with his background to act.

In her bones, Sylvie knew she'd live in Zeke's Bend for the rest of her life. It wasn't that she had to do it, it was that she wanted to do it. Sure, she'd like to travel and experience other cultures, but home would always be this small town with too many relatives driving her crazy because they had their noses in her business.

Zeke's Bend was the only place that she ever wanted to live. Zeke's Bend was where her family was, and she was established here. Her business was here. And she couldn't think of a better place to raise her babies. They were going to have an amazing life here, and it was going to be awesome.

She told all of this to Heath, sounding casual about it, but really, it was a warning. This was something he needed to know about her, and he needed to understand she would never change her mind about it.

This new wrinkle of Heath coming into her life had thrown her for a loop. When he said he'd come there deliberately to find her, she hadn't known what to say.

She was relieved that Heath hadn't asked her about the twins. She had been fully expecting him to, but then Momma had gone and basically said their father was someone else. What must Heath be thinking? Impossible to know.

When they finished the delicious lunch, they walked and chatted some more. She realized when she stopped at the front door of the daycare center, that she had mindlessly guided him there.

She was supposed to pick up the twins since she'd decided to take the rest of the afternoon off.

She studied Heath's face as she watched him put two and two together on where they were.

"I guess this is where we say goodbye," she said.

She knew that she still hadn't addressed what he had told her at the cafe. But what could she say? She had responsibilities now. This wasn't Chicago.

"Do we have to say goodbye?" Heath asked. "I meant what I said back there, Sylvie."

Heath's expression was intent, and she couldn't find it in herself to turn away from him. There was a part of her that was excited and wanted to see where this was going to go and if it was real.

"This is my home," she said. "I don't live in a fancy house or have fancy things. My life is simple and probably pretty boring to somebody like you."

She gestured at the daycare. "Plus, I'm a mom. I have two small babies. They put quite the crimp in a social life, but they're my life. You won't hurt my feelings by taking off before anything else happens. I won't hold it against you."

She looked away from him so he couldn't see the lie in her eyes.

Heath's finger dipped underneath her chin and dragged her eyes back up to look into his. "I want to get to know you better. I don't know how many times I have to say that, but I'll keep saying it until you're convinced I'm telling the truth. I know you're a mom, and I respect that. I'm not trying to take you away from time with your boys. I'm just asking for a chance to see if what happened in Chicago was a fluke, or if it might have meant something more if we hadn't been separated."

She was about to respond when she heard a chorus of voices call her name. She closed her eyes and said a silent curse. Then she turned as a trio of teenage boys jogged up to them. The boys were half out of breath, as usual, sweaty, as usual, and talking at the speed of light.

"Sylvie!" Tonio said. He was the ringleader of the small gang. Her other cousins, Neptune and Jackson flanked him. "Who's this?" He eyed Heath suspiciously.

Sylvie wanted to laugh at how his chest puffed up as he tried to look imposing even though Heath had six inches and probably a hundred pounds on him.

"This is Heath," Sylvie said. She didn't call him her friend this time, though. Tell the universe what you want, she thought. And she definitely wanted to be more than friends with Heath.

"These hooligans are my cousins, Tonio, Neptune, and Jackson," she told Heath.

Heath stuck out his hand. He smiled casually, even though she sensed his frustration at being interrupted yet again. Her family sure had a knack for it. The boys shook Heath's hand in turn.

"What's up, boys?" Sylvie asked as she looked at her watch hoping to indicate that she was in a hurry.

"We need some extra funds for a skateboarding rally in Rollinsburg next weekend. Meg said if you said it was okay, we could help clean up the shop a couple of times to earn a little green," Tonio said.

She should have guessed. The trio only made an appearance when they wanted something, usually cash. She did appreciate that they were willing to work for it, though. The Jones work ethic was firmly implanted in them.

"Sure, that's fine with me," she said.

The boys whooped and hugged her. She laughed and waved them off to send them on their way. "Make sure you're quiet when you're around, just in case the babies are sleeping."

They gave her a thumbs up sign and were gone. Sylvie turned to find Heath watching her with a cautious expression. The time had arrived for her to make her decision.

Sylvie understood the chaotic nature of life. She kept herself open for new experiences and dearly wanted to believe in the goodness of people's spirits. For a year, she'd been the most guarded in her life. It was as if she'd lost her will to trust, to open herself to anything or anyone other than her children.

She'd told herself it was the way it had to be. But looking into Heath's blazing green eyes, and swallowing hard at the passion she saw in them, she couldn't remember now why she'd ever closed herself off.

Maybe, she'd only done it because she'd been waiting for Heath to find her.

For the first time in a long time, Sylvie decided to go with her gut. And damn, did that decision feel good.

She smiled at the handsome man waiting patiently for her answer. "Don't say I didn't warn you. If you want to stick around and hang out with me, that means you have to hang out with my boys, too. That includes diaper duty."

"Bring it on," Heath said.

Then he gave her a thumbs up sign mimicking her cousins. She snickered.

Yeah, this decision was the right one. Fear be damned.

CHAPTER SIXTEEN

A WEEK LATER, SYLVIE STILL COULDN'T believe that Heath hadn't turned around and run for the hills. She watched as he walked around her living room attempting to burp Jadyn. He had tried bouncing up and down and patting Jadyn's back. Then he tried twisting side to side with a jerky bump at the end.

"That looks painful," she called to him from across the room.

"For me or the baby?" he asked.

"Both," she admitted.

"This burping thing isn't as easy as they make it look on TV."

She chuckled and made her way over to him. Heath handed her the baby without any argument. She started to firmly pat Jadyn's back and was rewarded with a small belch less than a minute later.

"Show-off," Heath said as he plopped down on the couch.

"It just takes practice," she said. She looked at Quentyn, who was in one of the two swings. He was alert, as usual, and seemed to be studying her as much as she was studying him.

She was still trying to figure out which baby was easier for Heath to try helping with. Both of them required multiple hands all the time. While Heath had seemed to take things generally in stride, she frequently saw the looks of panic on his face when he thought she wasn't looking.

"I'm going to go put Jadyn down for a nap. Can you keep an eye on Quentyn?"

"Er ... yeah," Heath said with an exaggerated eye roll. "It's not like he's going to get up and walk away."

Sylvie winked and shook her head at him. She headed to the twins' bedroom, thinking how amazing it was that Heath was still sticking around. He'd become a big part of her life in only a few days. It was scary when she allowed herself to think about it.

Most every morning when she got up, she would find him at her door. He brought coffee from the cafe and a croissant or donuts. He would help her go through her morning routine of getting the boys ready to go to daycare or to stay with Momma. Or, he tried, anyway. He may not have actually been of much help, but he was good entertainment.

Heath attempted to do every task she gave him, but it didn't take long for her to figure out that he had zero experience with taking care of little ones. It was obvious in the way that he held them as though they were pieces of fragile china every time she handed one of them to him.

He looked awkward and uncomfortable sitting with them in the rocking chair. The looks of fear when she asked him to do something on his own, like warm up a bottle or change a pukey onesie, were almost comedic. She hadn't dared ask him to do anything as complicated as changing a diaper for fear she'd send him into a panic.

He hadn't pressured her about their relationship. In fact, he hadn't said anything about their relationship status. So far, everything had seemed pretty aboveboard other than a few chaste kisses on the cheek when he would head back to his hotel every evening.

She wasn't sure if she was relieved or disappointed by his restraint. She didn't know what to make of it. That he still wanted her was unquestionable. She'd sometimes catch him looking at her with sizzling expressions that left no doubt about his desire for her. Why he hadn't acted on that desire kept her up at nights, tossing and turning, imagining all sorts of bizarre reasons.

Perhaps he was just doing what he'd said he'd do—getting to know her better. While they sat and cradled the babies and cooed them to sleep, they had quiet conversations about their lives. Sylvie didn't hold back and was as open with him as she'd been with everyone her entire life, with one exception—the babies.

She hadn't told Heath that he might be the father of her children. But he hadn't asked about it, and she wasn't going to volunteer anything. Perhaps he believed Sylvie's mother when she pulled that embarrassing stunt at the cafe, that her children were fathered by another man.

She wished she knew what Heath thought about all this. And then she hoped she never did. It was frustrating and awkward. The whole situation had been out of character for her all along. And it seemed with each passing day, it only became worse.

Sylvie was an ostrich with her head in the sand, and there was no doubt this was a poor strategy for survival. Sooner or later, the predator of truth was going to bite her on the ass.

After putting Jadyn in his crib, she made her way quietly back out to the living room. She didn't want to wake Quentyn if he had fallen asleep. That was when she heard Heath's quiet words.

He was kneeling beside the baby swing. She crept closer trying to figure out what he was saying.

"Hush little baby, don't say a word. I'm happy you're finally asleep. I'm exhausted and the stare down you've been giving me all night was creeping me out."

Sylvie stifled a laugh.

"How about this deal, kid?" he asked. "If you stay asleep for at least eight hours to give me and your mom some private adult time, I'll give you a million dollars cash."

Sylvie stepped into the room so he could see her. He smiled at her as she crept over to the swing and gently lifted the baby out, careful not to wake him. She saw the alarm on Heath's face and gave him another wink. She was an expert.

Humming a wordless tune softly next to Quentyn's ear, she moved back down the hallway and put him in the crib beside his brother. She leaned over and gave both of them a peck on the cheek and nuzzled their soft skin.

As soon as she was sure that both boys were out, she picked up the baby monitor and turned around. Heath stood in the doorway watching her. She couldn't read his expression. He moved out of the way as she exited the room, and then he followed her into the living room.

They sat on the couch, both of them sighing as they sank into the comfortable cushions.

"You're really great with them," Heath said. "I really respect that. My mom wasn't around when I was a kid, and even when she was, she never took care of me. She paid people to do that."

Sylvie had wondered about Heath's childhood. He didn't ever talk about his parents. She knew he was an only child. She knew he had gone to boarding school, but she didn't get the sense that he had any other family that he had been around in his youth.

It was an utterly foreign concept to Sylvie, the idea of not always having family around her. How strange. She'd grown up running around with Neesa and Phae. They'd constantly been getting in trouble with everyone all around them. There had always been family around and cousins to play with. She knew her own kids would have that experience too. That's why she was so excited about Phae's pregnancy.

"Well, thanks for saying I'm good with the twins," Sylvie said. "It's not like they come with an instruction manual."

"Somebody should really write one of those," he said with a light chuckle. "Of course, I never expected that I would need to read it."

Sylvie frowned. "Didn't you ever want kids?"

"No," Heath said.

The word fell between them like a blackout curtain.

He said no, Sylvie thought. He didn't want kids. Yet here he was with hers.

Heath gave her a steady look. "I have to be honest about it, even if I don't want to say it. I never wanted children because I'm certain I'll make a terrible father."

Sylvie was taken aback. "Why would you think such a thing?"

"I've had no example," he said, his voice too even, his opinion too detached while his eyes flashed a flicker of pain. "I know nothing about parenting because I might as well never have had any. I understand enough about human psychology, however, to know that people parent in similar fashion to how they, themselves, were parented. That could be me, and I would never wish that on any child."

Sylvie's heart ached. How unfair that Heath should not only have to live with the pain of his parents' neglect, but he also had to carry the burden of their poor legacy.

"Many adults had difficult upbringings," Sylvie said, "and they went on to be great parents because they knew exactly what they didn't want to do or be."

Heath gave a slight nod of agreement. "True, but I've read about this, and those kind of people are the exceptions, not the rule."

"Where did you read that?"

"Psychology journals, books, magazines, the usual," Heath said.

Sylvie realized her eyes were starting to burn a bit. Tears. She fought them back, knowing instinctively that Heath wouldn't appreciate them.

If her heart was aching before, it was close to breaking now. Obviously, if he'd done so much reading on the topic, this must be a gigantic concern in his life. She wondered how long he'd been researching it, how much he'd hoped for good news only to receive more of the bad.

Sylvie ticked off a mental check in her head: one more mark against science. It wasn't that Sylvie was categorically opposed to science, it was just that she thought people should keep their options open. It was a big wide universe out there, and not all of it could be probed and measured, made to line up neatly on a graph.

"Bullshit," she said.

Heath jerked backward. "Uh, what?"

"I call bullshit on science," she said, enjoying the way the word rolled off her tongue.

He barked out a laugh. "You can't call bullshit on that."

"Sure I can. I just did." She leveled a stare at him. "Listen, Heath. I haven't known you long, but I know without a doubt that you'll make a great father. I'm not saying you won't make mistakes; we all do. I've already made so many that it's embarrassing."

"Such as?"

Such as not finding out who my children's father is, she thought.

"Never mind that right now," she said. "Here's the thing. You've already given me the best proof that I'll ever need."

"And that is …"

"You'll be a great father because you're afraid you won't be. Get it? You care, and that's most of the battle right there."

Heath leaned in toward her, a glint in his bright green eyes, his dark hair shining in the light. "I want to kiss you right now."

She wanted to kiss him, too, so badly. But instead of doing it, she said, "Well, I guess you should probably get out of here soon. You can't keep hanging around Zeke's Bend forever. You said you run your own company, so your employees probably need you and stuff."

Heath looked at her as if she'd lost her mind. He was probably right.

But she couldn't help it. He said he wanted to kiss her and she'd gone all silly inside.

And the silly wasn't going away. "I'm sure somebody is going to come looking for you soon," she babbled. "Probably better check up on them and so on."

Sylvie didn't know why she was saying these things. It wasn't like she wanted Heath to leave.

He had said he wanted to get to know her better, and he'd been doing that. He'd seemed to accept that her children were part of the package, and that was what she'd told him she wanted. She hadn't wanted him to pressure her physically, and he hadn't. And now that she did want him to make a move, he finally had.

So, what the hell?

"They're fine without me," Heath said.

"Who?"

"My employees," he answered with a slight grin curving up one side of his sexy lips. "You were concerned about them."

"Right, I was."

"They're fine, I assure you. I was hoping that we could spend a little bit of time together tonight," Heath said. He put his hand on her knee.

Sylvie instantly felt a rush of warmth run through her body. She looked down at her hands and saw they were locked together. When did that happen? She pulled them apart and forced herself to relax. She took a deep breath and blew it out slowly.

"Erm ... look, I haven't ... umm ... I had the babies and ... well ... it's been a long time and ..." God, this was so embarrassing, Sylvie thought.

She was terribly attracted to Heath, but she was a mom now. Her body had changed in many ways since she'd last been with Heath. Her breasts were fuller, as was the roundness of her hips. She was insecure in a way that she'd never been.

But then she didn't have to think anymore because Heath took over for her. He lifted her chin and met her gaze. What she saw in his eyes made her tremble, and when he reached for her and pulled her into his lap, she didn't fight against it.

She balanced on his knee as he grazed her jawline with a feather touch. This was the first time they'd had such intimate contact since he'd shown up on her doorstep. He'd been so proper and respectful. A reserved gentleman.

Tonight, though, that reserve was gone. Tonight, something was going to happen, and his eyes promised it would be wild and wonderful. She tingled all over.

Then someone pounded on her door.

Sylvie started and Heath cursed.

"Don't answer," Heath said. "They'll go away."

The pounding got louder.

Sylvie leapt off Heath's lap and headed to the door. "Dammit. They're going to wake the boys."

"Oh, yeah, the boys," Heath muttered.

Sylvie rushed to the door and pulled it open. Her brother Will stood there with his hand up, ready to knock some more. His girlfriend, Zilla, was behind him.

"What are you guys doing here?"

"I need to talk to you ... now." Will's expression told her that whatever it was, it was serious.

Zilla was bouncing on the balls of her feet.

Sylvie glanced back at Heath. He'd gotten up to inspect who it was at the door.

"I need to talk to you alone," Will clarified as soon as he saw Heath.

She didn't want Heath to go. She knew that if he had kissed her, it would have just been the beginning. God knows all she had been thinking about for days was being with him. But Will looked really serious, and he wasn't one to make drama without cause.

"That's okay, I was just leaving," Heath said, taking the decision out of her hands.

He nodded at Will and Zilla then gave Sylvie a small smile. "See you tomorrow?"

She nodded at him. "Absolutely."

And then he was gone.

CHAPTER SEVENTEEN

SYLVIE MOTIONED FOR WILL N' ZILLA to come in. Will rolled his eyes.

Everyone called them Will n' Zilla, which Zilla loved. Sylvie's brother, however, claimed to hate it. Sylvie believed he secretly loved it as much as his girlfriend did.

Sylvie hit Will on the arm as he passed her. Hard.

"You could have woken the babies," she hissed. "You know better than to pound like that."

Really, she was more frustrated about the fact that her body hummed for something only Heath could offer. Now Heath was gone for the night and that spelled another night spent alone and unsatisfied.

"Ow!" Will complained before dropping into an overstuffed armchair. "I forgot."

"You forgot about your nephews?" Sylvie gently closed the door then stomped over to the couch. "You ever wake them up and I'll make the two of you get them back to sleep. Trust me, you don't want that duty."

"Quit bitching. I don't hear any yelling so they must be fine. Anyway, I have to talk to you about something. It couldn't wait," Will said.

Zilla perched on the edge of the couch cushion and fidgeted with her hands as she looked anxiously at Will. Sylvie wondered what the heck was going on.

"What is it?" Sylvie asked. "What is so important that you two had to barge in here and couldn't even bother with a phone call instead?"

"Did we interrupt a romantic interlude? If the action isn't happening, it might be because of your wardrobe." Will looked pointedly at her faded jeans and t-shirt. "Folks have been talking about how they've seen you around with that guy everywhere lately. Heath was his name, right? I thought you said he was just a friend."

"He is," Sylvie replied. So far, that was true. Nothing else had happened between them. She could feel a migraine coming on. She didn't want to get into it with her brother and his girlfriend.

She knew as soon as she told anyone anything it would be all over town anyways. As long as she said that she and Heath were just friends, she hoped that she could avoid most of the idle chitchat.

Of course, gossips would gossip no matter what, and there was nothing she could do about it.

Momma sure wasn't happy about Heath's appearance in Sylvie's life. In fact, Momma had taken it upon herself to call Sylvie at least once a day to remind her that she was supposed to be spending time with Alan, the father of her children.

Momma rarely hid her opinions, and on the topic of Heath, she believed Sylvie shouldn't be wasting her time on tomfoolery with some man that was going to disappear as soon as he got in her pants.

Sylvie's cheeks flushed whenever she thought about the conversation. She was almost thirty years old. She was a mother, so clearly she had had sex at least once. And yet the warnings from her mother made her feel like she was sixteen years old all over again.

And now here was her brother, her younger brother, grilling her about Heath. It was ridiculous.

"Leave me alone about him," she told Will. "It's none of your business, little brother. If that's what you came here to talk about, then—"

"I thought you said that Alan was the twins' father." Will crossed his arms over his chest.

Sylvie was thrown by the abrupt change. "Yeah. Wait. No. What?"

"I couldn't stand watching you working yourself to the bone while that jackass tooled around town in his new car with his new girlfriend and not paying a dime of child support. It wasn't right," Will said, chest puffing out with indignation.

Uneasiness rolled through her. "I don't know why we're talking about this. What's going on?"

"If Alan isn't the father, then who else would it be?" Will glared at her defiantly.

Zilla was wisely keeping quiet, looking everywhere but at them, clearly trying to avoid involvement in the conversation.

"Perhaps you should start at the beginning," Sylvie said. "I don't know why you barged in here, and I don't care. If all you're going to do is just regurgitate the same old stuff and berate me for not going after Alan for child support, then you're wasting everyone's time. It's getting late, and I'm tired."

Will spoke with a tone that combined accusation with triumph. "Yeah, I guess you would say that considering Alan isn't the father."

The world went a little hazy along the edges. Sylvie's mouth went dry and it was hard to swallow. "Why do you say that?"

"I'm your brother and I've been worried about you. I've also worried about my nephews, no matter what you think. I've watched you struggle to get enough money to make sure you can support them right. I know you're going to say everybody's helping you, and you're doing just fine, but I was talking to Esther at the electrical co-op a few weeks ago, and she told me you've been late paying your bill every month for the last six months."

Sylvie put her hand over her face. She had been doing her best, and she had paid the bills, albeit a little late. Now she knew that everybody was gossiping that she couldn't make ends meet. She cursed silently to herself. "Esther should respect her customers' privacy. My bills are my own business." She couldn't believe it.

"I knew if I asked you about it, you'd tell me to back off. You can't blame me for being concerned. So I decided that it was time that Alan started paying his fair share."

Sylvie realized that this train of logic was going in a bad direction, and she was terrified. "What did you do?"

Zilla stood up. Sylvie sensed that she wanted to play the part of the peacemaker.

"It wasn't a big deal, Sylvie. You shouldn't blame Will. It was my idea, and it was actually really easy. We just needed to get a little bit of Alan's DNA to have it tested."

For a peacemaker, Zilla sure knew how to drop a bomb. Holy hell. DNA?

Zilla twittered on. "See, once the paternity test showed that he was the father of the babies, you would be able to go after him for child support. The court would make him pay. We wanted to make it easy for you."

Sylvie finally sat down, her legs on the verge of giving out on her. She felt cold all of a sudden. "I think that you're going to need to tell me that again."

Will seemed to think that she was interested in the details. He started talking animatedly with his hands. "You know how Alan has a thing for good-looking girls? I had Zilla here distract him, and we were able to get a swab of his fluids."

Fluids? Sylvie shuddered. "I honestly don't think I want to know that level of detail."

"It was only his mouth," Zilla said, sitting down beside her and patting her hand. "Inside his cheek, like on the forensic shows on TV."

How in the world had Zilla managed to ... never mind. She didn't want to think about it. Sylvie's head pounded. "Seriously, just get on with it."

"Well, if you want me to skip to the good stuff, I guess I can do that." Will looked disappointed. His amateur sleuthing wasn't being appreciated, and he was clearly put out.

Sylvie thought there'd never been a time in her entire life that she more wanted to punch him in the arm.

She rolled her hand in the air to get him going again.

"Well, you know how Zilla works part-time down at the clinic? Once we got the swab, we sent it off to one of those mail order paternity testing places." Will paused for dramatic effect.

Then he pulled a piece of paper out of his pocket and opened it. He set it on the coffee table in front of Sylvie. "Read it."

Sylvie refused to pick it up. She shook her head.

"Go on," he said.

"Nope." Sylvie was now in full-on ostrich mode and no one could make her stop—

"Alan isn't the father of your babies," Zilla announced.

So much for ostriches, Sylvie thought.

She sat in silence, waiting while the news sunk in.

Alan wasn't the father.

Alan wasn't the father!

Good God.

She covered her mouth with both hands to hide her joy.

Heath was the babies' father.

She wanted to cry and laugh at the same time.

Why had she waited so long to find out the truth? This was wonderful news, the best news ever. It was a revelation, the greatest relief she'd ever felt. When Heath found out—wait a minute.

Sylvie flinched and dropped her hands, pointing a finger at her scowling brother. "You can't tell anyone about this, Will. You either, Zilla. This is important. You don't know how important."

Sylvie's mind raced with the impact of the news. She had to keep a lid on it until she could figure out a way to broach the topic with Heath. The conversation must happen sooner rather than later before Will 'n Zilla spilled it.

She had no idea the best way to do that, though, especially after today's conversation and knowing Heath's concerns about being a parent. Plus, there was the tiny detail that she'd never told him being the twins' father was even a possibility. She was pretty sure he wouldn't let her gloss over that fact.

"We've got to know, Sis," Will said. "If Alan isn't the father, who is? Were you stepping out on Alan, too?"

His words ignited a flare of disdain inside of her. "You think that I cheated on him? No way. I'm nothing like Alan. I can't believe you'd say that."

Unable to sit still any longer, she got up and stalked into the kitchen. She began wiping down counters that were already clean.

Will followed. When he spoke this time, his accusatory tone was gone. "I'm sorry. I shouldn't have said that. You're definitely nothing like Alan."

Sylvie stopped scrubbing and looked at her brother. He appeared genuinely sorry. "Okay. I just need you to not tell anybody about this until I say it's okay. I really, really need you and Zilla to promise me."

Zilla slipped in beside Alan and he put his arm around her tiny waist. They both nodded at Sylvie and pledged they'd keep her secret.

"I want you to know," she said, "it happened after I broke up with Alan. It's something that I'll take care of. Soon."

"So did you know all this time that Alan wasn't the father?" Will asked.

Now Sylvie was embarrassed. Part of the reason she had let everyone believe it was Alan was because she didn't want to admit to anyone that it could have been one of two men. She had sex with both of them during the trip.

"Never mind," Zilla said. "Leave her alone, Will. She's embarrassed."

Sylvie appreciated Zilla's defense. "It's okay. I've got to tell someone, sometime, right? I didn't know if it was Alan or someone else. With the timing, either man could have been the father."

"But you let us all believe that it was Alan, for sure," Will said.

"I think of it as not correcting your assumptions," Sylvie countered.

"Hairsplitting, and you know it."

She sighed. "You're right. The bottom line is this, I knew Alan could be the father, and the man who it turns out actually is the father didn't know that I was pregnant. That's why I didn't say anything." There, she had said it out loud. "Now I really need to be alone. I have a lot of thinking to do."

Zilla's face wore an expression of sympathy. She patted Sylvie's shoulder. "At least, you know for sure now, right? I know it must be hard to think about telling somebody they're a daddy."

Sylvie didn't want Zilla's pity. She didn't want anybody's pity or sympathy. Right then, all she wanted was some peace and quiet.

She looked at Will. "I appreciate what you were trying to do. But you were out of line and may have just made a bigger mess of things. Can you just give me some space to think about this and deal with it on my own? Please?"

Will finally looked abashed "Of course. I really only was trying to help you and the boys. That's how it started anyway."

"I know."

"I'm sorry to have barged in here and upset you. I'm glad we didn't wake the babies."

"Me too."

She let them out and then flopped down in her chair. She picked up the piece of paper that Will had left on the table. She couldn't believe it. Alan wasn't the father. Heath was.

It was a dream come true. So why was she more anxious than ever?

Part of her wanted to call Heath and tell him to come back so she could tell him the amazing news. The rest of her felt strongly that Heath wasn't ready to hear the truth, not yet anyway.

It was important that she did this right. Sylvie took out a pen and paper and started to think. She had a pro-con list to make, and it meant her entire life.

CHAPTER EIGHTEEN

HEATH SAT AT A SCRATCHED-UP table in the noisy Trapper's Tavern and guessed he should feel flattered that Kent and Leon wanted to take him out for a drink. He had been in Zeke's Bend a little more than a week, and he was starting to get to know Sylvie's family.

They were reluctantly getting to know him too. He ran into Kent, Phae's husband, on the street that afternoon, and the man had invited Heath on a boys' night out. Heath had agreed, mostly because he thought it was important to get to know the people in Sylvie's life.

When Kent said he'd invite Leon, Meg's husband, there was no way Heath could decline. Meg was Sylvie's business partner and was very important in Sylvie's life.

Heath wondered what he would be like when he got married. He admired the way that Kent talked about Phae as if she were the most important thing in the world to him. Kent was obviously over-the-moon happy about becoming a father soon, even though he downplayed it.

Part of Heath was wistful he'd missed Sylvie's pregnancy. It was a crazy idea to even cross his mind. Sylvie was already gorgeous but adding in the pregnancy glow had probably made her luminescent.

He shook his head and stared at his beer, watching the tiny bubbles stream upward to the surface, wondering about a fleck of something unidentifiable floating around in the golden liquid. The bar was pretty much a dump, a place that attracted locals who were serious about drinking and couldn't care less about basic hygiene.

He tried to ignore the fleck and looked around Trapper's Tavern. To say that it was a dive bar was an understatement, and as a result the it attracted mostly men. It was situated several miles outside of Zeke's Bend on a state highway.

Heath listened with a cautious ear all night to the conversations going on around him. Leon and Kent were currently caught up in a rowdy game of darts. Heath went out early. He'd kidded with them when they first walked in the door that he had absolutely no athletic prowess whatsoever, and Leon and Kent proceeded to take full advantage of it.

He took a sip of his beer and chuckled along with Kent as Leon threw a dart and missed the dartboard entirely. Leon blustered around about having something in his eye. Heath had no idea how he'd lost the round so quickly to someone who was obviously so horrible at it.

But then again his head wasn't really in the game. It was back in town with Sylvie. He'd made a move toward taking their relationship to the next level and been interrupted by her brother. He and Sylvie hadn't discussed it since it happened the night before, even though they had spent a few hours together this afternoon.

Kent gave a small whoop as he hit the dartboard with the final dart that won the game. Heath smiled and raised his glass in the air. Kent pulled the darts out and tried to hand them to Heath to start a new game, but Heath shook his head.

"No thanks, I think after these couple of beers, I'm more likely to take out somebody's eye than hit the dartboard."

Kent grinned. "If you're going to be hanging out with us more often, you're going to have to get better at darts. Every Thursday night is league night, and we have an opening for a floater."

"What makes you think I'll be hanging around long enough to join a team for league night?" Heath asked the question cautiously.

He was curious to know what Sylvie's family and friends thought about his continued presence in town. He had said that he was a friend of hers, but it seemed like it was pretty obvious to folks that there was more going on. Little did they know, not a damned thing they thought was happening actually was.

"Right..." Leon gave Heath a long look. "You're gonna try and tell us that you're not into Sylvie? Ho-ho! We know that look. You've got it bad, man."

Heath was chagrined. He thought he was covering his emotions for Sylvie better than that. "I don't know what you're talking about."

Kent lightly knocked shoulders with him. "It's okay. You're among friends here. The only thing is if you get involved with Sylvie, you have to put up with that asshole of an ex-boyfriend of hers. Especially since he's probably going to want to be part of the babies' lives, eventually."

Now, this peaked Heath's interest. He had heard rumors around town that there was an ex-boyfriend in the picture, and of course, Sylvie's mother had basically said as much. But he didn't know the details, and he didn't want to put off Sylvia by putting her on the spot about it.

He tried to sound casual when he asked his next question. "So what's with them, anyway? Sylvie never talks about him."

"Can you believe a guy would get a woman pregnant and not step up and take care of his children?" Kent seemed appalled by the idea.

Even though he hadn't known the man long, Heath liked Kent a lot. He recognized Kent right away as the genius behind Kenrik, a company Heath had once scouted and considered trying to purchase.

The rumor around town was that Kent had a small fortune stashed away and that he was a reclusive billionaire. Kent wasn't ever reclusive, but he certainly had a large fortune. He'd made a killing on the sale of Kenrik.

Heath wondered if, at some point, he might become the object of similar gossip around Zeke's Bend. The funny part about that, of course, was that he really was a reclusive billionaire. The irony wasn't lost on him.

Leon stepped up to the table and took a drink of his beer. "Alan's a chiropractor. He and Sylvie dated way too long. He's an ass. Never treated her right. Always chased around other women's skirts behind her back. He didn't even bother to hide it that well because everyone knew. I think Sylvie knew, too, but she wouldn't admit it. I don't know why she put up with him for so long. I think she was just being stubborn."

This was also interesting news. Sylvie had been going out with this man until last year.

"So what happened? What made her finally give him the boot?"

"She went on a trip with him," Leon said. "I don't remember where. And I don't know what happened. Meg went on and on about it, but who can listen to all that chatter? Ho-ho! Anyhoo, when Sylvie came back, she was done with Alan, and that suited all of us Joneses just fine. We were glad to see him go. Isn't that right, Kent, my boy?"

Kent nodded. "I don't know the guy, really, but he hasn't stepped up to his responsibilities, so I don't have much use for him."

"She went on a trip with him, you say?" Heath asked. "Does she travel often?"

"Nah," Leon said. "She's always working, just like the rest of us. Gotta make a living, eh boys?"

The pieces of the puzzle were finally starting to fit together. The trip must have been when he met Sylvie in Chicago. And if so, then it was when she'd broken up with this Alan character. It was all starting to make sense. A heartbroken woman would be a woman looking for perhaps a little bit of fun and a rebound.

And that's where Heath came into the picture. Fun and a rebound. Was that all he'd been? Not exactly a testament to his romantic prowess.

"Of course, then it turned out that Sylvie was pregnant," Leon continued. "Sachet can't stand that Sylvie is letting Alan off the hook. At the very least, he should be paying child support for those babies. I agree with my sister."

"So she's admitted that Alan is the father of the babies?" Heath asked the question with a great deal of trepidation.

"Who else could be the father?" Kent asked. He shook his head at Heath like he was crazy. "She hasn't dated anyone else since she broke up with Alan."

"I see." And Heath definitely did see. If Sylvie had been with him and with Alan that weekend, it was possible that everyone could be wrong about the man who fathered Sylvie's twin boys.

The conversation may have settled nothing for him, but it certainly had reopened a can of worms he thought was sealed.

"So, you have to tell us the story. When Meg found out I was going out with you tonight, she told me I had to get all the dirt." He took a drink and mumbled, "It's pretty much the only reason she let me come."

"Yeah, what's up between you and Sylvie," Kent asked.

"Just friends," Heath said.

"Ahem." Leon cleared his throat. "Meg told me that Sylvie's been acting happier in the last week than in a long time."

"Really?"

"She's whistling, Meg says."

Huh. Whistling. A warm swell of pride filled his chest, although the conversation itself was awkward. He wasn't used to having conversations like this with other men. He didn't think that men usually gossiped, but then again, he didn't know why he was surprised. So far, he'd observed that it seemed as if everybody gossiped in Zeke's Bend.

"We're friends, that's all," he said.

"What do they call it these days?" Leon blustered. "Friends with benefits? Ho-ho!"

Kent and Heath exchanged glances. Kent appeared to share Heath's opinion that Uncle Leon was quite the character.

Heath didn't answer Leon's charge, only shook his head and sipped at his beer, keeping an eye out for the floating fleck of whatever it was.

"You know what? I think I'm going to toss some more darts," Kent declared.

Heath silently thanked him for the save. Leon whooped for some unknown reason. Heath couldn't imagine getting that excited over a game of darts, but whatever floated the older man's boat.

As they played, the noise rattled through the whole bar and before long they'd attracted a surprising fourth—Will Jones, Sylvie's brother.

The four men split into two teams, Heath with Will, and Kent with Leon. Soon, the score was tied. It came down to the final minutes of the dart battle. Some fellow patrons of the bar stood around watching them play.

In an aside, Will nudged Heath's ribs. "Everybody around here said you don't play darts."

"I had some incentive." Heath wasn't going to say that the incentive was that he wanted to stop talking about Sylvie.

Thankfully, Will wasn't asking any questions about his sister. All the same, Heath knew Will was sussing him out, trying to get a handle on who he might be, what kind of man he was. Heath couldn't blame him for it. Heath liked to think if he had a sister he'd be protective of her, too.

Sometimes, though, when Will thought he wasn't looking, Heath would catch Will watching him with a speculative air. It was as if Will were trying to figure something out. It was strange and Heath did his best to ignore it.

Kent stepped up. He took his time at the line studying the board intently. People around them were taking bets, and he thought he heard someone call out a bet for fifty bucks on Heath and Will. Heath wasn't quite sure what to make of being the center of attention, but the fresh, fleck-free beer he'd been served was helping.

"So where did you say you were from again?" Will asked.

Heath was trying to focus on what was going on in front of him. He was going to be up after Kent's turn was done if Kent didn't hit the mark that won the game. "Seattle."

"Sylvie's never been to Seattle."

"I didn't know that."

Actually, Heath did know that. Sylvie told him that shortly after he arrived in town. It was a topic of conversation during one of their many talks where they discussed everything but what was going on between them.

"So where did you say the two of you met again?" Will asked, his tone far too casual to be real.

Now Heath's attention was on Will and he stopped watching the game. "I didn't say. We met online. Isn't that the way of it these days?" Will didn't look impressed. "Were you out trolling for women?"

"Yep. That's what I do. I spend all my time trolling for women on the internet and traveling halfway across the country to meet each and every one of them. Already got my next conquests lined up. They're up north, in Wisconsin."

Will's brows furrowed. "I assume you're kidding."

Heath laughed. "I don't have to troll for women, Will. They troll for me."

"Think pretty highly of yourself, do you?"

"No. But I am thinking I can't win with you, so I believe I won't be trying anymore." He turned back toward the game, making it clear that he was finished with the conversation.

"Huh," Will muttered.

Heath hoped that this would take care of the man's inquisitive line of questioning. He studied Will out of the corner of his eye. He rather wished now that he had let Sylvie create a cover story for how they met. She'd wanted to, but he had blown it off, not seeing why it would possibly matter.

Now he understood why Sylvie didn't want anyone to know they had met in Chicago. The nosy citizens of Zeke's Bend would be sure to make connections.

So many things were falling into place, and he still had questions, but there was only one that was important. One that would change his life.

Perhaps that was what helped focus his thoughts and allowed him to throw the dart that won the game.

CHAPTER NINETEEN

SYLVIE PUT HER HAND UP TO SHADE her eyes from the brightness of the sun high overhead. She cast a glance at the boys who rested in their stroller across the yard.

She yelled to Neesa, who was closest to the stroller, to put more sunscreen on the babies. Neesa waved back at her with an indulgent grin and a shake of her head, but Sylvie saw her move to comply.

Sylvie knew Neesa's amusement was because Sylvie had asked the same thing fifteen minutes prior. Sylvie didn't care. It didn't hurt to be overcautious about some things. She was their mother, after all.

She was hard at work near one of the vegetable gardens on Neesa's farm. She looked around her at the myriad of relatives moving in between the barn, the house, the garden, and the fields beyond and had to grin. It was as if an impromptu Jones family reunion had been organized on this warmer than average Saturday afternoon in February.

Her eyes strayed across the lawn to the tall, trim figure pounding nails to repair the fence at the far corner of the barn, a much-needed fix to ensure that Neesa's single cow didn't escape.

She sighed with a happy smile. There was no doubt about it. Her eyes would always find Heath, no matter where he was. Kent helped him, and Sylvie saw the two men laugh several times. It was nice to see him getting along with her family.

In the meantime, she and Phae were cleaning underbrush from an old fence line.

Neesa purchased the farm not too long ago. She grew specialty organic produce and sold it to a number of high-priced restaurants from as far away as St. Louis.

The farm had been in quite a state of disrepair when she bought it, which meant that Neesa got it for a steal. But it also meant that there were always projects to do to keep the place up, and Neesa already had a full-time job as a security guard at the college in Rollinsburg.

Neesa dreamt of making enough money from the farm to make it a full-time job, but it was far from a reality. That didn't stop Neesa from continuing to pursue her dream in the meantime, though.

When Neesa heard that it was going to be warmer than usual that weekend, she put out the call to the Jones clan to request that anyone with some free time come out and help her get some chores done. She needed the most help with the bigger jobs she couldn't do on her own like repairing the barn's roof.

Sylvie had volunteered to help, and Heath offered to come out as well. So far, he was proving himself surprisingly adept with a hammer and nails.

Momma was supposed to be keeping an eye on the babies, but she kept wandering over to one relative or another to gossip. Sylvie wasn't too worried, though, about the babies being left alone. Someone was always passing by the stroller, stooping down to smile and waggle their fingers at the boys.

Sylvie watched with a grin as Neesa skillfully ordered her ragtag group of troops to complete various tasks. She was in awe of Neesa's commitment to her business venture.

When they were growing up, Neesa was the one with the green thumb, a nurturer by nature. She was the most content when she was outside with her sleeves rolled up getting her hands dirty. That was far from Sylvie's favorite thing to do, and she grimaced as she pulled off a glove to inspect her ruined manicure.

"It should be illegal to ask a pregnant woman to do this," Phae complained nearby. "And everyone knows I can't garden to save my life."

Sylvie grinned. For all of Phae's moaning and groaning, Sylvie knew that there wasn't anything that Phae wouldn't do for Neesa. That was how Sylvie felt too. Plus, there was a little bit of guilt mixed in there for both of them. After all, Phae had found her Prince Charming. Sylvie had her babies. Neesa's whole world was her farm.

Lately, Sylvie wondered if perhaps she had something else to add to her gratitude list. So far, it had been almost two weeks since Heath's arrival in Zeke's Bend. They spent an increasing amount of time together, but she was still unsure of what it all meant.

Obviously, she knew that he didn't have to go back to work given his billions in his bank account, but more and more, friends and relatives had turned up the heat on her. It seemed everyone had questions about her gentleman caller and how long he planned to hang around.

From out of nowhere, rumors had started to fly that Heath was another reclusive billionaire who had somehow found his way to Zeke's Bend. Sylvie wished she knew where that rumor had started. It probably was the brainchild of the rascally teenage trio of Tonio, Jackson, and Neptune. And now, even some of the adults thought it might be true.

Of course, it actually was true, but they didn't know that. It irritated Sylvie that they should be so right when they didn't have the first clue about what was up.

Those who didn't think Heath might be a secret tycoon thought Heath must be an unemployed bum. They warned Sylvie to be wary of hot men who didn't have jobs. Fortune hunters, they said. Ha-ha. As if Sylvie had any fortune to hunt.

In all, it was downright tiresome, so Sylvie created a cover story for Heath. She told everyone that he had a job which allowed him to work remotely. So as long as he had his computer, he would be able to work from anywhere.

When they questioned her about what kind of job, she said he was a writer, doing research in Zeke's Bend. Everyone wanted to know what kind of research.

Sylvie wanted to throw up her hands. Answering one question only led to five more. She'd never been more put out with everyone.

Heath, on the other hand, was starting to have a bit too much fun with it. He began by hinting that he was doing research on small town police departments. Before the day was out, James offered to let Heath do a ride-along in his squad car the next day.

Heath accepted happily and went out often with James. It was something of a regular deal these days.

Then Heath began claiming that he used to cover the police beat for a Seattle newspaper. And now he was writing up exaggerated stories of his ridealongs with James to regale Sylvie with each night. They were hilarious, including a cast of the town's most eccentric citizens. If Heath were going to stay in Zeke's Bend much longer, Sylvie was going to have to help him find another hobby before he got himself in trouble.

Neesa rang the bell on the front porch to let everyone know it was time for lunch. Sylvie got up and dusted the dirt off her jeans and helped Phae get to her feet as well. She was eager for the break. She saw Momma start to wheel the stroller towards the house, and she and Phae headed in that direction, too.

Heath and Kent left their post, and Heath waved at her with a grin. She waved back and felt that flutter of anxiousness in her stomach. After the night that Will 'n Zilla had interrupted them, Heath hadn't made any other romantic moves on her. He seemed to be waiting for her to decide what she wanted to do.

She appreciated that, but it was also just making things more confusing. She really just wanted to know if he was for real or not, especially now that she knew he was the twins' father. She hadn't found the courage to broach the topic with him yet. She wanted to know how he would react, even though she couldn't know it until she told him the truth.

So she had been watching him and observing him with the babies, listening to the different cues he gave her about what he wanted out of life. He seemed perfectly content so far. But they hadn't spent a lot of time together just hanging out with the babies. If anything, he seemed to be avoiding them lately.

He took her out for dinner several times in Rollinsburg, and they went on a couple of day excursions as she showed him around the area. They always left the babies with Momma Jones or in daycare.

Heath had settled into the evening routine with Sylvie though he'd often arrive shortly before the babies' bedtime. Coincidence? She didn't think so.

Still, it was nice to just hang out with him, to sit next to one another on the sofa and watch TV. It all felt good and right, except when the twins were around. That part kept her from pulling the trigger on telling him the truth.

"Daydreaming again? You better watch that around Neesa. Get it out of your system during lunch. If you don't do a better job this afternoon and quit missing all those weeds, she'll have you hoeing out in the field," Phae said as she put her hands on her hips and stretched from side to side.

Sylvie chuckled. "Sorry, I've got a lot on my mind lately."

"Would any of those things have to do with a tall, handsome reporter?"

Sylvie stepped up onto the wide, wrap-around porch and glanced from side to side. No one else was close-by. Her face flushed warmly and she knew it didn't have anything to do with the heat.

"I have been spending a lot of time with Heath, if that's what you're asking," she said.

"I wasn't really asking. Don't have to. Everybody around town has been reporting back every single detail of what you two have been up to around town. I don't even have to drive in to find out the latest gossip. I'm getting texts, emails and phone calls all hours of the day and night. Maybe Heath should start writing *The Heath and Sylvie Gazette*. It'd sell out in seconds."

Sylvie groaned.

Phae put an arm around her shoulders. "Aww, I'm putting you on. It's not quite that bad. Remember, I'm your best friend. You have to tell me the good stuff first. And I'm nothing but a big fat pregnant lady now. No more romance for me." She made a ridiculous pouty face.

Sylvie heard a snort of outrage from somewhere close-by...Kent.

Sylvie laughed. "I have a feeling you see way more romance than I do these days."

She hadn't meant to say it like that out loud. She was perfectly content with the fact that Heath wanted to take things slow. She did, too. But she didn't want everyone else guessing that her bed was empty as ever. She'd rather they guess the opposite. Less embarrassing.

Phae raised an eyebrow. "What are you saying, girl?"

"Nothing. Nothing."

She turned as she heard the rumble of a car coming up the driveway. She recognized the car. A cherry red convertible. Brand new. The same one James ticketed the day Heath showed up in town.

Alan's car.

CHAPTER TWENTY

WHAT THE HELL?

"Uh-oh," Neesa said as she came out of the house and stood at Sylvie's side. "Who invited him?"

"I certainly didn't," Sylvie said as she crossed her arms over her chest.

"No one would have," Phae said. "Kent, what's he doing here?"

Kent stepped up and slipped an arm around Phae's shoulders. "No idea. I can't imagine he's here for anything good. Can you?"

"No," Sylvie said with the finality of an expert.

Everyone watched the car stop at the end of the circle driveway. Alan got out of the car.

Sylvie thought that he looked ridiculous. He was wearing khaki pants and a long flowing shirt that she wanted to tell him the 80s wanted back.

His hair was parted off to the side, and she could see he had been getting his fake tan on again. He looked like a dissipated "Miami Vice" Don Johnson trudging toward them, and she wondered how she'd ever been attracted to him.

When his glare settled on her, she returned his nasty look in kind. She hadn't spoken more than half a dozen words to Alan since their break-up, and those had all been stiff nods when they had inadvertently passed each other in the street.

The fact that he was at the farm couldn't be a good sign. And the way he was scowling told her this wouldn't end well.

"There you are, Sylvie. I've been looking all over town for you." His tone was nasty, accusatory, as if she'd been hiding from him or something equally ludicrous.

Sylvie stepped off the porch and met him halfway to the house. She realized that both Heath and James flanked her as she went. Any other time their protection would make her feel more confident, but she just wanted to make Alan to go away.

"They have these things called phones now. You might have tried using one." She couldn't keep the snark out of her voice.

"Har-har. I have a bone to pick with you."

"Oh, please. Why are you acting like such an ass?"

"Why are you breaking the damned law?"

"What's this about?" James asked.

"Stay out of this. You're not on duty," Alan sneered.

"I'm always on duty, little man. I'm the Sheriff."

"Whatever. Doesn't matter. There's only one lawbreaker here and that's your cousin there." He lifted his chin and tried to look tough. "I want to know how you thought you'd get away with it, Sylvie. I can't believe you would run a paternity test without my permission." His voice was loud and carried across the property. His face was turning red.

Sylvie's eyes widened. She hadn't expected that. Her relatives were everywhere. And not just her relatives, but Heath, too. She didn't know how to respond. Then she realized that Alan was just getting warmed up.

"Back it up, Alan," James warned.

"You know what? I'm glad you're here, Sheriff, because I have a complaint that I want to file against this woman." Alan pointed at Sylvie with narrowed eyes.

Sylvie wished for one crazy moment that she had something that she could bop him on the head with, to make him shut up and forget everything about that paternity test. It was a dumb thing to think, she knew, but right then, it was the only way she could think of to stave off imminent disaster.

"I've known ever since we got back from Chicago last year that you were going to try and pin those little bundles of joy on me," Alan said. "You illegally took DNA from me without my consent and ran a test, and I'm going to sue you for everything you're worth. I'll take your shop and every dime you have, and if you think for one second I'm going to give you one penny of child support for those little bastards, you're delusional!"

Alan didn't have a chance to say anything more because Heath charged forward and lightning quick, punched Alan square in the nose. He went down with a wail.

Sylvie rushed to Heath's side and grabbed his arm just as he was winding up again.

"Please, don't," she said. "He's not worth it."

James moved in between them and pushed Heath on the chest. "Stand down. I've got this." The Sheriff had taken over.

Alan was wailing on the ground, muttering curses and yelling about having Heath arrested and suing him, too. That was interlaced with more venomous spewing about Sylvie and her bastard babies.

It was a spectacle to end all spectacles, and a few dozen Joneses were present and accounted for on the lawn. Sylvie felt sick. It couldn't get worse than this.

She was wrong.

Will marched up and put his arm around her. He stared down at Alan with a distasteful look on his face. "Sylvie didn't have anything to do with that test. It was all my fault. I was the one who took your DNA."

Alan scuttled to his feet ignoring James's outstretched hand. One hand over his bleeding nose, he pointed at Will with his free hand. "You Jones' twerps are all the same. You think because there are so many of you around that you can bully people into doing what you want. But I'm telling you I will never, ever pay one dime of child support. I didn't want them, so I won't pay. And you can't make me."

"Well, that's just fine!" Will yelled.

Sylvie tried to grab onto his arm, but Will shook himself loose. "Don't, Will!"

Too late. There was no stopping what was about to happen.

Will delivered the coup de grâce. "Nobody wants your damned money! You're not the babies' father. The DNA test proved it! So get the hell out of here!"

The silence that fell was thunderous. Sylvie covered her face with her hands. She heard Alan muttering, but then it was as if he realized there was nothing else to say. She peeked at him between her fingers and saw him struggle to get to his car.

He spat on the ground and looked at her with hate-filled eyes. "I knew I dumped you for a reason. You're nothing but a backstabbing whore. Good riddance."

Then he spat on the ground again. James was barely able to hold Heath in check.

"Dammit, James," Heath said, "Let me go. No, come with me. We'll take turns."

"Can't do it, friend. Sorry," James said, struggling to maintain his hold.

Sylvie wrapped her arms around her stomach. She heard the twins behind her starting to cry. Even the babies knew something terrible just happened.

She felt as if her world had been torn apart. Then she saw Heath quit struggling. He twisted his head to get a look at her. She saw in his eyes that he knew the truth.

She would do anything to go back in time and change everything. Now it was out there for everyone, and Heath had learned he was a father in the worst possible way. She felt exposed. Raw.

James walked up to her as Alan's convertible headed back down the driveway. "I don't think you have to worry about him anymore." He said it like it was some kind of consolation prize, and in a way, it was.

But Alan Posner was the least of her concerns right then. She gave him a short nod, and James walked away grabbing Will by the arm, knowing that now was not the time.

Heath approached her obviously going to say something. The sound of a whirring motor interrupted him.

Great Aunt Elfleda buzzed between them on the walk. She sucked her teeth and scowled at Sylvie.

Sylvie shuddered, willing the elderly woman to disappear before she said whatever hurtful thing she was getting ready to say.

But Elfleda surprised her. "Sylvie, I'm pleased that man isn't those sweet babies' father. I'd been worried about them. Apples don't fall far from the tree, if you know what I mean. And we don't need any more bad apples in this family. I'm relieved, Girl."

"Uh, thanks, I guess?" Sylvie said.

"And you, Hoss." She rotated the chair to face Heath. "I don't know what you have to do with all this, but I want you to know I've got my eye on you." She pointed at her rheumy, but still sharp eye. "This one right here. On you. All the time. You've got a secret and I'm going to figure it out."

And with that, she whipped around and raced off toward the house again, ordering a frozen Neesa to get with serving lunch for everyone.

"Nothing more to see here, people," Elfleda ordered as she drove up the ramp to the porch. She stopped briefly in front of Sylvie's mother, who was standing on the porch next to her husband, Eli.

"That means you, too, Sachet," Elfleda said. "I see you're revving yourself up to have a go, but let it be right now. Eli, take your wife inside. Don't forget the babies. Let's go eat."

Her final order served to shake everyone out of their stupors. They all stopped staring and tucked their heads down, most of them abashed to have overhead such a private matter in such a way. They were used to hearing shocking gossip second hand, not first.

Heath looked everywhere but at Sylvie until everyone was in inside.

With a neutral expression on his face, he said, "I think I'm feeling a little tired. Must be the sun. I'm going to head back to my hotel now. We should talk … later."

He seemed to be in a state of shock. Sylvie didn't know what else she expected.

"Shall I come by about six then?"

Heath gave her short nod and walked to his car. She watched him go, wanting the earth to open up and swallow her.

This wasn't the reaction she wanted. She wanted him to want her babies. His babies. She wanted him to be happy he was a father.

She had completely messed everything up. She should have told Heath as soon as she found out Alan wasn't the father.

Heath drove away, not looking back for even an instant.

She slowly turned in her tracks. Phae and Neesa stepped onto the porch, both of them with expressions of sisterly sympathy.

They held open their arms and Sylvie ran to them, tears flowing down her cheeks.

CHAPTER TWENTY-ONE

HEATH SAT IN HIS HOTEL ROOM staring out the window. The afternoon hadn't gone anything like he expected. He had left that morning as simply a man. He had come home a father.

Even though he'd known for a while that it was a possibility, the way the truth was revealed shook him to his core. His thinking about being a father had been superficial. Now he was forced to go deeper.

He kept coming back to all the things that his father didn't do for him. Fathers were responsible for showing their children the ways of the world. They should protect them from its dangers.

They were supposed to teach their kids right from wrong and give them the tools they'd need to make good decisions in life. Heath was overwhelmed at the idea of shouldering such responsibility.

He wasn't sure if he could do it. He never backed away from challenges, but this was different from his usual dealings like corporate takeovers. This had ramifications that went far beyond the legacy of a company. He was talking about people, little people that were part of him. It scared him shitless.

The clock rolled toward six o'clock, and he waited for Sylvie with trepidation. He had to get this right. No matter what, no matter how unsure he was, it was important for her to understand that he wouldn't shirk his duty. The babies were his responsibility, too, and he intended to live up to that.

He managed to buoy himself up when the thought occurred to him that Sylvie could decide she didn't want her him in their lives at all. He wasn't sure how to feel about that. On the one hand, no more parenting problems. No more risk. On the other, no more Sylvie. He damned sure didn't want the latter. He wasn't so sure about the former.

He wondered if Sylvie knew he was her children's father, or if she'd only learned it that day, like him. And if she had already known, why hadn't she told him? These were troubling concerns.

He told himself she must have had her reasons. And there was no point speculating about what they might be. Sylvie had her own style of logic, a bold kind of faith in things that Heath lacked. He couldn't begin to second-guess her, so why even try?

When the knock on the door finally came, he employed the same calming techniques he used before big meetings. It was a combination of focus points and deep breathing, and it worked every time. Even now.

He opened the door. Sylvie wore a flowing skirt and a silky, colorful blue, print blouse that accentuated her full bosom. She took his breath away, as always. He'd never have the upper hand with this woman, he thought, not if she was going to insist on being so beautiful.

They greeted one another, a bit shyly. He closed the door behind her, and they went to the sitting area and sat in the two chairs that faced each other.

Sylvie seemed more uncertain than he'd ever seen her. Despite her beautiful outward appearance, she looked downright miserable.

He had likely played a part in that, discovering he was a father and reacting by running away. He had some fixing to do.

"Would you like something to drink? Some wine? Might take the edge off," he said.

She nodded. "Neesa's got the babies for the night."

Heath went and got the bottle of wine from the mini-fridge and set it on the table between the chairs. He grabbed the wine glasses provided in the kitchenette, and brought them over, too. He knew he was just making busy work for himself, but he felt anxious.

The irony of the situation was that he and Sylvie had been doing nothing but talking for the last two weeks. Unfortunately, they hadn't been discussing what they should have. Heath was afraid to press the issue, and she must have had her own reasons, too.

There was no avoiding it now, though.

He poured her a glass of wine and handed it to her. She looked grateful for the distraction. She took a long sip, and he realized that she needed the liquid courage as much as he did for what was going to come next. He poured a glass of wine for himself, and then he waited.

"You probably have questions." The way she said it was a statement and not a question. Probably because she knew as well as he did that it was the understatement of the year.

"How about you start at the beginning, and we'll go from there." He figured at this point the less he said, the better. He definitely did not want to say the wrong thing.

Sylvie took a deep breath followed by a sigh that seemed to come from the deepest part of her body. She looked up at the ceiling then closed her eyes tight. When her eyes opened, they met his, strong and true. "I didn't know for sure until last week that you were definitely the twins' father."

"Why didn't you tell me sooner?" he asked, trying to keep his voice even and neutral. "I thought they must be Alan's since that's what everyone kept telling me."

She looked down at her glass. "I don't know. It was silly of me, but I think I was scared."

"After all the time we've spent together? Why?"

"I felt all along that you were their father. I did. I had no proof, of course. Phae would have made fun of me if she'd known, and kept telling me it was just wishful thinking. But Heath, I swear, deep in my soul, every time I looked at my sons, I knew they had to be yours."

"And that frightened you because ..."

She set her glass on the table. "I don't know. Maybe because you weren't here, and then you were, and I don't trust easily. And this just was so big, so powerful. I can't explain it, what it's like to know something then have it come true. It kinds of shakes you up."

"You're talking about being somewhat psychic again?"

"Don't say it like that. Don't patronize me."

"I didn't think I was. I apologize."

"Well, maybe I'm a little sensitive about it," she admitted. "I realize that no one believes me."

"I don't know if you're psychic or not. But you have every right to believe it," he said, treading carefully.

"Thanks."

"How about we back up," Heath suggested. "You didn't tell me I'm a father because you were scared that your psychic prediction came true. Is that right?"

She nodded, reached for her wine glass, and took a drink. She made a "humph" sound and finally looked at him. "Okay, that's kind of a load of nonsense. I admit it. I guess I didn't tell you about being a father because I was hiding from the truth. I was afraid you wouldn't want to be a father, and that you wouldn't want me. I kept thinking if you had more time to get used to the twins, if you spent more time with me, then when you learned the truth it wouldn't seem so big and overwhelming. You have said, if you remember, that you don't want children."

He winced at the memory.

Sylvie hurried on. "Also, what we had was just a one-night stand, and I didn't want you to feel obligated to have to take care of the boys. I don't want you to think that you have to do anything at all. I have everything under control. I'm taking care of them just fine, as you've been able to see. So you don't have to do anything."

There would be plenty of time to talk about how he could help Sylvie with the babies, although he wasn't sure if he should be offended or appreciative that she appeared to be trying to give him an out.

"We've been together practically every day all day for the last two weeks," he said. "If you found out a week ago, there's been a lot of time for you to grasp how I might feel about it, even if I did talk about my concerns about being a good parent. I've been here for you the whole time, Sylvie. I accepted that the babies are part of the package. I understood what it meant to get involved with you, and I didn't back away from that."

Her brow furrowed. "I don't want you to feel like you're getting a package. The boys are a part of me and my life. They should be viewed as a bonus, not a kind of necessary evil."

Heath realized they had tread into very dangerous territory. He started to backpedal. "Of course not. What I meant is that when I came for you, I knew you were a mother when I saw the picture on the Internet. I knew that going in. I still wanted to be part of your life and get to know you better. That meant getting to know the babies, too."

"Just because you said that, doesn't mean that's actually true when push comes to shove, especially once you started being around them all the time. Those little babies are entirely dependent on me for everything. They take my time and attention and energy nearly twenty-four hours a day, seven days a week. That's not a small commitment, Heath, and if you're not ready for that, why would I force that on you? I've seen the fallout of what happens when a man doesn't want to be saddled with a family."

"What do you mean?"

"I mean my own father."

CHAPTER TWENTY-TWO

SYLVIE HAD ONCE SPOKEN TO Heath about her father, but briefly.

"A man might leave for any number of reasons, not just because he doesn't want the responsibility," he said.

"I wouldn't know. I can't imagine how he ever did such a thing," she said.

"Since your father left you, you think all men leave."

"It's not that simple. I get it. For all I know I'm meant to go it alone. It could be my fate and there's no point in fighting against it."

Sylvie was afraid of commitment, he thought, and a lot of that came from her past. She was a strong, proud woman. And though her nature was to be whimsical and spontaneous, her life experience had left her afraid of losing control. So she clung tightly to what was most important to her life—her children, her family, and Zeke's Bend itself.

"You're the twins' mother," he said, "and you're doing an amazing job. I don't want to get in the way of that. And I don't even know if you actually want me in their lives."

Sylvie's eyes widened. "Of course, if you want to be there, I want you there. I just don't want you to feel obligated. Kids are smart. They pick up on that kind of thing."

Heath knew that better than anyone, but he felt as if they could go around in this circle forever. "I don't feel obligated, Sylvie. I'm a big boy. I don't shirk my responsibilities, and yes, I do see this as a responsibility, but that doesn't mean it's a burden. There's a difference. In fact, it's all the difference in the world. You know that if you think about it."

She nodded. "You're right. There's a difference."

"I'm not sorry this happened, Sylvie. I don't regret Chicago for a moment, and I don't regret showing up here on your doorstep completely unannounced and getting to spend time with you and with my boys."

It was the first time that he had used a possessive when talking or thinking about the twins. It still felt awkward, but he knew that he'd finally said the right thing when he saw Sylvie's face relax.

"I wouldn't change it, Sylvie," he said. "I'm more than ready for whatever comes next."

She smiled and practically jumped across the small space separating them and flung herself into his arms.

He hugged her tightly as she wrapped her arms around his neck. He felt the delightful light touch of her kisses going up and down his cheek.

"You're going to love them," she said between kisses. "They are so wonderful. Heath, I'm so glad that you are their father."

A voice inside him mumbled that at least somebody was happy about it. Damn. He wished that voice hadn't said that. It wasn't true, not really. That voice was simply speaking for the part of him that constantly reminded Heath that he had no idea of how to be a father.

He gave some voice to that fear. "I don't know how to be a family man, Sylvie, so I hope you'll be patient with me."

Sylvie looked up at him with a soft smile on her face. She put her small, soft hand on his cheek. "I'll help you. You're going to be great at this."

Everything he'd been denying himself when it came to Sylvie was right in front of him. They'd figure the rest of it out. It couldn't be that hard if they were together. Right now, he only wanted her.

"I'm ready, Heath. I want this, too." She must have read the unspoken question in his eyes.

This was what he had been waiting for since he arrived in Zeke's Bend. He dipped his head to find her lips and she eagerly met him halfway. Their hands were all over each other, but it felt different from Chicago.

Heath experienced a wave of possessiveness that was new. This was the woman he cared about, the mother of his children. She was a fragile piece of glass and he wanted to wrap her up in his arms and take care of her so that she never had to worry about anything bad happening to her ever again.

The joke was on him, he supposed. He hired an escort service because he wanted to avoid precisely this kind of commitment. And then, in a twist he'd never expected, he saw Sylvie in a champagne-colored dress sitting on a stool in that bar. Nothing had been the same since.

The joke was on him all right. He had railed for so long against the idea of commitment that it had come back and punched him in the gut. But, as it turned out, he didn't mind at all.

It wasn't commitment he'd been avoiding. He was avoiding the expectations of women he didn't care about. That was why he hired the escort service. Sylvie, though, she could expect pretty much anything she wanted and he'd try to deliver it.

He gently stroked Sylvie's hair. He wanted to spend hours worshiping her body, but neither one of them could wait long. They'd been waiting for this, he'd been waiting for this, for over a year now.

He gently scooped her up, laughing at the way she squealed and kicked her legs. There was nothing in this world like holding Sylvie. He took her to his bed and lay her on it.

She rapidly unbuttoned and slipped his shirt off his shoulders. They made quick work of undressing each other. Every inch of her skin that he uncovered, he had to kiss.

He admired the slopes and valleys of her body, the smoothness of her skin, the swoop of her calves, the delicate ankles, and tiny painted toes.

Her body was slightly fuller now, and as Heath skimmed her curves, he relished the change. He took his time admiring her when she was finally naked in all her glory.

She seemed slightly embarrassed and some of her ardor cooled. She'd made as if to cover herself. He'd have none of that.

He grabbed her wrists and pinned her arms overhead "No. You're gorgeous. I want to see every inch of you. No hiding, baby. This is all mine, isn't it?"

She licked her beautiful lips and nodded, her glittering brown eyes drawing him down for a passionate kiss. He pulled back before he lost track of what he was about.

"Mine?" he repeated.

"Yes," she whispered, her eyes gone dreamy and smoky from his kiss. "And you're mine."

"Damned straight."

An animal sound emerged from him as he rose up to gaze down at her sexy form.

He looked over her glorious body and grew even harder. He moved against her and in a fluid movement he slipped down between her full thighs.

His eyes feasted on that part of her that he had tasted in Chicago, and he craved to repeat the experience. She moaned as his fingers slowly opened her slick folds. He loved how wet she was, the tactile evidence of her desire.

He groaned when his tongue first made contact with that small nub that made her hips buck against him. It took but seconds to bring her to release. She dug her fingers into his hair and pulled hard. He could see her head twist from side to side.

"Yes, baby," he told her. "Mmm, yes. That's it. Come for me again. Oh … yes."

When he moved up her body and centered himself at her opening, he propped himself above her and their eyes met. Sylvie wrapped her legs and arms around him.

As he pushed against her, slowly opening her wider and wider, she groaned and lifted her hips. She drew him ever closer, ever deeper.

She whispered things that he could hardly hear, and yet he understood the sentiment. This was the ultimate consummation of everything they had gone without for the past year.

It was a miracle they'd been brought back together. It was an equal miracle that, as he rocked inside her as deep as he could go, it was even better than his memory. The perfect joining. The fit of her, the way she opened for him. Exquisite.

He thrust into her harder and she met his rhythm. More. More. They wanted it that way. They wanted it in the same way.

He brought her to climax twice, holding off his own until Sylvie was gasping for air and raking her nails down his back. Then he let the wave overtake him and as they rode their release together, he watched her face and knew the truth.

All he wanted to do was make her happy.

That's all. Nothing else really mattered. Sylvie ... happy.

Sylvie's lips parted, releasing a sexy little sigh as she came down from her orgasm. His faded along with hers and he dropped down beside, pulling her with him so he could stay inside her. He pulled her leg up over his hip and stroked down her silky thigh.

"Mmm." He hadn't felt peace like this in forever.

She smiled at him and twirled a lock of his hair around her tapered finger. "I think we forgot something again."

So Heath wasn't the only one who had noticed.

"I assume you're protected?" he asked.

"I can't believe you'd assume anything." She laughed. "Don't look like that. I'm covered. I learned my lesson the last time."

He smiled wickedly. "Damn you're sexy when you laugh. I have another game for you. You've got two minutes, and then I hope you're ready to go again."

"You'll wear out before I do," Sylvie said confidently.

Heath winked at her. "What are we betting this time?"

CHAPTER TWENTY-THREE

SYLVIE'S LIFE CHANGED OVERNIGHT. Now that Heath was a part of it, everything about her daily routine needed to be revised. She was disappointed that Heath eventually returned to Seattle for some meetings, but he returned to Zeke's Bend for long weekends, spending every waking moment with her and the twins.

She understood that she couldn't expect him to move there permanently, although they hadn't discussed it, so who knew what might happen. When she was missing him during the week, she'd sometimes fantasize about him selling everything, giving it all up to come live in Zeke's Bend with her and the twins.

She didn't see any reason now to hide the fact that Heath was the babies' father from her family. Most everyone was fine with it, although some weren't impressed that they'd been led to believe the father was Alan. She tried to explain as best she could, but in the end, she knew they'd get over it. She was family and they had to forgive her.

For certain, the news hadn't landed well with Sylvie's mother. She demanded that Sylvie have a paternity test done to definitively prove that Heath was the father. Sylvie was annoyed. She only slept with two men during that time-frame and if the babies weren't Alan's, then they were definitely Heath's unless nature had gone whacky all of a sudden.

But Momma had been insistent. Sylvie gave in just to get some peace and quiet. Plus, she hoped once Momma saw the evidence in black and white, she'd accept that Heath would be part of their lives now.

Fortunately, Heath graciously agreed to the tests once Sylvie explained everything to him.

It hadn't been any surprise when the paternity test came back positive. Heath was definitely the twins' father. With that last bit settled, it started to make it around the Zeke's Bend rumor mill that Sylvie's babies were actually fathered by the reclusive billionaire that Sylvie had met in Chicago.

And that was another new development. With Heath's frequent travel, no one was buying his cover story of being a writer anymore. She didn't give any credence to the rumors, choosing instead to remain silent. People needed to get to know Heath for who he really was, a good man.

Nobody needed to know that he had billions of dollars. Certainly, to her, it didn't matter. She just wanted him. Everything else that came with him was nothing but window trappings.

He still hadn't come clean to her about his real name, and she wondered at it. She couldn't ask him, though. If she did, then she'd have to admit that she'd known who he really was all along. Probably it was best to let that sleeping dog lie.

The part that proved to be the most difficult and comical to navigate was Heath's interactions with the babies. He really was pretty hopeless with them. The little bit that he had learned during the first couple of weeks in Zeke's Bend provide to be woefully inadequate as Sylvie started to fully integrate him into everything that went along with taking care of the twins.

For being such a smart businessman, he was really a slow learner when it came to babies. She'd begun to think he was hopeless when it came removing an old diaper and quickly strategically positioning a new diaper to avoid getting hit in the face with a stream of baby pee.

The first time Heath got nailed by Jadyn, Sylvie had laughed herself half sick. Heath was a good sport, but not all that amused.

The second time it happened, she got it on video. Heath wasn't a good sport at all on that one, threatening she'd regret it if she showed the video to anyone. Of course, she'd shown it to everyone in town. And because he "punished" her in all sorts of delightful ways in her bedroom, she never did regret it.

There never was a third time, or if there was, it happened when Sylvie wasn't looking or taking video.

Whenever he changed a diaper without getting hit in the face, he'd strut around her house, all cocky with his success.

She couldn't resist it. "What? You want a sticker?" she teased. "I'll make one that says: "Kiss me! I didn't get a face full of pee today!""

He chased her around the apartment and gave her a relentless tickling that left her breathless.

After that, she tried to show him the best ways of taking care of two babies at the same time. She knew it was exhausting. She'd already been on the front lines doing it for four months now. But it was still all new to Heath.

She admired his perseverance. Even when she offered to help, he frequently said that he wanted to try and do it on his own. He proved to be stubborn that way. He said if she never let him do it, he'd never learn how to do it on his own. Heath was intent on being as hands on with the babies as possible.

Finally, he insisted that she go out and have a girls' night with Neesa and Phae. He said that he would stay home with the twins by himself.

Sylvie didn't want to hurt his feelings, but she had more than a few reservations. In the end, though, she agreed, telling herself she was being overprotective. After all, the man ran a business with a gross income higher than most countries in the world. If he could run that, he could take care of a couple of little babies for a few hours, surely.

She went over the list of everything that he needed to do and made sure he had Phae's cell, Neesa's cell, and the number of the restaurant they were going to programmed into his phone in case anything happened. He laughed as he cradled both boys in his arms and gently shoved her toward the door.

"Go, woman. We'll be fine. Stop worrying. Nothing can go wrong. I stopped using pins on their diapers ages ago."

She laughed and kissed her men on their cheeks, one after the other, two smooth baby cheeks and one rough and scruffy manly cheek. Yummy.

At dinner, Sylvie kept checking her cell phone under the table for messages.

Finally, Neesa protested. "Sylvie, come on. He's their daddy, and he's not the first man in history who has had to figure out how to take care of a baby. He'll be fine."

Phae looked less confident. "You say that now, Neesa, but I don't know what I'm gonna do when this baby comes." She rubbed her hands across her ever-growing baby bump. "I don't think Kent has touched a diaper in his life, much less changed one. He doesn't know the first thing about taking care of a baby. I just hope that he doesn't get too cocky and do something stupid."

This idea worried Sylvie, too. Heath often pretended to be more confident than he actually was when tending the twins. "I've been watching Heath, and he is learning. I know it's a lot to take in, but he's been great so far. I'm really proud of him."

"I still can't believe you got knocked up by a stranger in Chicago," Neesa said.

This was still something of a sore spot with her best friends. They were more than a little disappointed that she hadn't told them what had actually transpired between her and Heath in Chicago.

"Well, can you blame me? The way that rumors start around here, I didn't want to have to deal with it."

"But we're talking about us. Not *them*. You're supposed to tell us everything. I told you about Kent when we started dating," Phae said grudgingly.

"Like you had to tell us," Neesa said. "The man hired a marching band to woo you up and down Main Street."

Phae raised a brow. "Good point. God, that was so dumb."

"Oh, you loved every second of it," Neesa said. "Both of you are so lucky. Now you both have a man, and you both have babies, and I'm left out." She pushed the piece of cake she had ordered for dessert around on her plate.

Sylvie didn't know what to say. Even though Neesa said she was ready to settle down, Sylvie wasn't sure how Neesa would ever meet anyone. The woman worked all the time. She was even worse than Sylvie when it came to earning the workaholic label.

She reached over and put her hand on Neesa's. "There's a guy out there for you. Trust me. You just have to be patient. And anyway, do you see a ring on my finger?"

Neesa frowned and shook her head.

"So there you go. I don't, technically, have a man. I have a baby daddy."

The trio laughed heartily.

Neesa's laughter died away first. "I don't know what's wrong with me anymore. I guess I've got the baby blues or something."

"Yeah, well, here's my baby blues. Nuh-nuh-nuh-nuhnuh," Phae sang, striking the table with her hand in time to the familiar blues starter tune. "I got me fat feet. Nuh-nuh-nuh-nuhnuh. They're all swolled to hell. Nuh-nuh-nuh-nuhnuh. My toes look like sausages. Nuh-nuh-nuh-nuhnuh. And my ankles are hams."

They laughed uproariously, drawing the attention of half the restaurant. They didn't care. The fabulous Jones girls were having their first night out in forever.

Sylvie lasted about another thirty minutes before her anxiousness to get home returned in force. She told her cousins, and Phae didn't give her a hard time; she was exhausted, too, and sang a lick or two of the "pregnant lady I'm so sick and tired blues" before they paid up and headed outside.

Neesa walked Sylvie out to her car. They waved as Phae drove away.

"Do you think that you and Heath would be willing to come out to the farm and help me again this weekend?" Neesa asked. "There are a couple of odds and ends I'd like to have done, and the extra sets of hands and muscles would be appreciated. Every time I turn around something else is breaking."

"I'm sure Heath won't mind. I'll ask him."

"Thanks, Sylvie I appreciate it. If he can't, I'll ask someone else. I just feel like I've asked everybody for so much help already. My parents keep saying now that I just ought to sell it. But I'm hoping that this year, with some good weather, the crops will turn enough profit that I'll be able to switch to part-time at my security job."

"I thought you liked working at the college."

"I do. I just need more time on the farm if I'm going to keep expanding. And you know how hard it is in the summer and fall to keep up with everything."

Sylvie hoped that things worked out for Neesa. She wanted to see Neesa achieve her dream, and she wondered if this was the root of her cousin's melancholy more than the baby thing.

She gave Neesa a quick kiss on the cheek then slid into her car. During the short drive home, she listened to music on the radio and thumped her fingers on the steering wheel. She was anxious to get home.

There hadn't been any calls or texts or any indication that there was anything wrong at home, and she told herself that she had to trust Heath. They were never going to progress as a couple if she couldn't trust him alone with the twins for a few hours.

CHAPTER TWENTY-FOUR

SYLVIE PULLED INTO THE PARKING spot outside her apartment. Everything appeared quiet. She tiptoed up to the door and listened … nothing. She unlocked the door and opened it.

Heath sat on the couch with his tablet in his hands. There was soft music playing in the background that she could just barely hear.

He looked up expectantly and smiled. "You're home early. Did you have fun? How are the girls?"

She returned his smile. He really was a great guy, never having a problem with her spending time with her best friends. Some men weren't so understanding. Some men were assholes, she thought.

"I know. Yes. And they're just fine." She closed the door. She looked around the rooms. "Are the boys already in bed?"

She was surprised to see Heath looking so relaxed. Normally, when she got done with an evening of taking care of the boys and getting them to bed alone, she felt like her hair was on fire. She usually flopped onto the couch, turned on the TV, and stared at it mindlessly until her brain turned off.

"I'm not sure." He held up the baby monitor. "Doesn't sound like it."

Sylvie frowned and listened. Strange sounds were coming from the monitor. It was a squeaky sound with some laughing and … chatter? Her twins weren't old enough to chatter. Coo, maybe. Cry, definitely. But not chatter.

"That doesn't sound right," she said.

"They're fine. No worries at all. See? I told you I'd do good."

Heath stood up, walked over to her and took her into his arms. She relaxed against him. He smelled good, a delicious combination of musk and manliness. She jerked.

Suddenly, she wasn't tired anymore. Why did he smell so good, anyway? He should smell like baby powder and gruel and upchuck.

"What do you say I start the fire, and we sit here and have a nightcap?" Heath asked, his tone a low, sexy invitation.

"Mmmhmm," she answered. "What did you mean when you said it didn't sound like the boys were in bed?"

Heath nuzzled her ear, sending little shivers down her spine. "Baby, I've got no idea what you're talking about."

"You said, 'it didn't sound like it.' That makes no sense."

"Kiss me. That'll make sense."

She pushed against his chest. "I'm serious. Quit seducing me."

"Damn, you cooled down quickly."

"I was never warm," she said.

A couple of whispered voices came through the speaker of the baby monitor. She peered around Heath's shoulder at it. "What the hell?"

Heath grabbed her as she began to lunge toward the hall. "It's nothing. It's just your cousins."

As if on cue, three faces emerged in the hallway from the back of the apartment. It was her teenage cousins, Tonio, Jackson, and Neptune.

They told her "Hey" in their usual, half-bored, sly way.

Sylvie glared at Heath. "What are they doing here?"

Heath smiled and shrugged as if he hadn't noticed her annoyance. Then he walked over to the boys and took a roll of cash from his pocket. He peeled off some bills and handed them to each of the teenagers.

"Thanks, man. The twins went out easy, just like we told you they would. Easy money," Tonio said, shoving his money into his over-sized jeans. "We're set for the skateboarding rally this weekend."

"Yeah, totally easy gig." Neptune chimed in. "You gonna come?"

"I might," Heath said. "If the old lady will let me out." He made a quick head gesture toward Sylvie.

Jackson snickered. "Old lady."

Sylvie glared them all back into straight faces.

"Guess we're out of here then," Tonio said. "Call us again if you need more help."

"You want a ride?" Heath asked.

"Nah, we've got our boards."

They filed past Sylvie, giving her a nod and a partial smirk. She wanted to bonk their heads together. Who knew what other mischief they had planned for the evening?

"It's late and it's a school night," she said. "You'd better get straight home."

Tonio actually had the nerve to turn and roll his eyes at her.

"I mean it," she warned. "I'm going to call your mothers in twenty minutes and make sure you're home."

She ignored their groans and protests and closed the door behind them.

Sylvie looked at Heath in chagrin. "That wasn't exactly what we agreed to for tonight. You were supposed to do this on your own. No wonder you smell so good."

He cocked his head. "Thanks for the compliment, though I don't think I get the connection."

"It wasn't a compliment. It was an accusation."

"Oh. I must have missed that part."

"Seriously, Heath. You were supposed to have your first night alone taking care of the twins."

"And I did. I took care of things. I didn't get where I am in life without knowing how to delegate," he said.

He tried to take her into his arms, but Sylvie pushed him away.

He looked at her in surprise. "If there's one thing I've learned in business, it's that it's always best to surround myself with people who know how to do things better than I do. I'm not an expert in taking care of babies yet, as you well know. But, you can feel confident knowing that if you ever leave me with them, someone highly qualified will be taking good care of them."

"By people who aren't their father," Sylvie said she tried to keep the terseness out of her voice.

On one hand, she was kind of amused by the whole thing. She shouldn't have been surprised that Heath would recruit help. But, on the other hand, this had been his first test — and he'd cheated by hiring ringers.

"You couldn't even last two hours?" she asked

Heath approached her again with an abashed look on his face, and this time, she reluctantly let him take her into his arms.

"Come on, babe. It's not a big deal. So the boys helped me out. All they did was help me a little bit with bath time and getting them to sleep. I promise that I was involved almost the entire time if that's what you're worried about. I just couldn't help them get the babies to sleep since they use their special technique."

Sylvie jerked back. "Don't tell me that. Do I want to know what that technique is?"

"Why not? They wrap up the babies real tight and hold them while they jump up and down on the bed."

Sylvie gaped like a grounded fish. "Wh-wh-wh-what?"

"Sorry. That didn't come out right. The teenagers are the ones jumping up and down. The babies are the ones being held. It's kind of hard to say that correctly."

"And you don't see anything dangerous about letting three teenage boys jump on the bed with your babies? Seriously? They could have dropped the twins. Or worse." She had a vision of them dropping Quentyn, and watching Quentyn bounce off the mattress and sail toward the wall. She shuddered.

"They said they do it all the time. They called it the Jones special. I assumed you knew about it," Heath said, clearly confused about her reaction.

Sylvie took a few deep breaths to calm herself. It was okay. The boys were fine.

Oh ... my ... God. The babies. Were they fine?

She blew past Heath and rushed into the nursery. She flipped on the light and peered down into the crib.

Quentyn and Jadyn were sleeping peacefully, lying side-by-side, small smiles on their sweet, bow-like mouths.

"See," Heath whispered beside her.

Sylvie jumped, not having heard him enter.

"They're just fine," he finished.

Not wanting to wake the boys, they tiptoed back to the living room.

Heath had an I-told-you-so look on his handsome face.

"I should go back in there and give them a good look-over," she said, hands on hips. "They probably put the twins in pajamas that are the wrong size and they'll be uncomfortable all night."

Heath looked unconvinced. "You won't go in there, though, because you won't want to get them all wound up again."

Sylvie sighed. He was right. She threw up her hands in defeat.

"Fine. They're fine," she admitted grudgingly. "But still. I can't believe you hired those three. You do know that they're the biggest con artists in town, right? We've all got a pool about what they're going to be when they grow up."

"Yeah, I know," Heath said. "I'm in for 'charismatic dictators of a Caribbean nation.'"

"Good one. I've got 'dark net crime lords.'"

"That's harsh."

"Maybe. We'll see. They sure played you."

"No, they didn't," Heath said.

"Did you or did you not just give them each fifty bucks to put your babies to bed?"

He flinched. "I didn't think you saw that."

"Yeah, and if you actually think that anyone in this town lets those three teenagers bounce on beds with their babies, you really are pretty gullible."

"I can't believe it. There's no Jones special? Are you sure?"

"Well, not a hundred percent."

"They told me everyone in the family hires them to put their babies to sleep when they're fussy."

"Ridiculous," Sylvie said. "I've never heard of it. And I work in a beauty shop. We hear everything in there. Literally everything."

"I don't know." Heath shrugged. "I still think they were telling the truth."

"Doesn't matter. We're not hiring them ever again, okay?"

"Okay. But that's just for the Jones special, right? I can still hire them to change really disgusting diapers, right?"

Sylvie couldn't help herself. She laughed.

Heath took advantage and maneuvered her over to the couch. He pulled her down into his lap. She reached across him, though, and grabbed the baby monitor. He waited while she put it against her ear and listened.

"I can't hear anything," she said "Something might be wrong. It can't be good to bounce babies."

"Sylvie, Quentyn and Jadyn are fine. You need to learn how to relax and let other people help you."

Sylvie knew that he was right. Although there was a part of her that really wanted to go check on the babies, she had to let him see that she could release control just a little bit. They were both still learning and feeling each other out. She was going to have to give in at some point or another.

"How about you distract me then?" she asked in a sultry voice as she wrapped her arms around his neck.

"Oh yes, I think I have just the thing, Ms. Jones. One distraction coming up."

His lips found hers and, with that, most of Sylvie's doubts and worries were washed away ... for that night.

Chapter Twenty-Five

"ARE YOU SURE YOU'RE READY FOR this?" Sylvie had asked Heath the same question multiple times over the last several days.

Momma had invited her and Heath over to dinner at her house. It was going to be the first time that they all sat down to sample the idea of being a family. Momma still hadn't warmed to Heath at all and it made Sylvie nervous.

"I'm pretty sure I can handle your mother and stepfather for a few hours," he said with a smile as they pulled up in the driveway of her parents' house.

She knew that Heath was well aware of her mother's reservations about him, but he was taking it in stride.

He helped her undo the clasps and buckles of Quentyn's and Jadyn's car seats. Then he picked up Jadyn as she took Quentyn, and they slowly made their way up the sidewalk.

Sylvie's feet dragged. Heath had asked her several times why she was concerned about this particular dinner.

They had already gone out a few times with Kent and Phae and Will 'n Zilla. So far Heath hadn't buckled under the pressure, and he seemed to go out of his way to tell her how much he enjoyed all of the different Jones constantly dropping by the house, bringing food and other sorts of things they thought the babies would need. Her family was ever-present in their lives.

But that was also part of the reason she was reluctant to introduce Heath into this particular mix. Momma had been getting more vocal with Sylvie over the last several weeks about her distrust of Heath in general.

The closer Sylvie got to Heath, the happier they were together, the more unhappy Momma grew. Sylvie didn't understand. Her mother should be thrilled that Sylvie was happy. Heath was a good man and everyone saw it but Momma.

Momma just didn't understand why Heath didn't step up as a father of the twins sooner. She didn't understand why he showed up when he did and then didn't take responsibility for them right away. She said that he was secretive and that he was hiding something from Sylvie.

Sylvie couldn't admit everything to her mother because she didn't want Momma finding out Heath's true identity yet, especially when Sylvie herself wasn't supposed to know. It would bring up too many other questions and concerns.

She just wanted her mother to like Heath for who he was. She wanted Momma to acknowledge that since he learned he was the twin's father, he'd been there for Sylvie and Jadyn and Quentyn.

And he'd bought them so much, too. Every time Sylvie turned around, it seemed as if Heath was hauling in some new gift or other.

It started with flowers for her, which she accepted readily enough. Then the purchases became slightly larger things. He brought over toys and baby clothes. She didn't mind that so much either.

If she had all the money in the world, she would probably spoil the kids rotten, too.

It was when things moved into new electronics for her house that she had started to get a bit queasy. She was now the proud owner of a massive ultra-high-def curved-screen TV that took up most of one wall of her small home. And she still hadn't figured out how to control the sound system and the myriad speakers tucked in every nook and cranny of the living room.

And that wasn't the biggest thing. When her car broke down, he offered to take it to the shop and get it fixed for her. He came back driving a new Mercedes and handed her the title.

He said it was just good business. Her old car would cost more to fix than it was worth, so he just got her a new one. This car, he said, was the highest rated in its class and would be safer for her and the babies.

All the paperwork was in her name. It was hers. He said he'd handle the taxes.

She stood there in the alley behind her house, gaping at the gleaming midnight blue car. What she wanted to do was shove the papers right back at him and tell him to forget it. It was too much, and they were only dating. She couldn't accept such a huge gift.

But before she could do just that, she looked at him. He'd been standing there watching her with the most hopeful expression. He was all up on the balls of his feet, expectantly waiting. But for what?

His questioning smile answered that question.

He was excited to find out if she liked the car.

It was ridiculous, really. Who wouldn't like such a car? But to see him like that, to realize that he thought there was a possibility she might not like it ... there was no way she could let him down.

He hadn't bought her the car to try to buy her affections. He hadn't bought it to make her feel bad about being poor. He hadn't bought it because he thought she was a digger and would expect it.

No, he bought it for the purest reason of all: because he wanted to make her happy.

So now she drove a brand new Mercedes that had more than tripled her net worth overnight.

What woman wouldn't be happy with this man, she wondered. He made her feel so good. He was funny and sexy, and he made her heart pound. He made her feel like a goddess in bed and out of it.

And she liked, too, that he wasn't some pushover. He went toe-to-toe with her and held his own. But he wasn't a bully, either. He was just right.

And he was still learning about his sons, but then, so was she. It wasn't like she'd ever had kids before, either. They were doing it together.

There was still some air cleaning they had to do before she'd feel completely settled that their new relationship was real. Heath still didn't know that she knew his true identity. She didn't want him to think that she wanted anything from him from a financial standpoint or have him doubt the reason she would want to be with him.

She hadn't missed the considering looks her mother threw her way as she observed all of the new toys and trinkets appearing in their lives. That brought about more questions. Momma started asking more details about what Heath did for a living that he could afford all these things, and Sylvie avoided the topic like the plague, sidestepping the questions.

Then Momma wanted to know if Heath would ever be staying in Zeke's Bend for good, instead of just being around three or four days a week. To be honest, it wasn't a question that Sylvie and Heath had explored yet.

Their new family unit was still too new to take the pressure of too many expectations for the future. Sylvie enjoyed having Heath around and wanted him to spend as much time as he wanted with his boys. She didn't want to push or prod on any of the weightier topics that might impact what they had.

That wasn't Momma's way, though. Nothing could stop her when she had her mind set on something. So Sylvie had gone out of her way to try and keep Momma and Heath apart. But, at the end of the day, she could only do that for so long.

She looked over at Heath, a baby on one arm and a giant diaper bag slung over his opposite shoulder. It was a sight she enjoyed seeing.

Tonight, her psychic sense was tingling. She suspected the turning point had arrived. Things were either going to go really well or really badly. She crossed her fingers for the former.

Heath rang the doorbell and Eli Ford, Sylvie's stepfather, opened the door and greeted them.

Sylvie liked Eli, even if he was a little too earnest for her and kind of boring. He was a good man and he was very good to her mother. He and Sachet had only been married for about six years, but he'd loved her far longer than that. She'd made him wait for marriage until Sylvie and Will were both grown and out of the house. Sylvie never understood why Sachet did that, but it wasn't for Sylvie to question, she supposed.

Eli was a much-needed contrast to Sachet. Where she was flamboyant and often over-the-top, Eli's grounded calmness balanced her out. When Momma was on the warpath, Eli always found a way to make the peace. He had amazing patience with Sachet, doting on her and appealing to her vanity.

In short, he made Sylvie's mother happy, and that was all Sylvie could ask. Her mother had made some very poor choices about men in the past, so it was nice to see her settle down with a solid, stable man.

Eli smiled at them and automatically took Quentyn out of Sylvie's arms. "Look at you, boy! You're getting so big!"

They stepped inside, and Sylvie took off her jacket.

That was another thing that Sylvie liked about Eli. He was fond of the boys and treated them just like they were his own grandchildren without any question.

"Sachet is in the kitchen," Eli said. He bounced Quentyn on his hip. "I sure hope you're hungry. She's been cooking for what seems like a week."

Sylvie's sense of dread grew. Her mother sometimes cooked like a tornado when she was upset or frustrated about something. In times like that, she made enough food to feed an army.

It likely meant that Momma was just as nervous about the evening as Sylvie was. Or she had something on her mind, and that something would surely come to a head at dinner.

Sylvie took Jadyn from Heath as he put down the diaper bag and stripped off his jacket. They went into the living room, where they sat on the couch waiting for Momma to make her appearance.

Sylvie brushed her palms across her knees. They tingled. That never was a good sign. Well, it usually wasn't a good sign. You just never knew for sure. The second you thought you had your psychic gift figured out, something came along to shake up everything.

There was no way she was going to be able to sit still. Handing Jayden to Heath, she excused herself, saying she wanted to go see if her mother needed any help in the kitchen.

As Sylvie made her way to the kitchen, she listened for any signs of chaos. That was when she heard pots and pans being flung about. Uh-oh, Momma was definitely in a mood.

Sylvie stopped in the doorway of the kitchen and cleared her throat. "Hi, Momma. We're here. Do you need any help getting anything ready?"

"Oh, there you are. Here I was thinking you weren't even going to come in and say hello to your mother. It's not as if I've been calling you all week," Momma said barely glancing in Sylvie's direction.

Sylvie instantly felt guilty. For all of the issues there were between her and her mother, she had to admit that her mother was always helpful and willing to lend a hand when it came to the babies. She really did need to be more grateful about that.

She gave her mother a peck on the cheek and a quick hug. "It's nice to see you, Momma. The boys and Heath are in the living room."

"If you want to help, I could use somebody to set the table," Momma said in a slightly warmer tone.

They bustled about the kitchen not saying anything else. It had been almost a week since Sylvie had last seen her mother, which was an anomaly. Usually, her mother was constantly underfoot, asking to take the boys or pestering Sylvie, in general, at the shop.

It had been odd that after the last time she babysat the boys, she had only made a few phone calls to check on them. Sylvie wanted to ask her about it, but didn't know what kind of pot of hot tar she would be opening. She decided it was best to be silent.

Perhaps, Sylvie was overthinking the whole thing. Perhaps, there was really nothing wrong. Perhaps, Momma was finally getting used to the idea that Sylvia and Heath were together and hadn't intruded so Sylvie would have time alone with Heath.

Nah, that wasn't likely.

"When's Will coming?" Sylvie decided her brother's absence was safer territory for a conversation. Or, at least, a diversion from focusing on Sylvie's life.

Momma shook her head. "He's off with that girl again tonight. Something about some tournament or something she's playing in."

Zilla played on an intramural women's volleyball team at her college during the winter months. Will loved to go watch and cheer her on. Sylvie also thought that he liked to watch the other women on Zilla's team just as much. It was a team of Amazons in Sylvie's opinion. All of them were tall, athletic and had strong hips and shapely legs. She was surprised, though. It was the first time she had ever heard her mother snark about Zilla.

"Oh, that's too bad," Sylvie said.

She continued to set the table, thinking that it would have been nice if Will and Zilla had been able to come to dinner. It would have provided a buffer between her and her mother.

Will always had a way with Momma that Sylvie didn't. Being the youngest, he could smooth Momma's ruffled feathers in a way that no one other than Eli could.

"He might be around for pie later," Momma said.

Sylvie could see over her mother's shoulder that there were three different pies sitting on the counter. Considering there were only going to be four people for dinner, that seemed an ill omen. Way too much pie. Not good.

She thought again about Eli saying Momma had been cooking for the last few days and Sylvie scratched her itchy palm.

"Dinner's ready!" Momma yelled into the other part of the house, and Sylvie winced.

She thought again about how she hadn't been able to really prepare Heath in the event that her mother was on the hunt, out of control, ready to shoot first and ask questions later. Sylvie almost laughed out loud, her nerves nearly getting the better of her.

Whatever happened, Sylvie fervently hoped that Heath wouldn't decide that he would never see her again after that evening.

She shook herself. Momma wasn't out to ruin their relationship. She was simply concerned about Sylvie and the boys' welfare, which wasn't the worst thing ever.

Eli and Heath entered the dining room. Each man had a baby in his arms, and she watched Eli give her mother a small kiss on the cheek as he presented Jadyn for her inspection.

Momma gave Jadyn a quick squeeze, but her smile fell as she took in Heath. She muttered something under her breath as she moved to give Quentyn a similar greeting as his brother.

The whole thing was embarrassingly awkward. Heath tried to give Momma his hand to greet her as well, but it was clear when Momma sniffed and turned away that she didn't want to have anything to do with him. Sylvie felt a headache coming on and had a burning desire to tell her mother off for being rude to Heath.

Heath gave her a look that said he wasn't upset by what Sachet had done. Sylvie's cheeks were burning from the snub, though. She tried to remember her new positive attitude, to hope for the best. It was just dinner and it would be over in just a couple of short hours.

It was feeling more and more, though, that a positive attitude was a hopelessly naive approach to take with her mother.

CHAPTER TWENTY-SIX

MOMMA PUT THE TWINS IN A BASSINET Eli had set up so the babies could be close by while everyone ate.

After they were all seated, Momma reached out and grabbed Eli's and Sylvie's hands. Momma liked to say grace before the meal. Sylvie wasn't sure what Heath was going to think about this either.

Heath took her hand, and Sylvie saw the twinkle in his eye. Despite everything, he was enjoying himself. She knew that he and Eli got along well and talked about sports, cars, and all of the other things that men found endlessly fascinating, but most women did not.

After Momma said grace, everyone began filling their plates.

"Mrs. Jones … I'm sorry, Mrs. Ford," Heath said, correcting himself, "this looks delicious."

Sylvie grimaced at his screw-up. He was so used to everyone referring to her mother as Momma Jones that he forgot that her last name was actually Ford now.

She saw the look of exasperation cross her mother's face. Sylvie looked at Eli, but it wasn't clear if the older man had even noticed; he seemed so intent on the food on his plate.

"Thank you," Momma said. That was all.

That was when Sylvie started to realize that perhaps her optimism had been misplaced. The looks that Momma threw in Heath's direction definitely didn't indicate a welcome of any kind. And then, the fact that she wasn't saying anything at all was very uncharacteristic of her. Sylvie started to suspect a set-up.

"Good eating, Sachet. You are a dream in the kitchen. I'm a lucky man," Eli said.

Sylvie appreciated his efforts to get Momma was in a better mood.

They ate in silence. It was awkward. Heath made several attempts to draw her mother out in conversation, but each time Sachet answered with a single word. It was clear that she had no interest in being engaged in any conversation at all.

Heath shot questioning glances at Sylvie several times, but she could only shrug. If Momma wanted to talk, she would talk. So she and Heath started exchanging stories about the latest cute and/or smart and/or gross thing that the twins had done.

It didn't matter if it was a silly story about them rolling over, or smiling at them, or a new toy that both boys seemed to like. Sylvie was aware that really it was just the two of them filling empty air. Eli would occasionally stop them and ask a question, but it was always a mundane one.

Finally, Momma's head snapped up. Sylvie guessed that whatever she'd been holding back was about to come erupting forth. She sent a prayer out to the universe that all would survive the deluge, whatever it might be.

"So where did you say you two met again?" Momma asked in a snippy tone.

"Chicago," Sylvie and Heath said at the same time, in stereo.

Momma pointed her knife in Heath's direction. "You're not from Chicago, though. You're from where again?"

Sylvie's intuition was going crazy. Everything was turning bad. Damn. That'd teach her to think positively.

"I'm from Seattle," Heath answered politely, even though Sachet didn't deserve his politeness.

"That's right. So you have family there in Seattle?"

"Oh, I don't come from a big family," he said. He had neatly avoided the question and given a semi-answer as well.

"That's interesting," Momma said. "Because you look really familiar. I swear I've seen a picture of you recently."

"You wouldn't have seen him anywhere before," Sylvie said. "So Eli, how are things going at the shop?"

Eli opened his mouth to answer when Momma interrupted him. "No, no, Sylvie. I have seen him before. But the funny thing was the pictures said his last name was Collins. Not Cartwright."

Sylvie's heart dropped all the way down to her lower stomach.

Heath carefully placed his silverware across the edges of his plate. He didn't look at anyone or say anything.

Momma bulldozed onward. "And Heath Collins, as it turns out, is some kind of big shot, who makes all sorts of big business deals. So you're sure you don't know who Heath Collins is? Still gonna stick to this Cartwright lie?"

"I knew it would come out sooner or later," he said. "I am Heath Collins."

Sylvie couldn't breathe. Her chest had constricted or all the air in the room had somehow evaporated. She didn't know what to do to control the situation.

And that was when Momma rounded on her.

Sylvie's eyes widened at the catlike move.

Sachet pointed at Sylvie. "You've known all this time that he was lying to the whole family and you didn't say anything. I'm so disappointed in you, Sylvie Jones. You've known all this time and you didn't have the decency to tell your own mother the truth."

"That's not fair," Heath said, his face flushing, red streaking across his cheekbones. "I haven't told Sylvie my real last name either."

Sylvie hung her head. Heath hadn't hesitated to defend her while she had allowed her mother to attack him without stepping in to stop it. She felt like an ass.

And a liar. Again. Damn.

Once again, by hiding the truth, she had put herself in hotter water than ever.

She focused on the issue at hand. Right now, her mother was making a great big mess of her entire life.

"Where are you getting all this, Momma?" she asked.

Momma crossed her arms over her bountiful bosom and curled her upper lip in triumph. "I had to use your computer the other day to look up something for the twins on Web MD. I saw there was a folder on your home screen called Chicago. You've said you met Heath in Chicago, so I was curious and clicked on the folder. And guess what I found? All sorts of articles and notes about Mr. Big Shot Heath Collins. And they went back all the way to before the babies were born."

Sylvie couldn't look at Heath, couldn't bear to see his expression. She set her fork down with a trembling hand.

Momma went in for the kill stroke. "You knew who this man was this entire time, all through your pregnancy. And you never told us the truth. Shame on you! On the both of you!"

Sylvie dared to sneak a glance in Heath's direction. He was staring down at his plate as if he thought that he could find the meaning of life on it. He was very still.

Sylvie would've given anything to know what he was thinking. Likely it had something to do with betrayal and liars. She couldn't do anything about him until they were alone.

Anger bubbled up inside her. How dare her mother do this? What gave her the right? In no time, she'd worked up one hell of a whirlwind of righteous anger.

"I can't believe you went through my personal things," Sylvie told her mother. "That's wrong. And you can keep your opinions about me to yourself. This is my life, not yours, and I don't have to tell you everything about it. I'm sick and tired of you always making everything about you!"

"How dare—" Momma began, but Sylvie cut her off.

"My whole life you've done nothing but criticize my decisions and everything I've done."

"So you won't make the same mistakes I did," Sachet said.

"I'm not you, Momma. And I'll damned well make all the mistakes I want, whether they're the same as yours or not. Do you get that? You know, you act like the world owes you something because your husband drove off and left you at a convenience store with hardly a dollar in your purse."

"We're not talking about that right now."

Sylvie smacked a palm on the table, making her mother jerk back. "I'm talking about it, Momma. Daddy leaving us didn't just happen to you. It happened to Will and me, too. And I still remember what it felt like to stand out on that hot tar, watching you run around the lot, wailing about how you'd been abandoned and how we were all going to starve and die in the desert and how Daddy wouldn't give a damn."

"You never once thought about me and Will, did you, Momma?" Sylvie rushed on. This had needed saying for a long, long time. "Once you wound down, you just sat on that suitcase and didn't move again. It was Will and I, who begged for money from strangers so we could call home for help, and so we could get a room for the night while we waited for the wire from Grandpa to arrive. Momma, I was eight years old, and Will was only six. We were terrified and devastated. And you didn't help us at all!"

Sachet had begun to cry. "I did my best. Lord knows I did. I've never said I was perfect. I tried so hard, and I only ever want what's best. I want to be a good mother and I—"

"I, I, I. Always with the I's, Momma," Sylvie said, the adrenaline in her system beginning to wane. "That's the real problem. You don't care if Heath's last name is Cartwright, Collins, or Cooper. You only care that I've cut you off and haven't let you run my life anymore. I didn't tell you about this because I knew what your reaction would be. I knew how you'd judge me. Well, I'm done with all that. I won't be afraid anymore of your self-absorbed judgments that you try to disguise as loving concern. The truth about my private life is my own business and you can just back the hell off."

Momma jerked up, her thighs hitting the table and shaking it. Her voice boomed. "I can't believe I would've ever raised such an ungrateful child that would speak to me like this."

Eli stood up and put his hand on her arm. "Sachet, I think you might want to lower your voice. You don't want to cause the boys to fuss."

Momma shook off Eli's hand. She shook her fist at Sylvie. "I have never wanted anything but what is best for you, and for Will, and for my grandchildren. Forgive me for wanting to be helpful to you and to protect you from the horrible things in life that *I* had to deal with when it came to your father."

Sylvie wanted to rip her hair out. "I know, I know! You were the only one that got hurt that day. It's over now. It's been over forever. Move on. And anyway, I'm not you. I'm grown up. I'm a parent now, and I know what's best for my children."

Momma barked a nasty laugh. "You know what's best? Apparently you conceived these children out of wedlock during a one-night stand with a total stranger. I would hardly call that the best judgment in the world."

She got to her feet. "I don't regret that night for an instant. Your grandchildren were the result of it. If I ever hear you say anything else about that night, or if you ever say anything about it in front of my children, I swear on everything I hold sacred that not only will I never talk to you again, you'll never see your grandchildren either. Not as long as you live."

Now, Heath got to his feet. Sylvie could see by her mother's sputtering that she was settling in for an all-out brawl. Then, one of the babies started to cry and Sylvie instantly focused on Quentyn. She wanted to go to him and comfort him, but Heath was already headed that way.

Eli broke the standoff. "I'm going to take Sachet out into the kitchen for a minute. We'll cut some pie and have a little chat," he said. "Perhaps you two would like to do the same."

Sylvie watched Momma's mouth open as Eli dragged her out of the room. Sylvie hadn't realized Eli had it in him to be that forceful. She'd never appreciated him more.

She slowly turned to the silent man standing there staring at the bassinet and the crying baby. "Heath?"

Heath touched Quentyn and Jadyn. Quentyn quieted right away, comforted by his father's proximity.

"Is she telling the truth?" He asked the question in a cold, toneless voice.

"Which parts?" She was desperately trying to figure out how to delay the inevitable reckoning. She shouldn't do it, she knew but she couldn't help it. She was guilty, and she knew it, and she wasn't ready to hear the sentencing.

Sylvie had already seen glimmers that the boys were growing attached to Heath, which had made her so happy. She thought that the perfect family she had always wanted was right there in front of her.

And now it might all be slipping away.

Heath stared at the twins as if he were memorizing their faces. Dread filled Sylvie.

"Does it matter which parts?" he asked, not looking at her. "Did you really know who I was all this time?"

She had no choices. They had all been taken from her. There was only one direction left, and traveling it meant baring herself to the truth.

"Yes, I knew," she said. "I was seven months pregnant when I found—"

"I need some time," he interrupted. "I'll walk home."

Before Sylvie could protest, Heath had gone to the hall, grabbed his jacket off the coat rack and was out the door.

Chapter Twenty-Seven

HEATH WALKED FOR WHAT SEEMED like forever. It was warmer than normal for a March evening, but it was still below fifty. He carried his jacket on his arm. He didn't need it. It was as if the cold around him wasn't able to seep into his limbs because of the fire burning inside him.

He couldn't believe what happened. Momma Jones had sent the world spinning off of its axis.

Sylvie had known who he was all along.

The truth wouldn't click into place, so he kept stuttering over it. Sylvie didn't seem like the type of woman who would deliberately keep a man from his children, and yet that's exactly what she'd done. Before the twins were even born, she knew where to find him.

When he arrived in Zeke Bend's, she knew who he was, and still she let him pretend to be someone else. Had she played him for a fool?

Why would she do that? What could she gain from not telling him that she knew who he was?

He knew that he'd done his own lying, of course. He wasn't completely without blame. But surely giving her an incorrect last name and not confessing to being a billionaire wasn't as bad as not telling someone they might be a father.

Heath kept coming back the idea that Sylvie was suddenly a stranger to him. The Sylvie he thought he knew wouldn't have done this. So who was this woman, really?

Had she been putting on a façade for him, luring him in for financial gain, or something equally mercenary?

On a scale of who told the worst lie, she was far and away the victor. He hadn't admitted who he truly was. But she had not only known his identity, she'd also kept his possible paternity a secret. Yes, her crime was far worse than his.

If Sylvie were a gold digger, she was a seriously great one. He'd dealt with a lot of gold diggers in his day, and Sylvie was nothing like them. She didn't hang on his every word and agree with everything he said or go out of her way to do everything that he wanted her to do.

In fact, it was Heath who'd been going out of his way for her. Lately, he'd been contemplating selling his company and retiring to Zeke's Bend for her.

This was perhaps the biggest rub of all. His life was different because of her, and it was only because he pursued her. He'd been the one to keep searching, not her.

All that time, Sylvie had known exactly where to find him and yet did nothing about it. Why? Sure, she was proud, but this went far beyond that. This was denying a father a relationship with his children. There was nothing right about that in any universe at any time.

He circled around and around the streets of Zeke's Bend. Eventually, his feet took him where he knew they would ... to Sylvie's house. All the lights were blazing inside. She was home.

He felt a twinge of guilt for not helping her get the babies back and put them down for the night. He had started to get used to their evening routine. He was slowly, but surely, adapting to his role as a father.

He once had been so afraid of being a bad father that he almost gave up trying to be a good one. He still didn't know what a good father was like. It was something he still needed to learn. But, he was willing to try.

At least, he had been. Now he wasn't sure how anything would work moving forward. This was twice now that Sylvie had broken his trust. If she could lie to him about things so huge, what other secrets could she be hiding from him?

He approached her door with a heavy heart. The door opened as soon as his feet hit the small porch. Sylvie had been waiting for him.

Her expression was neutral. "Where have you been?"

He rubbed the back of his neck. "Around. I needed to think about things."

Sylvie opened the door wider. "Come in."

He turned sideways so he could pass her without touching. It was silly, perhaps, but he couldn't touch her right then. If he did that, he'd lose focus.

The thing that he hated was that he saw again how lovely she looked tonight. He had admired her several times on the way to dinner. He'd been excited about the opportunity to sit down with Sylvie's mother and stepfather and get to know them better. It was all part of creating a place for himself in this huge Jones family. Now he wasn't so sure if there was really a place for him in it.

"I want to explain," Sylvie started. She fidgeted with her hands as she stared downward at her feet.

They went and sat down at the kitchen table, facing one another as if this were an interrogation. The bright and cheerful primary colors on the walls and tiles were an affront to Heath's dour mood.

"I'm not sure that you can say anything that would change this for me. But you can go ahead," he said.

Sylvie grimaced. Again, part of him wanted to comfort her, but he held back. Fury was the main emotion roiling through him.

He used his calming techniques. Getting emotional wouldn't help. He thought, so far, he had done a pretty good job, even as anger had taken root inside him and began branching out like a weed in a compost pile.

"This probably won't make a lot of sense to you," she said. "I get that. But we've had a chance to spend time together, and I feel like I've gotten to know you. I didn't know you at all back then."

Sylvie paused and looked at him with a questioning look as if she wanted to make sure he was following her.

Heath felt they'd gone over this ground a million times since he arrived in Zeke's Bend. It seemed as if no matter what he said or did, Sylvie insisted on keeping him at arm's length by not admitting the depth of their connection.

She knew him as much as he knew her. Yet while he was scouring the world for her, she was hiding from him. She started hiding when she first met him.

"We got to know each other well enough that first night, as I recall," he said.

Sylvie tapped her fingertips on the tabletop. "I had just broken up with Alan and I was feeling crappy. You were so handsome and you wanted to take me out and wine and dine me with no strings attached—it was like a play, a fantasy. And that's all I let myself believe it might be."

"Because of you, or because of me?"

"You. I'm no one. You're the someone," she said. "Anyway, I know you think because we played that Private Yet Public game that we got to know each other. We did, but it was one exchange, a couple hours, a night. Not much to base a lifetime decision on."

Sylvie leaned forward. "Just to be clear, I haven't always known who you are, your real name. It was a random accident that I found out, and I was seven months pregnant at the time. After I read all the articles I could find about you, one thing stood out. Everyone always pointed out how ruthless you were. It scared me."

"So I'm ruthless in business. You have to be if you want to succeed. But what you and I had wasn't a business transaction," Heath said.

"Wasn't it? You were paying for my services as an escort and after we had sex, you tried to give me more money."

"I wanted to give you money to help you. It had nothing to do with business."

"We can't always know the reasons behind what we do."

"I have no idea what you're getting at. If you're saying I was subconsciously trying to turn the best night of my life into a business transaction, then you need to get a refund from whatever pop psychology course shafted you."

"Funny. You think I should have totally trusted you after knowing you for all of one night, and you don't think that's expecting too much? I'm only trying to explain my thinking behind the decisions I made."

Heath couldn't keep the bitterness out of his tone. "Those decisions being lies."

She held up her hands. "Yes, they were lies. I'm not trying to justify myself. I know I can't. Look, I didn't know who you were as a person, okay? And I was seven months pregnant and I can't tell you how weird you get when you're seven months pregnant. Not as weird as when you're eight or nine, but still pretty damned strange. We call it pregnancy brain, and—"

"I'll concede that you didn't know me if you'll get back on topic."

"Fine. Back then, I was afraid if you found out the babies might be yours, you would demand a paternity test. If it came back that you were the father, and as I've said, I'm pretty psychic so I had a powerful sense that you were the father. So I was afraid when you found out you were the father, you might want to take my babies away from me. I could never win against you and all the lawyer sharks your billions could buy. I couldn't risk losing my children."

He glowered. "I can't believe you ever thought I would try to take the twins away from you. That's preposterous."

"But I was struggling to get by, financially, and your world was so different from mine. I know who you are *now*, and I know that's not something you would've ever done. But I didn't know it back then. How could I? When it comes to my children and me, I'm always going to follow the better-safe-than-sorry route."

He stood up and began to pace the room. He looked at Sylvie. "Crazy."

Sylvie leaned back and crossed her arms over her chest. "Why is it crazy? You can do anything you want to do. You have so much money that you can swim around in it like Scrooge McDuck if you feel like it."

Heath almost laughed at the vision and that she would compare him to an over-the-top cartoon character. But her description only emphasized the truth of what Sylvie said: they truly were from two different worlds.

That didn't mean, however, that they couldn't find a way to bridge those worlds. Opposites attracted all the time. He refused her explanation and logic outright.

"I don't care what kind of person you thought I might be," he said. "At the end of the day, there was no reasonable reason for you to not get in contact with me and let me know I might be a father."

Sylvie's face fell. "Maybe. But Heath, I figured it was a long shot if you even remembered that night, remembered me."

CHAPTER TWENTY-EIGHT

HE WAS FLOORED. HE'D SEARCHED for this woman for nearly a year, and she thought he might not remember her? "I'm beginning to think that you and I had very different reactions to that night in Chicago. I'm realizing it meant far more to me than to you."

"That's a load," she said with some outrage that sent his anger up a notch. "I've got two new human beings in the nursery that would tell you otherwise ... if they could talk!"

"You know what I mean."

"I guess I don't."

"I guess you should."

She threw her hands in the air. "You're driving me crazy. You won't listen to reason!"

"Me? Seriously? What's your psychic side telling you I'm going to do next?"

"You're not very attractive when you're sarcastic. And stop pacing around like a caged bear. You're looming all over me."

Looming? He bit back his next retort. Someone had to be the adult here and he guessed it was him. He took a deep breath, steadied himself, and sat back down. "Let's take a moment to center ourselves, shall we?"

He thought she might argue, but after a pause, she nodded tersely. They sat in silence for a while.

Sylvie spoke first. "I want you to know that I realize I should have handled the situation differently."

Understatement, he thought.

"But hindsight's twenty-twenty," she said, annoyingly cheeky.

"That's incredible. So you admit you could have handled the situation differently, but you had no way of knowing that it was wrong at the time."

"Uh, well, I may have realized it could be wrong, too."

"Gee, that's gracious."

"You're being all smartass-y now."

"You're right. I apologize. And this isn't getting us anywhere," he said. "Let me tell you what I'm needing. How would that be?"

She sighed. "Okay." Her tone sounded more contrite.

"Good. I need to hear you say that you made a mistake. I need you to admit that not telling me I might be a father was a very unfeeling thing to do. I need to hear that you realize it wasn't just unfeeling, but unfair to both me and our children."

He ignored her frown and charged ahead. "I bet that if I hadn't shown up in Zeke's Bend, I would still be completely unaware I'm a father. I doubt I would have ever found out the truth, nor would my children. It seems like your hand has been forced every step of the way, and it's only when your lies are exposed that you finally break down and tell me the truth."

Sylvie's back stiffened. She had gone from contrite to angry. That made him the most furious yet. She had no right to be affronted. She was the one who had betrayed him with her lies. He'd done nothing but tell her the truth.

"At least, I've admitted what I did and told you why," she said, acidly. "I still haven't heard what you've been up to, have I ... Mr. Cartwright?"

It was a low blow from Heath's perspective though he'd been expecting it. "Lying about a name is not the same as lying about your children's father. And yours is sneaky because it was a lie of omission. It's far worse than what I did."

Sylvie stood up. "If you're wanting me to admit that I was wrong for what I did, you'll be waiting a long time. I don't think I was wrong. You seem to be forgetting that I didn't know until recently that you definitively were the father. Sure, I could've reached out to you, gotten you all upset. You probably would have thought I was a gold digger. And then, what if the paternity test had come back negative? Then I would've had my heart ripped apart for absolutely no reason."

It was the closest Sylvie had come to admitting how she felt about him. Heath was livid that she'd chosen this moment to come clean about it.

He'd been around her for weeks and he'd been tripping over himself to do everything he could to make her happy. All he wanted in return was to hear from her that she would let him in and that she wanted him to be a part of her life.

Now, at the worst time possible, was when she chose to finally toss him a crumb of acknowledged affection.

He shook himself. He couldn't let it be a distraction. "Whether you ever admit it or not, what you did is wrong. You didn't think about anyone else. It was all about protecting yourself from possibly being hurt."

Sylvie's chin lifted. "You don't get it."

He started to protest, but Sylvie stopped him. "Remember when you admitted to me that you didn't know if you wanted to be a father? How was that supposed to be the confidence booster that I needed to be able to say, 'Oh, by the way, Quentyn and Jadyn might be your sons.' It's not like finding out you're a father has filled some big, gaping hole in your life. Fatherhood was something that you didn't think would fit in the tidy, neat life you created for yourself."

Heath was shocked. Not only was she defending her decision not to tell him, but she was also attacking him. How had she managed to do that? "I had concerns, yes, but that doesn't mean my opinion would never change. I was worried for good reason, I believe. My inexperience, my own upbringing, never having had a serious relationship with a wo—"

"Was I supposed to figure all that out, Heath? God, my head hurts. You demand that I tell you everything, so that's what I do. And my reward for that is you telling me how my reasons are wrong, that my thinking is wrong. You're so damned arrogant. Try this question on for size. Why did you lie to me about your last name?"

That brought him up short. "You don't want to know that answer."

"Oh yes, I do."

"Fine. I did it because I wasn't sure how you would react to me after we'd been apart so long."

She snorted. "You're a hypocrite. That's just a different way of saying that you lied because you didn't really know me. You were afraid if I learned how rich you were, that I might just be with you because of your money—like all the other women who chase after you. You lied to protect yourself, just I did. Admit it, Heath. We're more alike than either of us realized."

A small voice inside him acknowledged that she was right, but a louder voice refused to listen. Heath was riled up and wanted justice, wanted her to admit that she'd wronged him.

He backtracked the conversation. "Just because I said I never pictured myself as a father doesn't mean I never wanted children or a family. I had legitimate concerns about fatherhood and about getting into a relationship with you. I've never had a serious girlfriend in my life."

"You didn't ever wonder if there was a reason for that?" Sylvie snapped.

"I think we're going a bit afield of the issue here," Heath said. His blood was boiling, and he knew if they continued, there was a chance he'd say something he'd regret.

"No, I don't think we are," Sylvie said. "You see my mistakes as something I did on purpose to hurt you. Your own mistakes, meanwhile, you don't think are mistakes at all. They're all perfectly reasonable things for a perfectly reasonable man to do. Unlike me, the flaky, psychic, unreasonable, bad—"

"Don't be so dramatic," he said.

"You didn't just say that. Oh hell no."

"I can't believe you're attacking me right now, Sylvie. My life choices up to this point have nothing to do with you or your life. Had you chosen to tell me that they might be relevant, we would be having a very different conversation. I don't know how you can expect me to trust you when our relationship has been built on a pile of lies. I don't know what's real or what's a lie anymore."

Sylvie looked as if she was biting her tongue hard. If the words that had been coming out of her mouth so far were any indication, he was sure that he didn't want to hear the rest.

"And sex," she said, as if it were a bad thing. "Like Momma reminded me tonight, our relationship is built on a casual, one-night stand with a stranger."

"Don't do that."

"You're not some paragon of virtue yourself, either, Heath. I mean, you wanted to pay me for that sex."

"For God's sake. Not this again."

"I'm sorry," she said, looking down her nose. "I just don't think that's being a good role model for my children."

Heath felt as if a blood vessel inside his head exploded. All he could see was red. "Well, we know now that they aren't just your children. They're mine, too."

Sylvie crossed her arms over her chest, and her back had stiffened to the point that he wondered if she were going to turn into a statue. "They are my children. I gave birth to them, I have been the only one taking care of them, and I will be the one to continue to do so. They're mine."

"They're mine, too."

"Only if I allow it."

"I think a judge would have something to say about that," Heath said, heavily laying on the threat.

Sylvie's mouth thinned into a line. "Are you threatening me?"

"I don't threaten. I tell you the way it is. If you think for one minute you can keep me away from my children, you're out of your mind." Heath had gone on the offensive now. All logic had evaporated. He was laser focused on one thing, and that was keeping his sons in his life.

Sylvie's face turned to stone. "I think it's time for you to leave."

"Fine by me. I need some time to think anyway. This conversation has been illuminating." Heath stood and stalked toward the front door.

Sylvie's wasn't quite finished. "Don't come back, either."

Heath spun and stared at her. A coldness tamped down his raging fire, the sensation he always got when he was challenged by a competitor in a deal or in the boardroom. He entered full-on, high-stakes war mode. "Think about what you're starting here. Think long and hard. I told you that if you think you can keep me away from my sons, you're wrong. This can go straight to court if I want it to, if you push me to it."

Sylvie didn't even blink. "Whatever. Take me to court. We'll see how that works out for you."

Heath pulled his checkbook out of his coat pocket. Since he wasn't sure when he was going to be able to come back, he wanted to make sure that, in the meantime, his children were taken care of and he'd done the right thing.

He quickly scribbled out a check for $10,000. He walked across the room and held it out to Sylvie.

She looked at the check blankly but wouldn't take it. "What's that? A bribe?"

A lick of flame fought its way through his icy control. "This is the start of taking care of my children. There's more if you need it."

Sylvie snapped the check out of his fingers. She slowly ripped it up then let the fragments fall to the floor. "I don't need your money."

He fought against the returning flames of fury. "They're my responsibility. I *will* help you take care of them."

Sylvie shook her head. "If you want to do something for the kids, put the money in a trust fund or something like that. I don't need your money, and I don't want it. I can take care of them all by myself."

Heath walked away, scribbling out another check. He laid it on the side table next to the door. Sylvie rushed over, picked it up and ripped it to pieces just like the previous one.

A nuclear blast shattered all that was left of his icy veneer. He was beyond furious. "You'll be hearing from my attorney," he hissed.

"Fine," Sylvie hissed back. "Don't let the door hit you in the ass on the way out."

Heath stomped out of the apartment. When he didn't see his car, he skidded to a stop, and Sylvie nearly did hit him in the ass when she slammed the door shut with a bang.

He heard the distant sounds of crying babies. Served her right, he thought.

"Enjoy getting them back to sleep now," he muttered.

He glanced around, wondering where his car was, then remembered he'd left it back at the hotel. He began walking. It would be good for him. He wasn't fit to see anyone until he cooled down.

If he could ever cool down again.

CHAPTER TWENTY-NINE

SYLVIE MAINTAINED A STOIC EXPRESSION and a tight rein on her emotions until she heard the light tapping on her door. She'd just gotten the babies back to sleep so she rushed to open the door.

It was Neesa, who Sylvie had called within moments of Heath stomping out of her life.

Sylvie felt guilty about calling Neesa so late. She had probably just gotten home from work when she got Sylvie's cryptic call that she needed her friend. But instead of putting Sylvie off until the next day, Neesa had gotten in her car and driven into town.

All of the emotions finally overwhelmed Sylvie, and she sniffled.

"Oh, sweetie, what happened?" Neesa asked. She stepped across the threshold and gave Sylvie a hug.

Neesa patted her back and told her that everything would be okay.

After Sylvie pulled away, Neesa gave her a sympathetic look. "I'm here now. Tell me what happened."

"I screwed everything up so badly that I don't think it can ever be fixed," Sylvie said. "And I'm so mad, too. I don't think I've ever been this furious ... ever."

"Let me make you a cup of tea. That will calm you down," Neesa said.

She pushed Sylvie across the room and settled her onto the couch. Neesa headed to the kitchen to boil water while Sylvie stayed in the living room, stewing, almost literally.

Neesa return shortly, bringing a steaming teacup over and setting it in front of Sylvie.

Neesa sat down beside her cousin and patted her shoulder. Sylvie took a sip of the tea, sighed, and blinked back an angry tear.

"Okay, spill it. Don't hold back. You'll feel better if you just get it out of your system," Neesa said, briskly.

"It's such a mess. You wouldn't believe it. Heath is Heath Collins, not Cartwright."

Sylvie figured it would be best to start at the beginning. Nobody knew about Heath's background. She wasn't going to go into the whole billionaire thing, but she didn't want to hide the truth from her closest friend.

"Heath Collins is a very successful businessman, and he has lots of money."

"We kind of figured that already. His attempt to pull off being a writer was weak. Did you ever read any of his fake articles? Horrible. The man would have been eating ramen noodles with those skills," Neesa said, waving a hand dismissively. "Collins, Cartwright, what does it matter? It's easy to get them confused."

Sylvie shook her head. "No, there wasn't any confusion here. He lied about he who was. And I lied about knowing who he was for a long time."

Neesa frowned. "I don't get it. I'm confused. How long have you known his real name?"

"Er, since I was seven months pregnant."

"Then I'm even more confused. If you've known who he was for a while, why didn't you tell him that he might be a father?"

It was the question of the day. The question of the year. Even Neesa went straight to the heart of it.

Sylvie knew deep down that she was a chicken. She had let her fears and insecurities get in the way of what was undoubtedly the best thing for her babies. She'd done a bad thing, and she was sorry for it.

She probably would have gotten around to admitting that to Heath, but when he kept coming at her with all that anger and self-righteousness. It put her on the defensive. And it bothered her that he'd pushed his own lies under the rug.

"I don't know. I think it has something to do with what happened with my daddy."

Neesa clucked her tongue. "Oh, Sylvie. That was a long time ago. I didn't know your daddy, but from everything I've heard, he was nothing like Heath."

"I know. But letting someone else into my life means losing control."

"Aren't you always the one claiming that the universe is a chaotic place and trying to control it is a waste of time?"

"Yeah, but this was different."

Neesa smiled. "If you say so."

"I mean I've done everything for Quentyn and Jadyn. They're my world. I'll always do whatever I need to do to protect them. It makes me feel sick to think that there might be someone in their life who would hurt them. Somebody who's supposed to love them the way I do."

Neesa wrapped her arm around Sylvie's shoulders. "It's part of sharing the responsibility of being a parent. It's part of being in a relationship with their father. Eventually, you have to take that risk. You have to let him in."

"Well, it doesn't' matter now. It's all over. I said some things that were pretty terrible to him. I accused him of being ruthless and cruel. I demeaned his work and his life. I basically called him shallow."

Sylvie was ashamed of herself. Now that she was outside the heat of the moment, she admitted to herself that she was partly to blame. There was no doubt about that. But at the same time, he hadn't been kind to her, either. His accusations still rang in her ears and stung in a way that made her skin itch.

"Heath has had a lot to deal with," Neesa said. "I think he might've come here thinking he was going to sweep you off your feet. Then, not only did he find out that you had the twins, but then he found out that he was the father of said twins. It's a lot to take in. You've got to give the guy credit for sticking around. He could have run for the hills.

Instead, he started to get to know you and all of us. That doesn't look or sound like a guy who would set out to hurt you or the boys."

Sylvie had to grudgingly admit that her cousin was right. She hadn't really thought about it that way. "I don't know, Neesa. When he left, he was furious. He talked about getting an attorney and taking me to court."

"Why would he say something like that?" Neesa looked shocked.

Sylvie grimaced. "It might have had something to do with me telling him I wasn't going to let him see the boys anymore."

Neesa gave a low whistle. She looked at Sylvie with an expression Sylvie knew well. Neesa was about to tell her something that she didn't want to hear.

"Sylvie, I love you. You're my best friend, well, you and Phae. So that's why I'm telling you this with deep love and with the utmost respect for our family and our friendship." She paused and then said with even enunciation. "You are an idiot."

Sylvie's brow furrowed. "I think that's a bit of a strong assessment, don't you?"

Neesa shook her head. "Nope. Heath is great. He did everything he could for you and the boys, everything you'd let him. He was itching to do much more. I see the way he looks at you, and I dream of having someone who'll look at me that way, too. You're so lucky."

Well, if she was going to put it like that … Sylvie admitted there might be something to it.

Neesa was far from finished with the tough love. "And why in the world did you date that loser, Alan, forever, even though you knew he was a total douche. We couldn't get you to let go of him for anything, even when he cheated on you with skank after skank. Now here's Heath, a terrific, handsome, and apparently, wealthy man who treats you like a queen and is, hallelujah, the father of your children. Why have you been pushing him away? It doesn't make sense. Why would you ever tell a man like Heath that you're not going to let him see his sons? That was just plain crazy talk. If you had stopped and thought about it for one minute, for twenty seconds, you would have known that you aren't the type of person who would keep someone away from their kids. That's just not who you are."

Neesa was right. The thing was, Heath didn't know that about her. "I was angry and said things I didn't mean. He was talking about how all we've done is lie to each other since the day we met, and how there's nothing about our relationship that's true. And it's always felt true to me, even when it wasn't. He hurt my feelings, Neesa."

"You love him," Neesa said in a singsong voice.

Sylvie swatted her cousin on the arm. "I do not. I like him, at least, I thought I liked him. But I don't love him. People don't fall in love this fast."

Neesa clucked her tongue again. "You have love written all over you right now. That's why you're so bundled up in all these emotional knots, and why you're so upset. You screwed up. You're human. That's what you need to tell him."

Sylvie moved back against the couch and shook her head. "Oh no, Neesa, I think we're too far gone for that. He's leaving town. I'd be surprised if he wasn't gone already. You weren't here. What we said to each other was nasty. It's not something that you can just forgive and forget. Like I said, there was talk about lawyers and courts and everything. He even tried to pay me off with a $10,000 check."

Neesa's eyes widened. "He gave you $10,000? Did you take it?"

Sylvie pointed at the shreds of paper on the floor near the door. "What do you think?"

"Can we tape it back together?"

"I don't think a bank would take a taped-up check."

Neesa sighed. "$10,000 would have made a nice little nest egg for you and the boys. You could have paid off a bunch of the debt from the shop and cut back your hours to be able to spend a lot more time with them."

"That's not what he was giving me the money for, Neesa. That money was for the boys, and he can put it in a trust fund just as easily as he can give it to me. I don't need his help, and I don't want it. Heath Collins can take his fat checks and go fly a kite."

Neesa watched her with a frown. "I don't think a judge would see it that way. If support gets ordered, you'll have to take it."

"Do me a favor and don't talk about judges tonight."

"You're a proud woman, Sylvie Jones. I really hope that doesn't come back to bite you in the butt someday."

Sylvie looked forlornly at her cousin and friend. "I'm pretty sure it already has."

CHAPTER THIRTY

HEATH STOOD AND STARED OUT THE massive windows that lined one wall of his Seattle office. He looked at the skyline which, at one time in his life, had brought him a sense of comfort. He had stood in the same spot and known he was on the top of the food chain. Now, he felt beaten, driven down to the bottom of the pecking order ... and he'd been the one doing all the pecking.

He'd made a mistake with Sylvie, a huge one. And he couldn't fix it or get past it. He'd seriously screwed up everything.

As soon as he returned to Seattle, he set his mergers and acquisitions team to work finding the next big company to acquire. Although everybody else was ready for a rest after the last acquisition, work was the only place where Heath could forget for a period of time about what happened in Zeke's Bend.

In the end, he did just what he said he would. He got his lawyers involved, but it was only to try to make Sylvie take his money. It turned out, that had been his greatest mistake.

Prior to first contact with the lawyers, Sylvie had grudgingly emailed him a few pictures of Quentyn and Jadyn. He had looked forward to those with greater anticipation than he'd admit to any living soul.

After the first call from his lawyer, though, the emails had stopped. He tried texting her and calling her, but he never heard back.

After a week of silence, his lawyer told Heath that he received a call from one Zachary Jones, attorney at law, from Zeke's Bend. He was apparently acting on Sylvie's behalf. Zachary informed them that Sylvie was submitting a motion to stop Heath from contacting her directly in any way. She wanted no contact from him at all.

This had infuriated Heath, but later, he thought he probably deserved it. Bringing lawyers into the situation for any reason after what they'd said to one another the last time they were together ... big mistake.

He missed Sylvie with a passion that made him ache sometimes. But he still couldn't get past her knowing who he was before the twins were born, and not contacting him.

He kept obsessing over missing out on the children's births. He'd gone online to see if he could have proven his paternity before the births (yes, he could have, and it would have been non-invasive).

So he could have been present at their birth, but because of Sylvie's lies, he wasn't.

He hadn't been there to help Sylvie through labor, to see the boys take their first breaths and hear their first cries. He hadn't gotten to count twenty tiny toes and twenty tiny fingers. He hadn't gotten clapped on the back and congratulated when he handed out cigars ...

He needed to quit thinking about it. Since when did he live in the past, in what might have been?

Heath sighed, knowing that he wasn't going to get anything productive done that afternoon. He changed into his workout clothes and headed downstairs to the on-site gym. He spent the next hour doing everything he could to exhaust his body to the point that his mind would stop obsessing over his and Sylvie's mistakes.

He zeroed in on the number of the incline and the minutes left as he ran on the treadmill. He focused on every weight and every repetition as he moved through the circuit of the strength-training machines. He narrowed his span of attention to just the absolute present moment.

It was the only way he knew how to forget about the fact that he had a family in Zeke's Bend that didn't want him.

He didn't know how it happened, but somehow along the way, Sylvie, Quentyn, and Jadyn had taken up residence inside his heart. Whenever he tried to label what they were to him, he could only come up with one word: family.

It hurt to be separated from them. He didn't know how he could make it right, and he believed Sylvie would never forgive him.

As he was taking a shower to get cleaned up, he recalled a conversation he'd had with Momma Jones a week ago. For some reason, as he was strategizing how to get Sylvie to talk to him again, he thought Momma Jones could be an ally. After all, he had heard her battling with Sylvie when he first arrived in town, trying to make Sylvie talk to Alan about being part of the children's lives. Perhaps, now that she'd had a chance to cool down after that disaster of a dinner, she might feel that he should be in the children's lives, same as she previously felt about Alan.

He considered calling Phae or Neesa, but he was certain they wouldn't appreciate him putting them in the middle. Besides, no matter how wrong they might think Sylvie was, they'd always take her side, no matter what. Heath wished he had friends like that.

It had taken him several days before he'd called Sachet, wanting to have all the angles worked out in his head ahead of time. In the end, the discussion had taken an unexpected turn.

"Mrs. Ford, it's Heath Collins," he said hesitantly when she answered the phone.

"Heath Cartwright or Collins? It's hard to keep up with all these last names," Sachet said. He knew right then that she was going to be difficult.

"It's Collins. It's always been Collins."

"All right then, Mr. Collins. What can I do for you? Make it quick. I've got a pie that needs to come out of the oven in a few minutes."

"I was hoping you might be willing to say something on my behalf to Sylvie. Let her know that I have the best of intentions when it comes to the twins, and I want to do everything I can for them."

"I don't get involved in my daughter's affairs," Sachet said. "Not anymore."

He remembered the set down Sylvie had delivered at the dinner, telling her mother to stay out of her life. "I understand, and I can appreciate that. Sylvie is a great mother, and I would never do anything like try to take the boys away from her. I know she's afraid of that, so I wanted you to hear it from me personally. At the very least, I want to be able to help out financially and make sure that Sylvie never has to worry about money."

Her voice raised an octave. "Financially, you say?"

"Indeed. I actually tried to write her a check before I left town, but she refused to accept it. I heard a couple of rumors that Sylvie might be struggling with her bills, and I don't want her to feel like she can't provide everything she wants for the boys. I can make sure she can give them anything she wants and it's the least I can do for her. For them. They're my kids, too."

Sachet was quiet for a few moments. Heath wondered if she had hung up. Then her voice came back full strength on the line.

"I tell you what, Mr. Collins. I do think that my daughter works too hard. It pains me to see that she's not able to spend as much time as she'd like with my grandbabies. So I do think you having some financial stake in their upbringing would be a good idea."

Heath almost whooped in delight and relief. "Then you'll speak to her for me?"

"I'll figure out a way."

Heath was so afraid to ask the next question, but since he had already had some success, he thought he might as well barrel onward. "You know, it would be a great thing if we could figure out some way for me to be actively involved in the boys' lives, as well. I know that I'm in Seattle and you all are in Zeke's Bend, but I would be willing to fly down there, at least, every other weekend to spend time with them. More, if we could make the timing work. I wouldn't impose, of course. But it would be great if I got to spend some time with them."

This time, the resulting pause was even longer than before. "Actively involved, you say?"

"Yes, ma'am." Heath had no idea what direction the conversation was going to go.

"From what I could tell from those articles I read, you're a busy man Mr. Collins. The babies are so little; they need someone stable in their life. That's why my Sylvie is such a good mother. There isn't a thing she wouldn't do for them. I don't know if it would be confusing for them, especially since they're so little, to have someone that comes and goes in their lives."

"Lots of children do fine with visitations from a parent."

"Well, I'm sure there will be lots of times when business matters will force you to miss those visitations. I think it would be nearly impossible for someone like you to have the kind of regular schedule you're talking about. Running a company is busy, important work. I don't think it would be right for you to be disappointing the twins all the time. It would be confusing for them. Don't you think?"

Heath couldn't believe it. For the first time in his life, he was going to be at a disadvantage because he was successful. But then he started to think about what she had said.

She was right. His work did take him all over the world at odd times and at a moment's notice. He could be called upon the next day to have to fly halfway across the world to have a meeting. His life was often chaotic.

Before he found Sylvie, he had acknowledged his life wasn't suited to having a family. He saw other successful men with families, and they rarely had time to spend with the people that should have mattered most.

His own parents had been distant in his life, and he never knew when they would drop in on it. Their neglect had really done a number on him. He didn't want his kids growing up like he had.

"Yes, it would probably be confusing," he said slowly.

"Well, then that's decided then. It's not a problem, Mr. Collins. I'll talk to Sylvie about you helping financially. I think that's wise. I need to go now. I just heard the oven alarm. You have a good day." She ended the call.

Reflecting back on the conversation with Sachet now as he dried himself off, he wished he had said something different.

He should have said that he was going to be the father that he never had. He would be there for the boys, and he would change everything about his life to be with them if that's what it took. But he didn't want to upend things for them if Sylvie didn't want him in her life.

She was a good mother. The boys would have a wonderful life because she was in it. He wanted her to be happy just as he wanted them to be happy. He didn't want to cause them pain or confusion. Even if he was their father, that didn't seem right. Especially, since he was their father.

He thought about this all the way back to his high-rise apartment. It wasn't until he got there that he realized with chagrin that he forgot to pick up something for dinner. He looked in the refrigerator. It was practically empty. The only thing in there was some beer and a small package of brie. He made a mental note to tell the housekeeper to go to the grocery store.

He thought about ordering some Chinese takeout, but he didn't even have the energy for that. He didn't do Chinese anymore. It always made him think of Sylvie's Chinese Take Out Casserole. He idly wondered if Aunt Charmaine ever admitted the recipe was Sylvie's sole idea and property.

That made him think of some of the other Joneses. He wondered if Will, Kent, and Leon had found someone to cover his spot on their darts team. And the triple threat, teenage terrors. Were they still into their old skateboards now that he'd given them new hoverboards?

Was Phae grumpier than ever? He worried that Neesa may have never found someone to fix her well pump. And Meg, and Rita at the diner, and Elfleda and James? What were they up to tonight?

His body was exhausted, but unfortunately, his brain was not. He took the brie and a bottle of beer and went to sit and stare out at the bay.

He soon pulled out his laptop, but instead of checking his email and looking at the latest analysts' reports, he pulled up the pictures of Quentyn and Jadyn he had saved in a file. He could already see reflections of himself in Quentyn's face. But what he really saw was how much they looked like Sylvie. He loved that they were going to look like her. They were getting the best parts. That was all he could ever want for his kids.

He leaned back and closed his eyes. He just wanted to sleep. He wanted to sleep and wake up and have the whole situation completely gone away as if it had never happened.

Heath was woken up by the sound of his cell phone ringing. He picked it up from the table and stared at it. The display told him it was a caller from a number he didn't recognize.

He wiped his eyes to get rid of the last remnants of sleep and then hit the answer button. "This is Heath Collins."

"Hoss? Is that you?" the scratchy voice on the other end of the line asked.

CHAPTER THIRTY-ONE

HEATH GRINNED, KNOWING EXACTLY who it was and really pleased to hear from her. He couldn't resist egging her on for a second. "Excuse me, ma'am, who is this? Do I know you? There's no 'Hoss' here."

"It's Elfleda Jones, and don't be pulling any shenanigans," came her bossy reply. "You should thank your lucky stars that I managed to find your phone number in Sylvie's cell phone. Cell phones. Hmph. A device truly meant for the younger generation. I feel like I'm all thumbs when I'm trying to mess with that little screen."

"Oh, Aunt Elfleda. Of course, I know you. To what do I owe the pleasure?" He couldn't have been more pleased, in fact. This had to be a good sign.

"It's no pleasure, sonny."

Okay then, not a good sign. Damn.

"Listen up. You need to get back to Zeke's Bend right away."

He waited for an explanation, but it was as if she didn't feel the need to offer any reason. But that was Elfleda, Jones family matriarch. She said jump and everyone asked how high. But he wasn't a Jones, so he'd be needed a reason why.

"What's happened? Is something wrong? The babies? Are they okay?"

Elfleda sighed. It sounded as if she dragged it up from somewhere deep inside her tiny, shrunken body. "I'm surprised you haven't heard and aren't already here. It's shocking. Aren't you some kind of a hotshot big deal? I would've thought you'd have somebody watching your family affairs down here."

"What's happened? What should I already know about?"

"The accident, of course."

Heath shot to his feet, heart pounding. "Accident? What accident? Is Sylvie okay? Quentyn? Jadyn?"

"The boys are fine. They're with Sachet. But the prognosis for Sylvie isn't so good, I'm afraid."

Heath took a step forward and felt the world shift on its axis. He had to grab onto the chair to keep his balance. "But she's going to be okay soon…"

There was another pause. Elfleda sounded very sad. "I don't know much other than things don't look good, Mr. Collins. She's taken a turn for the worse, and she may not be with us much longer."

Heath blinked stupidly. He was frozen in place. He didn't know what to do. For the first time in his life, he was completely helpless. "What can I do? Tell me how to help her."

"I already told you. Get your ass back to Zeke's Bend! Sylvie needs you. I don't know what happened between you two, but you need to make sure that when the time comes for her to cross over, she can do it in peace."

"I don't understand." Heath's mind refused to work. He couldn't process the idea of Sylvie crossing over because that meant … no, he wasn't going to think that way.

"She needs to know that her babies are going to be taken care of by their father," Elfleda said. "You need to tell her that. You'll probably get into a fight with Sachet over custody, but you'll win. You're those children's father. If you can't parent with Sylvie, at least, you can do it when she's gone."

With that, Heath's brain kicked back into gear. He began to formulate a plan.

It would be hours before his plane could get him to Sylvie's side. He had to get there as quickly as possible. Even as he was talking to Elfleda, his fingers started moving over his phone's keyboard, sending an urgent text to his private pilot.

"I'll be there as soon as humanly possible," he told Elfleda.

"Hurry, young man, and think about what I said. Sylvie might not have that long after you get here. You want to make sure that she's able to cross over in peace knowing that you'll take care of your children."

The line went dead. He stared at the phone wondering how his life had completely gone off the rails so quickly. He was a fool to leave Zeke's Bend. He was a fool to let anything get in the way of his happiness with Sylvie.

He loved her, and he never told her that simple truth.

And he realized that somewhere in the back of his mind, he had believed he would one day rectify things with Sylvie. It was just a matter of time. Now, perhaps, that time had run out.

He was the biggest fool on the planet.

THE FLIGHT TO ZEKE'S BEND AND the drive to the hospital in Rollinsburg felt like it took an eternity. In all actuality, Heath had made even better time than he expected.

He jotted notes on the long flight, thinking about the ways that he could divest his company so he could spend all of his time with the boys. They were his priority.

He couldn't care less about making money anymore. He already had more than he could spend in a hundred lifetimes.

He made plans to call real estate agents in Zeke's Bend. He didn't want to take the boys away from their extensive Jones family. He would do right by the boys.

It was hard to think about Sylvie. He called and called the hospital but the nurse just kept saying she couldn't give out info if he wasn't Sylvie's husband or parent or sibling, etc. It was maddening.

None of the Joneses whose numbers he had were answering their phones. He must have left a hundred messages begging, then demanding, they call him.

It killed him he had no news about Sylvie. He would have called in a team of experts from all over the world, but he couldn't do that if he didn't know what kind of experts he needed. Elfleda had told him everything ... and nothing.

When the hired car arrived at the hospital, Heath shot out of it like a cannonball. He careened into the waiting room and dashed up to the front desk. He ran his hands through his hair as the nurse took her time ending her phone call.

What if he was too late? He couldn't be too late. Sylvie was going to fine. Just fine.

The nurse finally hung up and he asked for Sylvie's room number. It took a lifetime for her to look it up on her computer. He asked how Sylvie was doing and the nurse said she really couldn't say, whatever the hell that meant.

She did give him Sylvie's room number, though, and he took the stairs to the fifth floor because he didn't want to wait for the elevator.

When he emerged from the stairwell, flinging open the fire door, he searched for signs to get his bearings. Left or right? Or straight ahead? Which way?

His heart slammed against his chest wall, and he had a hard time comprehending the different colored lines on the floor and the arrows on the wall.

A dark cloud of foreboding swept over him. He prayed that he wasn't too late. He finally found the right direction and dashed down the hallway to the left.

He skidded around a corner and found himself right in front of several members of the Jones family. They looked at him with considerable surprise.

He recognized Phae and Neesa sitting in a couple of seats lined against the hallway wall. Will was there with Eli Ford and Aunt Elfleda was dozing in her wheelchair which was parked near Phae.

"Heath?" Eli asked.

Elfleda's head popped up, coming awake quickly for someone so elderly. She peered at him calmly, the only one who didn't appear surprised to see him. A wide, satisfied smile stretched across her wrinkled face. Heath had no time to ask why Elfleda was acting Cheshire Cat-ish.

Heath glanced at everyone. "Where is she?"

"Right there," Phae said, pointing at room 534.

"Is she ... awake?" Heath asked, not able to say "alive."

"No, not yet," Neesa said. "But ..."

Heath didn't wait to hear any more. She was alive, and that's all that mattered. The love of his life might be on death's doorstep, but for now, she was still among the living. He still had time to make things right.

Despite what Elfleda had said, Heath had already decided that he needed to do what he could to make sure that Sylvie had a fighting chance. There was no way that he was going to leave Sylvie's fate to a couple of suburban doctors.

He pushed his phone at a gaping Will. "Listen, I don't know your sister's condition, and I can't wait right now. So what I need you to do is call my assistant, Jamie. She's expecting your call and this is all set up."

Will looked confused. "Why would I—"

"I couldn't get anyone in this damned place to tell me about Sylvia's condition. And none of you were answering my calls!" He glanced around and thought Phae and Neesa hung their heads slightly, as if guilty.

Will shrugged. "Yeah, uh, well—"

"That's not important now. Call Jamie, speed dial two, and tell her about Sylvie. In fact, if you could find her doctor and get him on the phone with Jamie, that would be best. As soon as Jamie knows the score, she'll call the best doctors in the field and stop at nothing until she gets them on flights out here. So do that. I've got to see Sylvie."

He left a befuddled-looking Will holding Heath's phone as if it might bite him. He had no more time.

He burst into Sylvie's room and immediately saw Sachet sitting there holding Sylvie's hand. Sylvie was sleeping. Several monitors surrounded her bedside and an IV drip ran to her arm. Her color wasn't great, but she didn't look too terrible.

He couldn't see any bandages or other evidence of trauma, but there was a blanket over her and that might be covering up her wounds.

Sachet looked up at him, finely-plucked brows raised. "What are you doing here?"

If she was here, then where were ... "Where are my sons?"

"With Meg. What are—"

"I need you to leave," he said in a quiet voice that brooked no argument.

A look of consternation crossed Sachet's tired features.

"No, I don't think so. I'm not going to leave my daughter."

"I'm going to say this as nicely as possible, Mrs. Ford. I need you to get the hell out of this room right now. I want to speak to Sylvie alone. I'm not asking."

He expected Sachet to argue with him again, but to her credit, she nodded in understanding.

She stood up and stepped aside. Before she left, she said, "I realize I've made a lot of mistakes with my children, especially my daughter. But I do love her more than anything. I want to do right by her, and I want her to be happy. If you make her happy, then I've got no complaints."

She patted his arm in a disarming, motherly way and then quietly took her leave.

Heath was astonished. He had expected more of a fight. Perhaps realizing she could lose her daughter had led her to a breakthrough about what was really important.

Kind of like Heath, himself.

Chapter Thirty-Two

Heath slowly stepped beside Sylvie's bed. He looked down at her. She appeared to be sleeping peacefully. He reached over and gently touched her hair, smoothing it away from her face. She looked like an angel.

He was reminded of the very first night he saw her in Chicago. He had known then that she was the girl he was supposed to marry. Fate had hit him over the head with the message, so why had he been so stupid and let her go?

He had her and a family ready made for him, and then he let a gross misunderstanding come between him and what mattered most.

He'd been stubborn. He realized that now. She'd apologized, in her own way. And he wouldn't let it go. It was his fault their argument got out of hand. He hated when moments of brilliant insight came at the worst possible times. Perhaps even coming too late.

He sat down next to Sylvie's bed and took her hand in his. He stared at it. It was so small and delicate, so refined. He loved the shape of her fingers. They were tapered perfectly down to the tips of her painted nails. She had the hands of a princess.

He held that hand against his cheek and tried to pass some of his strength to her through the connection of flesh-to-flesh.

All he ever wanted was take care of her and the boys. He heard Elfleda's voice in his head, demanding he finally tell Sylvie the truth. He needed to tell her the words that would give her peace if she crossed over.

God no. But just in case, he couldn't let her leave him without hearing his feelings for her.

"Baby, I'm here." He figured that was the best way to start, although she was unconscious. He knew that she might still be able to hear him, even if she were in a coma.

"You're going to be just fine, Sylvie. I have the best doctors in the country on their way here. Just hang in there until they get here." His voice almost broke so he stopped talking for a moment to pull himself together. The last thing he wanted was to upset her.

There was so much he wanted to say. He was a better man because of Sylvie, and he had foolishly never told her that. Instead, he backed her into a corner and forced her to fight her way out because she was afraid of him.

In the end, he acted exactly like the person she feared he would be when she learned his name. He couldn't blame her for wanting to stay away from him. Hell, he didn't want to be around himself, either.

"You don't have to worry about a thing, Sylvia," he said. "I don't want you to worry about anything but getting better. I'll take care of the boys. I can do that, thanks to the way you helped me learn how to be a father. I'm sorry for everything that I said during that god-awful argument. I didn't mean it, not really."

"I screwed up. Royally," he said, emphasizing the word. "I know I'm not the best example all the time of a model parent, which I know you were worried about. But I love the boys. I do. So much. I don't know why I didn't tell you that before."

He stroked her arm, her skin warm against his touch. "Quentyn and Jadyn aren't just a responsibility to me. They're part of me, and I love them all the more because they're part of you, too. Those two little people are the best parts of us. And I'll make sure, no matter what, that they grow up and make their mother proud."

Heath had to stop then. A welling of emotion filled his chest, making it hard to take a deep breath. His words came out strained, as though they had to fight their way out of him, had to squeeze past the big lump in his throat.

Sylvie started to stir. Heath's hand tightened on hers as her eyes fluttered open. He could tell that they didn't quite focus on him, though. He imagined she was deep in the throes of the drugs that they were giving her to dull the pain.

"Is it over?" Sylvie croaked.

"No. Nothing's over. Everything's ahead of us. You're right here with me. You're safe." He smoothed her hair away from her forehead.

Sylvie looked confused. "Water?" Heath immediately searched for the water cup. He found it and brought the straw to Sylvie's lips. She sucked on the straw gratefully, and then she pulled away with a nod to him.

Too late, he feared maybe he shouldn't have given it to her. He jumped up and dashed to the door.

He flung it open and smiled at the gathered Joneses. "She's awake! She's talking!"

Everyone nodded and seemed pleased enough. He thought they weren't as thrilled as they should be. Maybe … oh, he didn't know and didn't care.

"I gave her some water." He looked at Eli, who was the only person there other than Elfleda who'd look Heath in the eye. "Was that okay? I didn't think."

Eli stepped in front of him and gave him a solid, manly squeeze on the shoulder. "It's just fine, son. She can have water."

Heath blew out a long breath of relief. "Okay, then. I'm going back in. You might want to tell the doctor she's awake."

"We will, son," Eli said, the low voice a beacon of calm for Heath.

Heath quickly returned to Sylvie's side.

"Everyone's so happy you've come back to us," he said to her, taking the water cup from her hands and setting it on the side table.

Her expression was confused again. "Come back? Oh yeah. What are you doing here, Heath?"

"I can't believe you need to ask me that, sweetheart. Aunt Elfleda called me and told me about the accident. Don't you worry about anything. You're a fighter and you can overcome anything. I'm here to help you and I've got specialists on the way. Just stay here with us. Don't leave."

"What are you talking about? Accident? Did they drop me on the way to the operating room or something?"

Heath wondered if she had a concussion. Brain trauma could account for her memory loss. "It's okay, baby. Don't worry about it."

Sylvie tried to sit up, but she groaned as she twisted and grabbed at her side.

Heath moved to help her just as a nurse bustled into the room.

She gave him a short nod and pulled the file from the end of Sylvie's bed.

"Good, you're awake, Ms. Jones. How are you feeling?"

Heath thought the nurse sounded a bit too chipper for his taste. Was this the way they acted around people who were dying? He was going to have to have a talk with the hospital's administration.

"I think I'm okay. I tried to sit up, but it really hurt." Sylvie pointed to her side.

"Not surprising. It burst before the doctor was able to get it out. You're a lucky lady," the nurse said.

Heath fixed the nurse with a questioning glance. "What injuries did she sustain in the accident?"

Sylvie and the nurse had puzzled expressions.

"What accident?" the nurse asked.

"That's what I asked," Sylvie said in a whisper. She looked like she was in pain.

The nurse moved immediately around to the other side and started switching out the IV bag.

"Give that a few minutes, dear, and you should start feeling better," the nurse said in a soothing tone.

"The car accident," Heath repeated the words, wondering if he was in some kind of alternate reality.

Sylvie shook her head at him. "I wasn't in a car accident." She looked at the nurse with raised brows.

"I don't think you were in an accident. It doesn't say anything about that on your chart."

"That's … bizarre," Heath said.

"I started having bad side pain while I was at work," Sylvie said. "I'd already had it before, and I guess I waited too long. The pain was so bad I couldn't move. It was pretty scary it was so painful. Momma had the boys, so Meg took me to the hospital. Turns out the pain was from my appendix."

"It required emergency surgery," the nurse said. "If you would have waited any longer, and that burst at home, you would have been in really bad shape. You could have died." She smiled at Sylvie, who looked aghast. "Like I said, you're a lucky lady."

Heath rocked back in his seat. She'd had her appendix out. There was no accident. He blew out a sigh of combined relief and restraint.

Great Aunt Elfleda.

Chapter Thirty-Three

SYLVIE FELT THE EFFECTS OF THE drugs starting to take hold, enjoying the loopy sensation. She thought she might also be a little loopy thanks to the tall, handsome man leaning over her trying to plump her pillows so she could sit up.

She couldn't believe he was there. Maybe he wasn't and this was an anesthesia-driven hallucination. She hoped not.

She inhaled deeply and savored the scent of his cologne as he reached across her to adjust another pillow on her other side.

She winced as she twisted to get a better angle, the stitches pulling at her side. Instantly, Heath was touching her forehead and stroking her arm asking her what he could do to make her feel better.

"I'm okay," she said as she resettled in the bed. "Thanks."

"Ask me for anything, and you'll have it," Heath said. He stared into her eyes, and she saw pain there. Pain that she had caused.

"I'm sorry for how things were left between us," she said.

Heath held up his hand to quiet her. Then he leaned over and stopped any further words with a gentle kiss on her lips.

It felt better than the IV drug. If he was going stop her from talking like that, she definitely wanted to talk some more.

She reached up and touched the scruff on his cheeks. Although he looked just as devastatingly handsome as she remembered, he looked exhausted. There were dark hollows under his eyes.

"There's nothing for you to be sorry about," he said. "I was a complete jerk about everything. I should have tried to see things from your perspective, but I was too tied up in my own. I'm so sorry that I didn't listen to you. I can be … stubborn when I get dug in. And that can make me unfair."

"You're a good man, Heath, and you're not the only one who can be stubborn. I shouldn't have compared you to my father. That was wrong. And I should have apologized when you asked me to. I should have been honest with you from the beginning. I was a coward, and I'm sorry."

Heath gently stroked her cheek. When he looked at her like that, she felt like they were the only two people in the world.

"Once again, there's nothing to be sorry for. And you're not a coward. You've never had any problem standing up to me. And you took on raising two children on your own while running your own business without a complaint. You went toe-to-toe with Momma Jones at that dinner … and won handily, I might add."

Sylvie smiled.

"You're so beautiful," he said. "You had a right to be afraid of what might happen, especially when it came to your children. I regret so much, Sylvie. I said so many things I didn't mean. My only hope is that you can forgive me and we can try to work things out between us. I promise to be better, to listen to you and to cherish our differences as much as our similarities."

Sylvie's eyes drooped against her will. She felt so sleepy but wanted to hear more. "I want … to …"

Heath pulled up the covers and tucked them gently around her. "Shh, sleep now. You need your rest. I'll be here when you wake up."

She drifted off, the ache in her side relieved by the IV, the ache in her heart relieved by the man stroking her hair.

WHEN SYLVIE AWOKE, SHE LOOKED STRAIGHTAWAY for Heath. There he was, leaning back in the uncomfortable-looking chair.

His long legs stretched out in front of him. His eyes were closed and his breathing was even. She thought he was asleep.

She glanced at the side table and saw her cup of water. She reached for it and the instant she moved, Heath jerked into an upright position, blinking his eyes rapidly.

"What? Oh, you're awake. Can I get you something?" he asked.

"Yes, water, please," she said, sorry she'd woken him. He looked so tired.

She drank her fill and he fussed around her. He called a nurse who came in and checked her over, said she was doing well, asked if she wanted something light to eat. Sylvie ordered some soup, but only after Heath had volunteered to go get her whatever she wanted from wherever she wanted. The hospital soup would be fine, Sylvie assured him.

When they were alone, Sylvie asked how long she'd been asleep. He told her four or five hours was all. She glanced at the window and saw it was dark outside.

"Where are the twins?" she asked.

"They're still with Meg. And there are plenty of Joneses that keep coming and going, asking about how you are and everything. I'm not sure who all is out in the hall right now. Do you want me to tell them you're up for a visit?"

She smiled. "It's really nice of them to come, but I just want to see you right now."

"Sylvie, that means more to me than you can know."

"Oh, I pretty well know. I mean, you're here and that tells me everything. It always should have."

He swallowed hard. "Do you remember my apology, before you fell asleep?"

She nodded. "Yeah. I don't know, though, why you thought I was in an accident."

"That, is quite the story," he said.

"Good, tell me."

He did, explaining how in essence, by terrifying him, Aunt Elfleda had made him realize what a stubborn fool he'd been. And because of this, he couldn't even be angry at the meddling old woman.

"Basically, Aunt Elfleda saved the day," he said.

"I feel horrible that she did that to you," Sylvie said. "Telling you I was dying. You must have been so worried."

"I was. I'll never forget it. I'm so grateful you're okay. Now that it's over, I'm far more upset by the fact that it took an old woman's scheming to make me realize what I was missing in my life. There is nothing quite like a life or death situation to make a person see the light."

"Well, Elfleda does fancy herself quite the matchmaker," Sylvie said. "She says it's only because of her that Meg and Leon are still married, though I don't know the story behind that."

"I bet it's a good one," Heath said.

"She must really like you. She usually only gets involved in this kind of stuff when she thinks somebody is worth her trouble. Her words, not mine."

"I'm pretty sure everybody was in on this thing, except maybe your mother and stepfather," Heath said. "No one would answer their phones when I called for updates, and I'm betting that was because Elfleda ordered them not to. You should have seen your brother's face when I told him to call my assistant and tell her your condition so she could bring in specialists. He was flummoxed."

Sylvie laughed and then winced. Heath immediately touched her shoulder. "Are you okay?"

Sylvie nodded. "I'll be good as new in no time."

"I'll make sure of it," he said, putting his arm around her.

Sylvie leaned against his chest. Everything felt right in the world when she was in Heath's arms.

"I can hear your heart beating." She pressed her ear against his chest. "It sounds like it's beating really fast." She put her hand next to her cheek on his chest and enjoyed feeling his heartbeat under her fingertips.

"I have to say that you missed quite a speech before you came around. I should've had someone here recording it. I basically ripped open my soul in front of you."

"What did you say?" Sylvie asked.

She couldn't remember hearing actual words, but as she had been regaining consciousness she had understood that Heath was there waiting for her. And then she felt the warmth of his hand around hers. It was exactly the way she wanted to wake up. It was the way she wanted to wake up for the rest of her life.

Heath gently pulled away from her. He moved so that he was looking her in the eyes. He took her hands and softly kissed the tops of each one. Sylvie's psychic sense kicked into high gear. Whatever Heath said next was going to change her life.

"I'm sorry, baby. I'll be right back. I have to use the bathroom." He let go of her hands and went into the small corner room that she assumed was, indeed, the bathroom.

Sylvie sighed. That wasn't exactly the earth-shattering news she'd been waiting for. And that was why she always claimed to be a little bit psychic, not completely psychic.

When Heath returned, he settled back in beside her bed and took her hands in his again. "You wanted to know what I said to you while you were still sleeping. There's no way I could repeat it word for word even if I tried. But it went a little bit something like this, and now it's modified, of course, since I know that you're not dying."

She smiled and nodded. Only in her family would anyone do something as crazy as Elfleda did.

Heath paused, obviously gathering his thoughts. "I'll just keep it simple. I love you, Sylvie Jones, and I was a fool for not telling you that before this very moment."

Sylvie's soul sang. There it was, the words that would change her life. So her psychic sense was just off by a few minutes, that's all.

She started to respond, but Heath kissed her softly again. She was starting to get the drift.

"Let me finish," he mumbled against her lips. "You are the most impatient woman," he said with loving affection.

"I love you because you are everything I've ever wanted in a woman, Sylvie Jones. You are beautiful, smart, and kind. I see how you are with your family and friends, and it reveals your good heart. And you're a fantastic mother. You're the kind of mother I wish I'd been lucky enough to have. It humbles me and honors me to know that you are the mother of my children. In fact, I wouldn't mind having more … children, not mothers."

Sylvie giggled. She wouldn't mind having another child with Heath. He raised his eyebrow and she quieted down because there was more.

"All of this is my long-winded, clumsy way of saying that I am not going to let you go, ever. Sylvie, would you do me the honor of marrying me?"

For once in her life, Sylvie Jones was speechless. Heath's sparkling green eyes were passionate and hopeful all at once. And she realized she should probably say something, and fast.

She put her hand on his cheek again and felt the jump of his jaw muscles beneath her fingertips. "Heath Collins, I love you too. I love, love, love you. And I have for a long time, but I'm an idiot and never told you. I would be honored to be your wife."

Heath gave an excited whoop and he pulled her into his arms. She couldn't stop the groan of pain caused by her pulling stitches and he instantly let her go.

"I'm so sorry, baby. I forgot," he said, looking stricken.

Sylvie shook her head. "It's okay. Already gone. Happiness is my pain pill right now."

He kissed her again, gently this time. It was so sweet and tender she had to blink back tears. She'd never felt cherished in her life, but this man cherished her. It was incredible.

She leaned against him and sighed against his lips. That's when she heard the clearing of a throat from across the room.

Sylvie's face flushed as she realized her mother was standing in the doorway. Momma had a look on her face that Sylvie couldn't read. Eli stood behind Sachet, and he had a wide grin on his face. She wondered how long they'd been standing there.

"Can I come in?" Momma's question wasn't directed at Sylvie, though. She was asking Heath's permission, and her tone was uncharacteristically docile.

This was a new development. It seemed Momma was uncertain around Heath. Something in their relationship had shifted.

"Of course, you can come in," Heath said. He made no move, though, to slide away from Sylvie.

Momma approached the bed slowly. She lightly touched Sylvie's shoulder. "I'm so glad you're okay, sweetie. How do you feel?"

"Like I'm on top of the world," Sylvie said. She was getting married to the man of her dreams. They were going to become the family she'd always wanted.

"May I have a word with you, Heath?" Momma asked.

"Of course, but there's nothing that you have to say that you can't say in front of my soon-to-be-bride." Heath's arm snaked around her shoulders. He had a possessive tone in his voice that Sylvie liked.

Momma nodded with a slight grimace. Sylvie couldn't tell if she was happy about the news or not.

"Heath, I'll be the first to admit I misjudged you. All I ever wanted was for my daughter to find someone who will take good care of her and the twins. I realize now that you are that person. I'm sorry if I made you feel unwelcome in our family. You are most welcome."

She offered her hand to Heath. He stared at it as if he didn't know what to do with it. Sylvie wondered if Momma might have so upset Heath that he was unwilling to forgive her. The tension level went up in the room considerably as they all waited for Heath's reaction to Momma's peace offering.

Momma added, "I'm a Jones woman at the end of the day. We're stubborn and strong-willed. That's what you'll get being married to my daughter, too. She's also the kindest and most forgiving soul. She'd have to be—she forgave me." She looked at Sylvie, who nodded and smiled gently.

"She helped me recognize that being with a man doesn't make you weak," Sachet continued. "At least, not when you're with the right man." She cast a glance over at Eli, who watched her with open adoration. "Being with the right man makes you stronger than you can ever be on your own."

Heath stood up then, still seeming not to acknowledge Sachet's outstretched hand. Sylvie was about to say something when he moved, quick as lightning, and took Momma in his arms, surprising all of them. He gave her a massive bear hug that left Momma laughing and batting at his big biceps.

Heath let her go. "I look forward to having you as a mother-in-law, Mrs. Ford."

Sylvie clapped her hands in delight. She sat up straighter in the bed. "Now the real question is, where are my boys? I miss their faces."

"Now that you're awake, Neesa is going over to pick them up from Meg's house," Momma said.

Heath smiled down at Sylvie. "I'm excited to see our boys too. I missed them more than I imagined possible."

Sylvie sniffled and rubbed her nose. He said *our boys*.

"Ours," she agreed.

EPILOGUE

SYLVIE LOVED PHAE AND KENT'S HOUSE. Kent had renovated the old Belleterre Mansion and turned the place into a glorious blend of Victorian architecture and modern technical wizardry. Whenever she was there, she loved to study the intricate carving in the woodwork and imagine who might have created it so long ago. And the robot that roamed the house doing general housework was beyond fascinating.

Phae sat in her favorite easy chair, her roly-poly belly looking ready to pop. She was close to her delivery date now. "Thanks for coming over for dinner, Sylvie. I needed the distraction." She rubbed her belly and no other explanation was needed.

"You know I love hanging out with you," Sylvie said. "And they seem to have their own bromance going on over there."

They looked fondly at their husbands. Heath had spread out the blueprints for the renovation they had planned for the decaying docks down by the river. Kent bent over beside Heath, both of them studying the paper avidly. They were talking away about details that flew over Sylvie's head.

"They sure are into that," Sylvie said. "I don't know what they see in it, but I'm glad they have each other to talk it to death."

Phae grinned. "I don't mind talking about it either."

"Great. I'm the only one who doesn't get it."

"Oh, you get it well enough. You just don't care about it. You're all artsy and everything, not into construction details."

Sylvie considered that. It was true ... mostly. "I helped design our new house. It's taking forever to get in all the finishing details, Phae! I don't know how you could stand waiting while Belleterre was redone."

"Yeah, it's tough. Oh! He kicked." She smiled down at her belly. "Or she kicked. Whichever."

"You know, you made me lose ten bucks to Aunt Chelly," Sylvie complained. "I bet her you would have given in by now and found out if you're having a boy or a girl. I can't believe you're still holding out."

"It's exciting, not knowing. And it gave me the excuse to buy lots of extra stuff for the nursery and everything, so I have the possibilities covered."

"If I'd known you were using it as an excuse to buy baby stuff," Sylvie said, "I never would have accepted Aunt Chelly's bet."

"That's okay. We all know you can afford to lose a little cash now."

Phae and Sylvie had long since confessed to one another that their husbands were embarrassingly loaded. It was nice, finally, to have someone with whom to share their secrets. They had told no one else, including Neesa.

Of course, anyone who cared to do it, could search Heath on the Internet and find the truth. When Heath had divested himself from the company he had created, there had been some buzz in the financial news. Heath had somehow stifled it. How, Sylvie didn't know.

The thing was, Heath and Kent just wanted to be regular citizens of Zeke's Bend, and the best way to accomplish that was to pretend they were no different from anyone else. And at their core, it was true. They were just a couple of married men who loved their wives. Same as a bunch of other guys in town.

Phae brought Sylvie back to the topic of her baby. "It's driving Neesa crazy, not knowing what I'm having. She's already made up babysitting schedules for you and me both and seems to think that it's necessary to know my baby's sex for the schedule to work properly."

"She's just trying to get you to spill the beans."

"She refuses to accept the fact that the pods are empty. There are no beans to spill."

Phae's maid came in and announced that dinner was ready, effectively ending any more speculation about Phae's baby.

Later, when dinner was over and they were gathered in one of the small, charming sitting rooms, having coffee out of the most exquisite, tiny cups Sylvie had ever seen, Heath leaned over to Sylvie and whispered in her ear.

"Penny for your thoughts?" he asked.

She nuzzled against him and murmured a choice word or two. She wanted him to know exactly what she was thinking, and it had to do with the big, empty bed waiting for them at home.

"Geez, can you guys save the mushy stuff until you get home, at least?" Phae said teasingly. "You newlyweds are—"

"Wonderful," Kent supplied with a wink.

"That's not what I was going for," Phae said.

"Remember, you were once a newlywed."

"That was forever ago," Phae teased. "We're an old married couple now."

Sylvie pushed Heath away and grinned. "How funny is it that we should wind up like this, Phae. Both of us old, married ladies. Who'd have thought?"

"I don't know about you, Kent, but they don't look like old ladies to me."

"Oh, go on," Phae said. "Seriously, go on. I'm huge as a house."

"But you're not old," Kent quipped, ducking when Phae threw a pillow at him.

Sylvie and Heath left not long afterward, knowing Phae needed her rest. And anyway, Neesa was babysitting at Sylvie's new house and probably needed to get home soon so she could work the next day.

Heath had situated their house on thirty acres of land outside town. She didn't know how he did it, but he'd somehow gotten the whole thing built while they were on their honeymoon. They'd only been gone six weeks, so Sylvie shuddered to think what it cost him to get it finished so quickly.

It was a spectacular mansion, two stories, surrounded by sprawling grounds that took half a dozen gardeners to maintain. The house itself was an eclectic mix of styles, bits and pieces of Sylvie's favorite styles, masterfully blended together to create something new. Sylvie loved it for its color and playful grandness.

Neesa was waiting up when they got home.

"The boys are sleeping soundly," Neesa said. "They're the best."

"They didn't give you any trouble?"

"What trouble? They're just being babies," Neesa answered.

Because it was Neesa saying this, Sylvie knew the boys must have been a trial. Neesa never said a thing against children, but Sylvie could read between the lines.

She hugged Neesa. "You're the best, you know that?"

"Mmmhmm. Hey, what days are you going to be at the shop this week?"

"I'm taking clients by special appointment on Tuesday and Thursday afternoons for now," Sylvie said.

"Great. Make me an appointment, will you?"

"Sure."

Meg had taken on a bigger portion of Shear Stylin's clientele, and they had hired another stylist because business was booming. Sylvie figured she'd ramp up her hours again when the boys went to school in a few years, but right now she was taking the opportunity to spend more time with them.

Since she married Heath, she didn't have to work unless she wanted to. And as it turned out, she did want to. She was a talented stylist and she loved it. She didn't want to give it up.

Heath went upstairs to check on the babies while Sylvie walked Neesa to her car.

It was a warm June night and the crickets were chirping along with night birds and the shrill trills of cicadas.

"Think about the loan we offered," Sylvie said. "It could really help the farm."

"I know, but I can't take it," Neesa said. "It's gotta make it on its own or it's not something I should be doing, right?"

"I've been getting a heavy psychic tingle around you lately, Neesa. Something big's going to happen for you soon. Maybe it will be a huge order from one of your fancy restaurants, so big it'll set you up for a year."

"Well, I'll bet my money on hard work instead of psychic tingles, Syl. You know how I am."

Sylvie shrugged. "You don't have to believe in it for it to work."

Neesa shook her head. "Okay, okay. And hey, I really appreciate you offering to help. It means a lot. I'll talk to you tomorrow." She got in her car and waved her arm out the window as she drove away.

Sylvie meandered her way slowly back into her house, stopping to adjust a piece of decor here, picking up a baby toy there. She found Heath in their bedroom, stripping off his shirt.

"Mmm, you're looking pretty good for an old married man," Sylvie said, admiring his toned abs.

"You're not suckering me into calling you an old married woman. I'm not that easy."

She chuckled. "You don't know how I'd react to that."

"The hell I don't." He tossed his pants aside and pulled on the sexy pajama bottoms Sylvie loved to see him in. "So what's the schedule for the rest of the weekend?" Heath asked as he sat on the edge of the bed. He patted the mattress.

She sat down and he draped an arm over her shoulder. "We're due at Momma's and Eli's on Sunday for brunch, and then we have tea with Aunt Elfleda and the rest of the elderly crew in the afternoon," Sylvie said.

"I'll make sure to save up all my charm for Sunday then," he said with a chuckle. He drew her closer.

"Sooo, are the boys out good?" Sylvie asked.

"Indeed, they are. Completely tuckered out from ordering their Aunt Neesa around all evening."

A wicked grin spread across Sylvie's face that went nicely with her wicked thoughts. "Remind me to give them a little ice cream tomorrow as a reward."

Heath ran his fingertips down her bare arm, making her skin tingle. "Tell you what. I have a new game for you. Want to play?"

She was excited. A new game. "What is it?"

Heath pulled her closer and kissed her deeply. Desire flared inside her.

When he pulled his lips away, Sylvie saw the twinkle in his eyes. "I call it Happily Ever After."

"What are the rules? How do you win?" Sylvie asked breathlessly.

"I'm pretty sure I've already won," Heath said with a sly smile. "But I'm willing to share my winnings if you're very good."

"How do we play?"

"First round is whoever gets naked fastest gets to pick out something sexy for the other one to wear."

Sylvie thought about what Heath would look like with just a silky tie on and nothing else. Yum. Then she looked at his pants. "Hey, that's not fair. You've only got your pajama bottoms on and I'm still fully dressed."

"I'll give you a ten-second head start. Ready, set, go!"

She laughed and leapt to her feet, yanking her dress up and kicking off her shoes. Heath counted down from ten.

"… three, two, one." he called.

Sylvie was frantically trying to undo her bra.

Heath stood up and dropped his drawers in one smooth movement. "I win!"

"That wasn't fair."

"Yeah, it wasn't."

"Do over."

"Nope," he said. "No do-overs. You forget how ruthless I am. Now, where's that tiny pink number you bought in Milan?"

"No way. You cheated," she insisted, eyeing his very naughty, very stiff and naked manliness.

"Guess I'll have to hold you down and rip the rest of your clothes off," he threatened, puffing out his chest and waggling his eyebrows.

She squealed and began running toward the bathroom.

He was hot on her heels.

He snatched her before her feet ever touched the bathroom tiles. He swooped her up into his arms and carried her to their bed.

"Hey," Sylvie said, playfully pummeling his brawny chest. "You didn't say we were playing Pirate and Wench. You said we were playing Happily Ever After."

"Baby, that's exactly what we're doing."

She grinned. He was right. They'd be playing this game forever.

And like Heath, Sylvie knew she'd already won.

After all, there were no losers in Happily Ever After.

MIA'S OTHER BOOKS

Mia has other great romantic comedies. Don't miss Phae and Kent's story in the first book of the *Fabulous Jones Girls* series: *Billionaires Don't Like Nice Girls*. It's a rom-com with a touch of steam.

Under cover of darkness, a mysterious hero silently prowls the streets of Zeke's Bend. Labeled Captain Nice Guy by the small-town press, he selflessly performs kind deeds for those in need. No one knows the identity of the man behind the mask.

During a visit to his aunt's home, tech tycoon Kent Holmes has an embarrassing midnight run-in with the local superhero. Kent longs to unmask the pesky guy who left him tied to a laundry pole, but gets distracted when he meets sexy hairdresser Phae Jones. She's beautiful, sassy and strong, his perfect woman, and nothing will stop him from winning her.

Phae knows she's not perfect. She has the secrets to prove it, but she won't reveal them to anyone, especially not Kent. He's the hottest man she's ever met, a witty and passionate billionaire whose kisses curl her toes and make her heart pound.

He has too many expectations. She has too many secrets. Something has to give and it starts with a simple question only Kent thinks to ask—

What if Captain Nice Guy is actually Captain Nice Girl?

Approximately 280 pages long. Available in Paperbook format and for your Kindle. Can be borrowed for free with your Kindle Unlimited subscription.

ABOUT MIA

Mia Caldwell has been fantasizing about stories of "Happily-Ever-After" since she was a little girl, and now that she's all grown up her "Happily-Ever-After" stories have taken a steamier turn!

After graduating from college Mia still wasn't quite sure what she wanted to do with her life. Bored with her day job as an administrative assistant for a non-profit, she started writing stories on the side and sharing them with her friends. They gave her the push she needed to share them with you!

She lives in New York with two rascally cats named Link and Zelda, eats too much chocolate and Chinese take-out, and goes on way too many blind dates. She's still waiting for Mr. Right, but in the meantime she'll keep dreaming up the perfect man!

Made in the USA
Middletown, DE
25 May 2016